B.D.PEDERSEN

RE-EARTH

Edited
by

June Pedersen

ISBN-13: 978-0692725894
ISBN-10: 069272589X

PROLOGUE

Talk about strange events and odd happenings, these events take the book. Over the four and a half billion years the Earth has been in existence, the continents on the face or surface of the Earth have moved around like they were on a race track. Well maybe a slow-motion race track. Anyway, it's been around for a long time and during all that time the continents have moved all over the place.

Now it doesn't seem like anything of particular interest in this day and age, but when you take into consideration what happened to Duke Ridgeman over the past year your ideas of a free roving continental system come into question. What if the continents did not simply float around the world at their own will? What if the movements of the continents were controlled in a much more spectacular way?

Now hold on there. Don't jump the gun and start looking at me like I was a nut or something. I'm not a nut, but after witnessing the events I'm about to tell you about you will surely think I am a true nut case. Hell, I felt that way myself when I first ran into this thing. This strange thing is so far outside of reality, unless you actually saw it you would never believe it. My name is unimportant. Just know I was present while Duke and his second in command were dealing with the Six Lakes Project. I witnessed all I'm going to relate to you and still I find it unbelievable.

This is a story about twenty-three people, including two of the support personnel who had been infected by some creature from Lake One. These were innocent people who unknowingly became pawns in a process that would change the whole of the Earth's surface, and displace millions upon millions of people all across the Earth. The really spectacular thing about this whole crazy thing is there was no loss of lives as a direct result of the event itself. I will say this; there were some deaths by people trying to profit from the event and taking advantage of those millions who were displaced.

Things started to happen in the State of Texas as a young woman was driving across the state heading for home for a holiday vacation from college. All she was doing was heading home and then all hell broke loose and she ended up being the first victim of this bizarre event. She did not die; no, she faced something more terror filled and life changing.

It started as an earthquake and ended with a flood, but a flood so strange and unbelievable you simply had to be there and witness it to even begin to understand it. Come to think about it, the earthquake was just as strange and mind boggling.

But the real issue we are faced with concerning this odd and strange happening is it happened. Second is the fact we, of this planet had no control over it, nor would we. The beings who set this up, started it functioning, and then left never to return to this place again, had built into our world, unknown to us, a process of change we could never have imagined. That's right, before you jump to any wrong conclusion, the movement of the surface continents of the Earth is controlled by an alien machine on auto pilot.

Yes, there is natural continental movement, but this system enhanced the natural and directed the actual directions the continental drift or movement would take. Once set up and running there was no reason for them to remain and they, the aliens, left.

However, they did not leave until after they had planted the new occupants of the planet. Once the seeding was completed, they moved on never to be seen or heard of again.

Until this point in time. Once this process was put into motion there was even more coming. What we were witnessing was beyond anything our imagination could create. It was beyond anything Duke had ever thought possible. You guessed it, they're coming back and Duke found himself right smack dab in the middle.

Don't believe me, well hang around long enough so I can give you a little more information, and after I'm done if you don't want to believe then that's all right with me. The important thing is you stay clear of the split line for the continental United States and the other split lines targeted for the other major continents of the world.

It's all the advice I'll give you right now. I need to fill you in on what's happening and then maybe; just maybe you'll understand I'm serious about this whole thing. Maybe I had better start from the beginning. In reality, it's no big secret. Who the hell could hide something like this?

After all, you were all there and you witnessed the re-terraforming of Earth. What you didn't know or understand was the ways and means the re-terraforming took place. This is the story I'm about to relate to you. If I'm right, I'll answer a lot of questions you've had running around in your heads since the re-terraforming actually took place.

Now's your chance to learn the inner story of what happened. We almost became victims of an actual invasion and will make you stand up and take notice.

Chapter One

DEPRESSION LAKE ONE

LeAnn Larson was on her way home for some time off before starting the fall quarter at the college she was attending in southern California. She was heading across the State of Texas on Interstate 10 and making good time, the weather was clear and warm, just the way she liked it when driving. She had been on the road for about six hours and was running a section of I-10 as straight as an arrow and flat as a board. She could look ahead and behind and see nothing but a straight ribbon of concrete running off into the horizon in both directions.

It was a quiet afternoon with little or no traffic on the interstate. She was listening to her favorite music and of course she was playing it loud. She had not a single care in the world and was looking forward to getting home to her family. It was a sixteen hundred mile run from Irvin,

California to Springfield, Missouri. She had planned on a three-to-four-day trip home, wanting to take her time and relax a bit before all the hubbub of family reunions and preparing for the next semester.

It was about this time, five minutes after three in the afternoon when she noticed a cloud of dust ahead of her. It drew her attention because of the size in both height and width. The thing was huge and was a deep dark brown color. It seemed to sit there and not go anywhere. What the hell was it anyway?

It was then she realized there was a huge cloud behind her as well and both were growing. This was not right, there was something really scary about this whole thing. Mainly because she had nowhere to go except straight ahead or back the way she came and they were both blocked by the dust storms. She had automatically taken her foot off the gas and the car was slowing down. She was so transfixed with the view of the clouds in front and behind she didn't notice the car coasting to a near stop idling along at about five miles an hour or less.

Just then the whole of the world changed before her eyes. She felt a sudden jolt throwing her car to the right and it kept going. She managed to brake the car to a stop but it was still moving to her right at a right angle to her direction of travel. It then dawned on her the road itself was moving along with her and she was along for the ride.

It was everything she could do to remain upright. She was thinking this thing had to be ending before too long. The movement of the car was too violent for her to stay upright much longer.

How far she moved, she had no idea, but she knew it was a considerable distance. When the car came to a halt, she was lying across the seat with her head against the passenger door. She felt as though the car had been taken several miles from its original locations before finally coming to rest.

As she pushed herself up and started to look around, she could see dust in every direction, huge clouds of dust floating everywhere. The next thing she noticed was silence. There was nothing except the running motor of her car. Not even a sound of the wind that is normal for this part of the desert.

As the dust started to clear she was able to see the landscape around her and it had changed. Before this happened, any mountains she had seen were miles off in the distance. Now there were mountains all around her and they were massive. She was sitting in the bottom of a bowl with no way out. Her best guess was she was sitting in the middle of this new bowl-shaped valley and the distance from where she was at and the base of the mountains was around two miles or so.

The bottom of a bowl, where the landscape had been flat as a griddle ten minutes ago, was now bowl shaped. She sat there looking around her, fearful of leaving her car yet knowing she needed to.

Everywhere she looked there was the new mountain range sitting where none had ever been before. It had all changed and changed radically from what she had been driving through a few minutes ago. Besides, the rest of the road was gone, it had disappeared. It ran about fifty yards from her car and it was land. It, the road, was gone.

It dawned on her she was alone out there in the middle of this new bowl and there were no roads out of area Where I-10 had once been was now just this section she was sitting on. She walked to the end of the road and could see it had been sheared almost as if someone had cut it with a saw. The whole of the landscape had moved like a conveyor belt for whatever distance she had come.

As she stood there looking out over the new landscape, she could hear a sound rolling across the land toward her. As she stood there, she could see a low dust cloud forming and coming at her, there was something about that cloud she was familiar with. She had seen dust action like that before but could not put her finger on what it was that caused or created it. It was the noise that finally got to her and she knew then what was happening, it was water, my God, its water.

LeAnn turned and ran for the car and when she got there she looked back and sure enough she could see the leading edge of the flow of water coming at her. She got in her car and rolled the windows up not knowing anything else she could do. There was no place to run or drive, so all she could do was sit and wait and hope she would be protected by her car.

As the ground started to move a great depression formed out in the desert area bisected by I-10. The land was going through a total reformation with a section almost a half mile wide being split off from the rest of the land and being pushed to the south perpendicular to the highway. That part of the quake was not natural. Something about it said this was not the way the land shifted when it was reformed.

As the mountain range started to form around the depression a series of underground streams started to open up and flow onto the land. The amount of water ultimately started entering the depression was forming up into a massive flood and would soon encompass the entire depression and fill it to the rim of the mountain range around it. One lone car would be left sitting on short section of I-10 sitting dead center in the lake. The car becoming the burial crypt for LeAnn Larson, she would not reach home for the reunion after all.

The Texas depression would soon become a round lake not unlike the five others that would form up in the region between the Mississippi River and the Rocky Mountains. The six lakes would form a perfect line running north and south and were separated equally between the Mexican and Canadian borders. The first lake would be found one hundred thirteen miles north of Lajitas, Texas and would be four miles in diameter. This would put depression lake twelve miles south west of Balmorhea Springs, Texas and would be known as Depression Lake One.

Depression Lake Two would be found two hundred twenty-six miles north of Depression Lake One, sixty-one miles southwest of Clovis, New Mexico and again it was exactly four miles in diameter and the exact same shape as Depression Lake One.

Depression Lake Three appeared two hundred twenty-six miles north of Depression Lake Two, and just three and six tenths miles southeast of Tyrone, Colorado. Again, the terrain conformed to the size and depth matched the other two lakes.

Depression Lake Four again was two hundred twenty-six miles north of number Three. It was located six and a half miles northeast of Briggsdale, Colorado. Again, it was the same size and structure as the other three lakes.

Depression Lake Five was located just four and a half miles southeast of Osage, Wyoming. The mountains where the lake appeared were totally reformed to accommodate the lake size, structure and position. It was again two hundred twenty-six miles north of Lake Four.

Depression Lake Six was the final lake and was located fifteen and six tenths miles northeast of Glendive, Montana. As with the other five lakes it reformed the land around it knocking down mountains and building its own mountain range around it so it formed the same round lake four miles across. It was also located a hundred thirteen miles south of the Canadian border and two hundred twenty-six miles north of Lake Five.

What had happened had never been seen or discovered anywhere in the world's history. A geological phenomenon was so unique, so odd, nothing like it had ever taken place or been seen anywhere on Earth in all the Earth's history.

Though the materials they were formed from may be different, the physical structure of each lake was identical to the other five lakes. This was true right down to the height of the mountain range around them and the formation of the peaks. It was almost as if a giant had walked the face of the Earth with a walking stick and as he stuck his stick into the land it formed each lake exactly like the others.

The lakes were not in the center of the continental United States but were offset with the line of lakes being about a thousand miles from the west coast and about fifteen hundred miles from the east coast.

All in all, it had taken about twenty-one minutes for the six lakes to form. Actually, for the depressions to be made into the Earth. It then took right at ninety-two hours for the lakes to fill, almost to the minute. There was no overtopping or river drain off from the lake. It achieved its level, the same at each lake, and then stopped there. This entire event happened with such precise timing scientists felt it was much more than an act of nature, by what they had no idea.

It took the government three days to get people to the locations of all six lakes and to start some kind of organized study of what had happened. It was during this process they determined each lake was exactly five hundred feet deep and the thing most interesting was in a rather short period of time the water cleared up, so clear you could see the bottom of each lake.

LeAnn's car was one of the first human

casualty scenes located. Even stranger yet was the fact the conveyor belt effect had taken place in each depression and had placed a human made structure or item dead center of all the depressions.

LeAnn's car was dead center of Lake One. Lake Two had a hunting cabin at its precise center. Lake Three had a farm house, Lake Four a railroad bridge, Lake Five a mining structure and Lake Six a National Park Ranger Station. How the hell all this fit in was anyone's guess at the time. The one other unknown was the number of people who had been in each structure as the waters flooded into each depression.

The hunting cabin was used mostly during the season and since it was not that time of year, the probability of anyone being in it was low. The farm house was known to be occupied by a family of eight. They were trying to determine where each family member was at when the event took place.

They were sure no one had been on the railroad bridge at the time, but knew there had been people on the mining property.

Last was the park ranger building and they had received radio confirmation from the occupants at the time of the event there were six of them there. They had not been able to confirmed visually as yet.

It was on the fifth day Duke Ridgeman arrived at the scene of Lake One. Duke was a trouble shooter for the government's geological survey system and the individual in charge of the research units at each lake. It was his job to review any and all oddities and come up with a reasonable determination as to why things had happened like they did. In fact, he was the head and Chief Scientist of the Six Lakes Project.

The first thing he did was take a helicopter run over Lake One for a good close-up look. He was impressed with the uniformity of the structure of the depression and its actual size.

As they approached the center of the lake, he saw the car sitting on the bottom on the lone section of I-10. As he looked at the car it crossed his mind it had been confirmed there was a young woman in the car and as yet no one had gone down to try and recover her body. He made a mental note of the issue and then signaled the pilot to continue the tour of the lake.

As they flew along over the water, he noted the water was absolutely flat. Even the turbulence of the helicopter's blades failed to disturb the surface. He had the pilot move down closer and it still remained absolutely flat, not a ripple in sight. Strange, I've never seen anything like it. It's almost as if the surface tension of the water was at a high level. It was, in itself, a rather odd and puzzling observation.

The chopper pilot kept circling over the lake as Duke sat there looking down into the water. He had been to many disasters over his years in the service, but this one he could already see was going to be unique and involved.

Satellite imaging, which had been done upon the completion of the lake's formation, showed the layout was unreal. The size and placement of each

17

lake was specific and balanced. Nothing in nature, he had experienced, ever is as perfect and uniform as these six lakes appeared to be.

As they flew over the water, he felt his stomach start to hurt. He knew he was going to be working overtime on this one and still felt what he was seeing so far was only the beginning. Where things were going to go from here, he had no idea, but he knew there was more to come, a lot more.

He needed to get on the water and do some testing to determine just what it was he was observing. Twenty minutes later they had landed and Duke was talking to the on-sight manager Dennis Adams. "Dennis, I'm going to need a boat as soon as we can get one here. Do you have any close by, if not right here right now?"

That was Dennis' job, getting the right tools to the right place when needed. "We have a boat down at the main camp and as soon as the access road is finished, we'll bring it up and launch it."

"Thanks Dennis, how long before they finish?"

"I would say about an hour and a half to two hours."

"That's perfect. I think I'll just wait here and go up with the boat when things are ready.

Duke started to go over what he had seen as the helicopter came in on the ridge overlooking the lake. He noted the formation or structure of the mountain range around the lake. It actually looked more like a dike than a mountain range. It was uniform in shape and structure and the back side angled away from the lake at a fairly shallow slope with no out cropping or any breaks in the landscape. It was a perfect boat launch layout.

This gave the responding emergency teams the ability to run access roads to the rim quickly and with little problem. In addition, they were able to set the rim areas up with facilities so those working the lakes could remain close by at all times. Larger and more involved facilities were located at the foot of the ranges where the access roads started.

Dennis had been an emergency response professional for twenty-three years and he was used to bringing the right tools to the right place at the right time, just as he had done here at Depression Lake One. As the road crew finished up the approach road to the launch area, Dennis walked over to Duke. "Duke we have a twenty-foot open craft and it can be in the water in less than ten minutes. We hadn't tried to launch a boat until someone from your unit arrived. We're ready to go whenever you are."

"All right Dennis let's get that thing on the water. I want to see how it launches and how it reacts to being on the lake's surface." Duke was grabbing his gear and heading for the truck. "I don't want the vehicle to touch the water so just back it far enough so we can push the boat off the trailer and onto the water."

Ten minutes later the crew was backing the trailer toward the water. Duke and Dennis were standing just feet from the boat as it slides by them toward the water. As the wheels of the trailer touched the water a strange thing happened, the wheels rolled out on top of the water, and in addition they stayed dry.

Duke yelled at the driver. "Stop, don't move anything in any way."

He stepped over to the edge of the water and lifted his foot and placed it down on the surface. It was firm and could hold his body weight. He then stepped out onto the surface and stood there looking down into the water. "What the hell?"

He started to step back off the surface but couldn't move his feet. The fear hit him square on and he knew he had made a big mistake by stepping out on the surface without doing some preliminary checks first. He noted he could move his feet inside his shoes, but he could not move his shoes, so he reached down and untied the laces to the shoes and then stepped out of the shoes and back onto the shore.

Duke was dumfounded, all he could do was stand there. Dennis then called out to the driver of the truck to pull the boat back up into the parking area. The driver put it in gear and gave the truck the gas but she didn't move. He gave more gas until the tires were spinning in place, but still, he could not move the trailer off the surface of the lake.

Dennis had the driver stop and then had the trailer unhooked from the truck and had the truck pull up into the parking area and park. They all stood there looking at the situation. The boat and trailer were stuck in place as were a pair of Duke's shoes. Duke turned to Dennis. "What is the density of water?"

Dennis stood there looking at the boat and trailer. "I have no idea."

"Well Dennis, at seventy degrees Fahrenheit water has a density of 1 gram per cubic centimeter with a gallon of water weighing 8.33 pounds. I want to try something. I want an item denser than water, something like a steel ball. Have you got any here?"

"As a matter of fact, we do, how about a boat anchor?"

Duke was busy looking at the water. "That will work perfect. Would you have someone bring it over here?"

One of the crew members climbed up on the trailer stinger and retrieved the ball anchor from the boat. Duke took it and stepped over by the water's edge and set the anchor down on the surface and it sat there. He stood there looking at it and then bent over and took a closer look. "The ball anchor was not sitting on the surface of the lake but was in fact sitting in an indentation. He looked over at Dennis. "Watch this."

Duke reached down and pushed the anchor and it rolled across the surface, but there was a clear and definite indentation as it rolled. "What's the weight this of anchor?"

"Duke, it's a standard anchor we use on all our boats. It weighs twenty-five pounds."

Duke was clearly in a state of bewilderment. "Well, Dennis, water or whatever it is can hold the weight of a twenty-five-pound anchor is denser than the water itself. This is one strange situation.

21

"Look at the tires of the trailer, they are causing an indentation as well and when I was in my shoes, they did the same thing. tells me whatever this stuff is, it is a semi-solid of some kind. Has anyone tried to take a sample of this lake yet?"

Dennis was shaking his head while watching Duke and the others. "Duke, we had not done anything sample taking as yet. Most of our time has been spent setting up the facilities before you scientists started showing up."

Duke was nodding his head in understanding. "All right let's see if we can get a sample and then do some playing around with it."

For the next hour Duke tried every way he could think of to get a sample of the lake material so he could run some tests on it, but he could not penetrate the surface. After he had finally decided he was not going to be able to get a sample, one of the crew men stepped up with a shovel and started to dig a hole along the edge of the water or whatever it was.

As he got the hole dug, he then shoveled out the remaining soil from between the hole and the edge of the lake and the lake flowed into the hole. He then shoveled more dirt back building a dike between the hole and lake and the sample separated from the lake.

They still could not penetrate it, so they took a shovel and picked the pocket of water or whatever it was up and placed in a bucket and they had their sample.

Duke turned and started walking away from

the lake and then at about fifty feet from the lake stopped and turned and looked back at the lake. He reached down and picked up a stone and threw it out into the lake and when it hit the surface it sank and plunged out of sight. He stood there watching the rock hit and then sink. His mind was spinning, that made no sense at all. There had been no splash or sound, the rock hit the surface and sank.

He stood there and then he reached down and picked up another rock and tossed it onto the lake close to where the anchor was sitting and the rock hit the surface and stayed right there. He picked up another stone and threw it as far out onto the lake as he could and it hit the surface and immediately sank.

Nothing was coming to him. He was looking at a boat and trailer sitting on the lakes surface, a pair of shoes, a twenty-five-pound anchor, and a couple of rocks all sitting on the surface which could not be moved. Then he threw two rocks out onto the lake and they sank immediately. He could not understand what he was seeing and he had no idea where to go from there.

Just then Dennis walked up beside him. "What do you think?"

Duke looked at him in frustration. "What the hell should, I think? I don't have a clue as to what is going on here and I simply cannot think of any idea as to what I should do next.

"All I know right now is I have a lake four miles in diameter sitting in a depression that came out of nowhere and did so in around twenty minutes time. In addition, it is at least five hundred feet deep

23

and what we thought was water is actually something else, what I don't know.

"But what is really chewing on me is we have six of these things running north to south almost dead center of the country. There is nothing I can think of to explain how these lakes came about, what they came about for, and what is going to happen now that they are here.

"But I can tell you this much, they are here for a reason and a purpose and this is what we need to determine. We need to know what they are made of and hopefully from that we will be able to make a determination as to the purpose or reason for their being here.

"Dennis is there any place around here where a guy can get a cup of coffee and a pair of shoes?"

Dennis smiled and directed Duke to his truck. "Yes, there is, come on we can go over to the mess tent and sit down and start to think this thing out. What size shoe do you wear? I'll have someone bring a pair over to the mess tent for you?"

Five minutes later we were sitting at a table working on a cup of hot coffee. Duke's mind was charging over the information he had developed so far, but he was making little headway in coming up with an answer. The scale of the project was massive. Six lakes totaling around seventy-five square miles of lake surface, not to mention six mountains that came with the depressions, eventually becoming the lakes.

Then consider the six manmade structures located at the bottom center of the depression lakes.

24

"What the hell is all this about, what does it mean?" Duke set his coffee down and then sat back and looked across the table at Dennis. "First things first, these are not naturally occurring events. All six lakes were intelligently made."

Dennis sat there looking at Duke. "What? You're telling me those lakes were made and were not an act of nature?"

Duke was nodding his head and looking him in the eyes. "Yes, I am Dennis. Nature simply does not produce things with the size, the shape, the depth, the substance in the depressions, and the precision of the depressions, they all speak to an intelligent origin."

That had surprised Dennis and he was having a hard time assimilating what Duke had just said. "But Duke, where or how could something like all this be done or carried out in the time frame and in the manner in which it was done? I mean, it's something that is impossible for any intelligent being to do in the time frame they developed in. On top of that, if it was intelligent, then who are they and where are they?"

Duke had made his point and now he was starting to think about the fundamentals of their problem. "I can't answer your question Dennis, but I am sure this is not an accident and I am sure it was intelligent. Beyond what I've observed and said, I'm at a standstill. In addition, I don't really understand or know why I feel this way, but something is telling me, my assessment is correct.

"Has there been any more information

25

coming in on the number of people who were lost in the lakes during their formation?"

Dennis reached over and picked up a sheet of paper and looked at it. "Well, we know there was one person in the car in Lake One. Lake Three has three people in the farm house. The other five have been located and have been moved to a motel where we can keep track of them. In Lake Four they spotted a railroad crew of four at the base of one of the main structural piers. They're near the tool shed located next to pier one on the east side.

Nothing on Lake Five as yet and Lake Six had a total of six people in the Ranger Station at the time of the incident and was confirmed when they radioed out just before the water hit.

"There's a notation here said the radio operator seemed to be calm and controlled when making the flood report.

"That's strange, you would think there would have been a level of panic involved but the notation said the person was calm and controlled."

Duke sat there a minute thinking over what Dennis had just related to him. He knew he was on the right track. How, he could not say, but he knew. He then turned to Dennis. "There will be a total of twenty-one people in all six of the lakes. Each lake will have the number of people based on which lake came first, second and so on.

The lakes started in the south with Lake One which had one occupant, and then Lake Two will have two occupants. Then Lake Three which had three occupants and so on, for a total of twenty-one people held captive at the bottom of all six lakes."

Dennis was nodding his head as Duke finished talking and he then agreed with Duke's assessment as to the number of people and the order of the lakes. "Duke, you said held captive not lost or dead, but captive. If this is true then it had to be intelligently created and not an act of nature. And if these lakes are intelligently made then what is their purpose."

Duke sat back and thought a moment and then looked at Dennis. "There has to be a reason for these lakes appearing the way they did. There must be some process or target they were created for. If nature did not make them then someone did and someone has a specific reason for these lakes.

"The problem is who are they? Where are they? And what the hell are the lakes for? I'm afraid we're just beginning to experience and see this thing develop. Dennis, I don't know how I know what is actually happening, but I know now this is not an accidental act of nature and there is purpose and a plan behind it.

"I have a bad feeling about this whole thing and I think we had better start figuring things out soon or we're going to have more surprises coming down on us than we bargained for. One thing I'm certain of, we must deal with this issue as one single issue and not six separate ones. These lakes are tied together and tied in such a way nothing will happen in one without it happening in the others as well.

"We need a complete understanding of each lake and their relationship to one another. What are the same features and what features are unique to each lake? This I'm sure of, all six lakes are basically identical but each lake will have its own uniqueness."

Puzzlement slid across Dennis's face as Duke sat there speculating on the lakes and their sameness. Duke looked at him, at the same time realizing what he had just said. Dennis finally leaned toward Duke. "Do you know and understand what you have just said. Duke, there is nothing we have discovered yet that would indicate what you have just said."

"I know, I know and I'm just as confused as you are. Dennis, there is something here, something so strange, so powerful, and so dangerous I am finding it almost impossible to understand. Yet, I keep getting these thoughts; these feeling and I don't understand where they're coming from.

"All I can tell you is I feel certain what I have related to you just now is factual and will prove to be just as I have related it."

Duke was now sure he was in over his head and what was coming was good reason for him to find some way and means of backing out of this situation. There were just too many unknowns and he did not feel he was in a position where he wanted to deal with them.

All right, that was the way he felt but was not going to be how things went. He knew he was in the pan and no one else was going to take his place. So, if this was the case then he had better get things moving and figure out some process to start to build an understanding of what was going on.

He was looking at an event had produced six new lakes and he had this feeling though they looked identical they were in fact not. What the differences were at this point he had no idea, but he now knew he had to make that determination before anything could be done to gain a better or clearer understanding as to what was going on.

He had no idea as to what his time line was. All he knew was he had to move and it had to be now. The first move would be the building of a knowledge base on the six lakes and any and all their unique issues. To do this meant he would have to go to each lake and conduct an observation of each one to try and determine what anomalies there were for each lake.

The problem was time and he knew he had limited time, but still an investment of time in a preliminary look at each lake would be needed. There was no getting around it a survey had to be done.

Chapter Two

MYSTERY OF THE LAND

How long has the North American Continent been in existence? In its current locations in relationship to the earth. We know about continental drift and the overall changes in the geology of the world over the four billion years it has been here, but, what about the last few million years and the current location of the North American plate?

Is there anything about this part of the world that would lend some sense of understanding to the events taking place over the last few days and weeks? There has to be something in all history to help them address this situation. Damn, it was more than aggravating to stand there and look at the lake and not have the slightest idea as to why it was there and what forces, natural or intelligent, brought it into existence.

As Duke sat there talking with Dennis and

realizing this was a bigger issue than he had ever thought when he first arrived, he had a thought. He needed to go and see the other five lakes and he needed to do it right now. There was a reason, even though he was not sure what it was, he knew there was a reason for him to make this trip.

Duke turned to Dennis. "Dennis, I'm going to make a run north to see the other five lakes and take a little time at each one to see if something, anything comes to me as to what it is about these lakes that seems to give me a sense of familiarity. Would you like to come along?"

Dennis had been sitting there watching Duke grappling with the issue before him and he had clearly heard Duke's invitation. He sat up and leaned toward Duke. "Duke what is it? What is getting at you on this thing? If you really feel it would serve a purpose to go to each lake then yes, I will go, but right now I don't see it."

Duke was looking directly at Dennis now knowing in order for him to gain an understanding as to what was going on, he needed to see the other lakes. "Look Dennis, I have been mulling this over in my head and it dawned on me nothing is ever identical. No matter what it is, whether man made or natural, two things which appear to be identical are not. Some place and somehow, they are different whether in plain sight or microscopic.

"What I want to know is what the differences between the six places are besides their locations and the number of people in them, there has to be something and that something will give us our answers. We know about the structures or items at the bottom center of each lake, but there is something else we need to see and understand before things begin to come together for us.

"Dennis, it's the land. It's the location on the land that is the key to what is going on here. It has to be recorded there in some manner and way we have never seen it before and need to see now.

"No, I'm positive we must look at this event from the perspective of all six lakes, not just one. Each lake has a purpose and a place in this puzzle and this is what I am going to find and figure out. Are you coming?"

Dennis stood up, looking at Duke not in a questioning manner but in a thoughtful manner. He too knew there was something tying the lakes together beside the north south line they made and their size. "I think Duke I better come along. I have a feeling we will need each other in this search of yours and I believe we will be called on in the not-too-distant future to provide some answers to the powers to be."

Meanwhile they had both got up and headed for Dennis's office where they could discuss Dennis's concerns and start to plan their trip. As they entered his office tent the two of them had determined they needed to make the trip as a team. Dennis moved around his desk and sat down as Duke sat in the chair across from him.

Duke then shifted gears and started to plan the trip. "All right then. Who is your second in command here?"

Dennis pointed up at the organization chart next to his desk to a woman's picture just below his. "That would be Betty Baxter. She's the most experienced individual we have here at the site and I totally trust her."

Duke looked over at the chart where Dennis was pointing. "Good, if you like her qualifications, then I think she will be able to run this end of the project just fine. I'm appointing her as administrator of Depression Lake One. And, you're going to be my second in command of the whole project."

Dennis reached over and picked up the phone and called Baxter and informed her of her new title. They waited the five minutes it took her to get to Dennis's office and the three of them sat down and went over their plan to make a trip to the other five lakes.

Duke wanted Betty to be fully aware of the situation at hand and to keep in close contact with both him and Dennis. Over the course of the next two hours the trio had laid out the plan of operation and Betty had been fully briefed as to her position and areas of responsibility.

By the time they were done Duke was clearly pleased with the skills and commitment Betty had demonstrated during their planning phase. It was approaching lunch time and so the three of them decided to continue their discussion over lunch and after lunch Duke and Dennis would head out on their inspection trip of the other lakes.

Duke's helicopter was sitting on the landing pad up on the ridge of the lake. They had Betty drive them up to the landing pad and the two of them took their bags to the helicopter and had them loaded on board. Duke then remembered he wanted to take a few shots of the lake for use when they got to the other locations.

Duke walked over to the helicopter and pulled his camera bag out, then returned to the edge of the lake and started taking photos of Depression Lake One. He started with wide angle shots of the full lake and the surrounding country. Then shots from the rim looking in at the water and then shots looking out at the sloping sides of the rim.

He then moved on to close ups of the water and the anchor and wheels on the surface of the water and the indentations they made, then the rock making up the landscape forming the rim around the lake. With each photo Dennis made a log entry describing the direction of the photo in relationship to the compass and the camera setting for each photo.

At this point the only oddity they had witnessed was the issue with the water. was one yet to be explained and may never be. Hopefully they would eventually come up with an answer that would bring everything into focus and explain what was going on.

Duke was standing by the chopper looking back at the lake. He had an odd feeling thing were just starting and this thing wasn't static but was active and preparing to become even more active.

He was having a hard time dealing with his feelings, not the normal everyday feelings one has

34

when starting out on something new. These were a feeling of forebodence. A feeling there was more, much more and what it was he had no idea. He didn't know if we would be up to what was coming.

By the time they had finished taking the photos and Duke going through his mental process; it was just before four in the afternoon. He looked at his watch and considered the time to make the run to the next lake and the fact there would be little day light by then, and decided not to start their trip until the next morning. They returned to the truck and moved on down to the base camp and settled in for the night.

The fortunes of war, and for that matter, other endeavor's come at unpredictable times and this was one of them. The fact they decided to wait one more day would bring the issues they were grappling with into clear focus. It would reinforce the purpose of visiting the other five lakes and also define their target.

The evening was spent going over what it was they were really wanting to see or find as they toured the other five lakes. There is one thing about speculation, it helps one hone his purpose and all the confusion and false ideas can be seen and analyzed and if need be set aside. It sharpens the target and focuses their purpose.

At about nine o'clock that evening they walked over to the mess tent and sat down for a late meal before calling it a day. As they sat there, Duke started to go over the totality of the events leading up to this point. "As the records showed, the quake produced these lakes thirteen days ago and lasted for around twenty to twenty-three minutes. In time six depressions came into existence in varied locations running north and south across the whole country.

We actually have a few witnesses stated they saw the various structures moving along on what they described were conveyor belts of ground to the points where they came to rest, which turned out to be dead center of each depression.

"Shortly after the quake ended, water started to flow into the depressions and it took around ninety-two hours for them to fill and come to a depth of five hundred feet and then part two would start. Everyone in those structures and the one car died in those places and are still there to this day. Right now, it is estimated around twenty-one people died."

"Duke paused at this point. There was something wrong with what he had just said and he needed to go over it in his mind. "Wait, I said twenty-one people had died. Yet, earlier today I was saying those people were being held there in those locations at the bottom of the six lakes and there would be twenty-one of them.

"I don't know why but I don't think they are dead. No, those people are being held. How I have no idea, but they are not dead I'm sure of that." He sat there puzzling over what he had just said. "I can't explain why I feel this way I just do. This is part of the overall issue, there are things I feel, and I know this is one of them.

"I was assigned the duty to analyze Depression Lake One and the overall administration of the research of all six lakes to try to determine how and why they formed. I quickly determined it was going to be much harder than simply coming to the scene. Dennis, does that describe the situation fairly well?"

Dennis looked up and nodded his head. "Up to now it does quite well. You left a lot of the details out, but those are recorded and we can compare the other lakes against those data when we get there.

"However, I do have one concern and that is your feelings about whether those people are dead or not. Duke, I have been watching you and I have to tell you I have seen a change coming over you in the few hours since we met till now and it concerns me.

"Now my concern is not one of distrust or anything like that, I just want you to know whatever is going on here has and is impacting you. I also must say it is not a negative impact but one which has understanding to it, for now that's all I have to say."

Duke was satisfied with their progress and had finally reached a point where his mind was comfortable with the prospects of making this trip. When he first proposed the trip, he was thinking more in the line of just seeing for himself, but now it was much more. There was a link here and he knew what he did at one lake he needed to do at the other five. Everything needed to be tied together step by step.

The next morning, they boarded the helicopter for the two hundred twenty-six miles jump to Depression Lake Two. As they lifted off and came up over the rim of the lake, they were surprised to see the boat was floating out on the lake and the trailer had sunk at the launch point. Duke told the pilot to land.

As they exited the helicopter Duke walked over to the water's edge and looked down and saw his boots sitting on the bottom. He picked up a rock and dropped it into the water and it splashed and sank to the bottom. The two of them looked at one another and then Duke stepped into the water and reached down and picked up his boots. It was water, just plain old simple water. So, what was the stuff yesterday that would not let anything sink into it?

Duke had a thought. "Dennis, what was the air temperature yesterday when we tried to launch the boat?"

At first Dennis had not heard him. He was concentrating on the lake and how it had changed. He then realized Duke had asked a question. "It had been warm around here all week and was around ninety degree at that time."

"All right, what is the air temperature right now?"

Dennis pulled his cell phone out. "Well, it's seven o'clock in the morning and it's around forty to forty-five degree."

Duke was clearly seeing something the others had not yet tied into. With his plans changed. "I think I want to hang around here today and see what happens around one or two this afternoon. If I'm right we are going to see an interesting happening around that time. We'll plan our trip north for tomorrow."

Dennis was nodding and turned and signaled the helicopter pilot to stand down. "All right Duke, I'll send the helicopter back to the base and we can stay here and start taking samples and making notations."

Duke reached out and touched Dennis's arm. "Oh, and Dennis, have the helicopter pilot send a couple of lab techs up here. I think we are going to need them as this thing develops. Make sure they bring their full sampling kit with them as well."

About half an hour later the team arrived and Duke met them at the back of their truck. "People, I need a complete collection procedure for this whole area. I want rock and dirt samples taken on the dry ground in the area of the boat launch.

Then I want samples collected from the lake bottom along with samples of the water and make sure you get samples from multiple areas, like the edge of the water then six feet out and then six more out from four or five sample areas. Do it now while you still have the opportunity.

"After the initial samples are taken, I want samples collected every hour until you can't collect anymore."

Dennis heard what Duke had just said. "What do you mean 'Until you can't collect any more'?"

Duke looked at Dennis. "That's what I said. When you get to the point where you cannot collect any samples or when it starts to get difficult to collect them, I want you to call me immediately. Got that?"

"Yes Sir, Mr. Ridgeman, we understand."

Duke took Dennis and they started to walk to the east around the rim of the lake. They walked maybe three hundred yards and stopped. Duke walked over to the edge of the water and tapped the surface of the water with his foot. It was still fluid and acted like water.

Dennis was still somewhat confused by Duke's actions. "What are you looking for Duke?"

Duke was in a deep state of concentration and then turned to Dennis. "Dennis, I got to thinking about the condition of the water yesterday and then seeing what it did this morning. I think, if I'm right, the water is temperature sensitive and as the air temperature increases, the density of the water will increase along with it, ultimately reaching the same level it was yesterday when we first experienced it."

That hit Dennis from a direction he had not anticipated. "Duke this can't be, as water increases in temperature it becomes less dense and actually expands before boiling and then going into a gas state."

Duke was nodding his head in agreement with Dennis's statement. "I agree with what you're saying Dennis, but this stuff is not doing what is normal and we need to know if it does the same thing today. If it does then we have one hell of a mystery on our hands and our coming visits to the other five lakes will have considerable meaning."

Dennis was beginning to understand where Duke was coming from. "Right, I understand what you're getting at. So, we stand by until we see if it repeats today or not. Then we head out tomorrow and see if the other lakes do the same thing."

Duke could see Dennis was starting to get it, but there was more. "Yes and no Dennis, if it does what I think it is going to do then we check the other lakes for the same thing or some other anomaly unique to each individual lake. I have a feeling the other lakes will not act the same as this lake and if this is true then all rules are off. We will have our hands full trying to scull this thing out."

By noon the tech people were starting to notice a change in the lake water. It was getting thicker as the temperature went up, which was exactly what Duke had felt would happen. The question remained was just how thick it would get as the temperature rose. The forecast for temperatures that afternoon was around ninety-six degrees, so they would simply wait and see.

By five o'clock the water was almost a solid and the temperature was ninety-nine degrees. When they looked at the samples taken, they too were almost solid. Duke then turned to the tech. "I need you to take the first sample you took and place it in a heater and bring the temp up on it until the water is a complete solid, like hard as ice."

An hour later they checked in with the tech and she was just taking a look at the sample in the heater. The heater had been run up to a hundred twenty-five degrees and the sample left there for five minutes. When she pulled it out the water was crystal clear and hard as rock and there was no heat or cool feel to it. When she set it down on the counter and left it, as it cooled down from the hundred twenty-five-degree level it remained hard until after it dropped below 100 degrees and then it started to soften up.

By the time the water temperature reached fifty degrees it was liquid again. So, we knew below fifty it was liquid and above one hundred it was solid. In between it ran the transition from liquid to solid as the temperature rose and the reverse was true. In the last three days we had learned the water of Lake One was not normal. The fact was it was unlike any water anywhere they could imagine. What it had to do with the lakes being there and what their purpose was, remained to be determined. All Duke knew was things were just starting to get interesting.

Those feelings had been working through his mind while there at Lake One and were still working on him. What he didn't know was as he moved north, they would become more intense and more informative. Duke didn't know it, but he had become the central conduit for information in a bizarre and terrifying adventure.

They had discovered the anomaly for Depression Lake One, now to Lake Two.

Chapter Three

THE OTHER SIDE COMETH

"Hello General, is this line secure and are you available to talk?"

"Yeah Mike, this line is secure and I've been waiting for you to call. Things have been moving fast around here and I think we're a little behind the game right now."

"General, I know, but this is an event that doesn't happen every day. Is there any information as to how these mountains came to be and who is in charge?"

"Right now, they have Duke Ridgeman in charge of the actual scientific response to the region. They're calling it the Six Lakes Project."

"What can you tell me about this Ridgeman?"

"Mike, he's probably the best the government has for this kind of an event. He's a scientist and he will concentrate on the Six Lakes. He has no background in military experience and his authority is limited to the project and nothing else.

"I would say we have plenty of time to set things up and prepare for a takeover. I would suggest we hold back and not move too soon. Let him carry out the majority of the research and discovery actions before we move on anything.

"The fact is Mike, there's nothing there for us to take over. My best advisors feel the Six Lakes are not natural and that some force has produced them, but we have no information as to what the force is or who is responsible for them."

"Do you have anyone on the scene?"

"That is affirmative. We have a man at Lake Five. We were fortunate to get him assigned as the lead scientist on that Lake and he is keeping my staff informed on a daily basis.

"Right now, he is waiting for a visit from Ridgeman and his second, a Dennis Adams. Once he is able to sit down with them, he should be able to glean something from them that will get us on the right track as to what is coming."

"Then you're on top of this thing?"

"That we are Mike. I'll keep you informed as to what is happening. Right now, it's a waiting game and we need to be patient and let things take their normal operational steps."

"Do you have anyone else in that area?"

"We have one security officer at Lake One who is monitoring Ridgeman and any activity taking place there and throughout the project. I don't want to touch that operative and run the risk of his being discovered. He'll be ready to act whenever I notify him.

"All right General, but I want you to understand my group will not tolerate any screw ups. This is our best opportunity to make the move of a lifetime and we're not going to permit dumb moves or actions by anyone.

"Oh-by-the-way we have set up a number of strike teams on this side of the lakes to be ready to move when you decide to make your move in Washington. Right now, we don't have a target, but we're preparing for something.

"Things like this just don't happen and that means there is something behind this and we plan on being at the head of the list in taking control of this project when the major discovery does come through."

"Mike, don't jump to conclusions about this thing. Right now, our best information tells us this is just getting started. It is our belief once Ridgeman finishes his tour of the Six Lakes Project; we will have a better understanding as to what is happening.

"Everyone here and over there on the west side has put a lot of capital and effort into this thing and we're on the verge of reaching the goals we have been working on for years. If the Six Lake Project will help us in reaching that goal then we will use it.

"My main forces are coordinating their actions at this time. We have Stryker Units moving under the guise they are carrying out special training activities. Once in place they will be in the best possible positions to move in and take control of their assigned target areas.

"Fort Lewis is ready and they have set this up for a quick and direct intervention when and if the order is given. We have the President isolated at this time while he deals with the Six Lakes issue and that will give us here in DC the ability to move quickly and directly when the move order is given."

"All right General, I think we have it covered. We appreciate your efforts and feel we have the right man in the right place to carry out this project. My associates and I are pleased with your work and I can assure you our support for you and your position is solid.

"Please get back to me when this Ridgeman has finished his tour and we can see where we are and what our next move should be."

"Will do Mike. Oh, by the way, I want to clear one area up right now. If and when we move, I want to be sure your strike teams are aware of the fact my Stryker Units are authorized to carry out their actions, and any other groups assisting fall under their direct control. Is that clear?"

"Absolutely general, there is no place for showboating. You're plans are developed and we'd be stupid to try to do anything outside of your plan. General, we want success as much as you do. I can assure you everyone knows their place and if anyone steps outside their level of authority you have our permission to deal with them."

"Thank you, Mike, that helps a lot. I'll get back with you once Ridgeman finishes his tour."

"Thank you General, we'll talk later."

The General turned to his aide and nodded his head. There was a smile forming on his face. He had just ensured when he moved he would have the ability to deal with the cartel group head on and quickly.

Right now, they were important to him, but once the move has been made, they will be useless to his overall plan and that means they can be eliminated. Why would he want to have a drug cartel backing him once he has control of the country? They would expect favors from him all the time and if they think he would permit the making of a new nation for them on the west coast of this country they have another thing coming.

No, when the time comes, he will control the west coast and this cartel will be completely destroyed to the last man. He is doing this because this nation lacks a decent level of leadership. It is floundering in the political back waters of greed and corruption and he feels it is his place to bring that to an end.

In time he will reinstitute the constitution and place the government of this nation back into the control of the people, but only after he has eliminated the corruption and political bigotry that exist there now. A lot of politicians are going to die in this house cleaning and that includes the President, the Vice President, all of congress and in particularly the political parties who are trying to control congress and run this nation.

He raised his hand to get the aides attention. "I need you to send a notification to General Smith at Fort Lewis and advise him of our current state of affairs. Be sure to include the information on this last phone call with Mike. Have him initiate "Score Board" immediately."

As Mike Sandburg hung up the phone after his talk with General Halverson he sat back and placed his hands on the back of his neck. He looked over at his second. "I don't think I like this General Halverson. He seems to be a little too sure of himself and a little overbearing. Know what I mean?"

His second was walking back and forth across the room in front of Sandburg's desk. "Mike, I don't trust him as far as I could throw this building. There is something really out of place with that guy. I think he is planning something for us we don't want to be any part of."

"You're probably right, but right now we need to play along with him. I need you to contact our people at Fort Lewis and see if they can come up with any information as to what their Stryker Units are going to be doing and where they are going.

"Also, I need to get our people at the Six Lakes Project to start to collect all the information they can on what is going on and who is doing what.

"Some time in the near future we are going to have our hands full dealing with the General and gaining control over the project as well.

"Our friends to the south expect us to be successful and if we're not, you know damn well what that means for you and me. They don't take favorably to failure and especially when there is a lot of money involved."

"Mike, I think we're jumping the gun. We really don't know what the Six Lakes thing is all about. It may be just what it appears to be and that is six lakes forming at the same time and nothing more. If there is anything else behind it, there is no way of us knowing at this time. I suggest we sit back and wait. Right now, patience will be a virtue."

Mike stood up and walked around the desk and over to where his second was standing. "Steve, I trust you and value your council. Right now, I think you're right and I also think we need to do some homework in the event, something more involved is going on here.

"I want you to go to work on what the General may be thinking and planning for us. I still don't trust him and I would bet we, you and I and the cartel, are going to be pushed out of this thing in the end. We need something that will give us a chance of taking control of things in this region, this part of the country."

"All right Mike, I'll get on that. But I need to caution you we cannot under estimate the General or any of the others on this side of the country. Everyone is for themselves and they will do just about anything to maintain their positions. This could get ugly."

"Steve, I know that but I think we're on the leading edge of this and if it goes the way I hope, we'll have the upper hand when all is said and done.

Chapter Four

DEPRESSION LAKE TWO

The following morning Duke and Dennis boarded the helicopter and headed out for Depression Lake Two. They were looking for a single anomaly that would be unique to each lake and that lake alone.

With Lake One it had been the density of the water and so Duke considered the fact any anomaly would again have to do with the water. Just what he should expect he did not know. Water could appear in many forms and so far, he had a liquid that changed in density as it heated up, in this lake it could or would be something else.

As they came in on the landing pad at Lake Two, he could see they had a team in a boat out on the lake working over the hunting cabin sitting on the bottom of the lake, five hundred feet down. It appears they had a video camera in the water and were trying to determine if anyone was in fact in the structure.

They could also see teams working around the lake taking soil and water samples. Like Lake One they had a main assembly area at the foot of the slope and a staging area on the rim by the lake.

As the helicopter came in to land, they could see a vehicle coming out to the landing pad to pick them up. When they got out of the helicopter the driver of the vehicle was out and standing by the front left fender waiting.

As Duke and Dennis approached, she stepped forward and introduced herself as Mary Bigalou, the lead scientist for Depression Lake Two. They spent a few minutes talking and hearing a short briefing from Mary as to how the research was progressing.

They got into the truck and headed to the main base and a more in-depth briefing on the progress there at base Two. As they drove the half mile to the base Duke was busy looking over the terrain and trying to get a good mental picture of this lake and its surrounding geology.

Clearly as they flew into the area, they could see the lake itself was an exact duplicate of Lake One. From the ground it was the exact same as well. They went to the main tent and Mary went over their current situation.

When asked about any outstanding anomalies she sat there for a moment. "So far Duke, we have not seen anything you could call an anomaly. We have spent most of our time collecting samples and running surveys of the depression itself."

Duke then asked about the water. "Mary, as the temperature increased during the course of the day have you noticed any unusual action or reactions of the water itself?"

She thought about the question for a few seconds and then shaking her head. "No, the water has remained the same from morning to sunset. We noticed no unusual reactions to the temperature at any time."

"When do you go up to the lake each day?"

She again thought for a few seconds. "Duke, we usually go up around eight in the morning and start down about an hour before sunset."

"I noticed you had a boat out on the water. Did you have any problems launching your boat?"

"No not at all. Frankly our time here has been rather uneventful."

By the look on Duke's face, you could see he was getting a little frustrated by there not being any noted anomalies with the lake or the water. He knew in his mind there had to be something, but so far he was drawing a blank and it was clearly frustrating him.

"Mary, you noted no change in the density of the water as the air temperature increased?"

"No, none at all, its density has remained stable and has shown no changes."

Duke sat there shaking his head. "That doesn't fit with what we think is taking place at all six Depression Lakes. Down at Lake One the water density changes as the air temperature goes up. It actually reaches a solid when the air temperature

53

gets to a hundred degrees or higher."

Mary was listening closely to what Duke was saying. "That sounds nuts. How could that happen anyway?"

He was looking at Mary. "That's the question we are addressing, Mary. There is no reason or rational behind why it would do that, but I can assure you is does

"So, we decided to take a trip to the other five lakes and see if we can find any similar or different anomalies that involve each individual lake."

Duke then turned to Dennis. "Dennis, do you have anything to add at this time?"

"Duke, I think you've covered it all. The only thing I can say is we were totally caught off guard when we discovered what was happening to the water. But there is another issue and it is the placement of those six man made items in the center bottom of each lake.

"We don't have the slightest idea as to why, and when we look close at the land around each item and then trace the location of those items we could tell, each item has moved to their current location. Why that and who or what did it?"

Both Duke and Dennis sat there watching Mary react to the question. She sat there shaking her head. "Yeah, we wondered about that as well. It just doesn't make sense those items, when you consider their size, could or would be moved as they were.

"Right now, we are taking a close look at the Hunting Cabin to try and determine how and why it is where it is. We know this much, it was moved, but it was not picked up and moved. We are sure, it appears the land around it literally moved into its current position."

"Like a conveyor belt?"

She looked at Duke. "Yes, I guess you could say it that way, like a conveyor belt?"

"Mary, are you not sure of this observation?"

"Duke, I don't disagree with your observation of the movement of the land to its current location, what I find difficult is how the process was initiated and worked. If the land moved that way then it means a huge mass or volume of land was moved as well.

"What happened to the land moved out of the way and where did the land come from that came in behind as the cabin moved. We can see the clear break in the land where it separated as the cabin was being moved. The interesting thing is we can trace the movement all the way north to the rim of the lake and all the way south to the rim of the lake. It's clear there was land movement and it was a uniform width and it ran from rim to rim.

"Next, when you look on the outside of the rim, there is no indication of land movement at all so this tells me the conveyor ran between the north and south rim and must have stopped at the edge of the rim or under the depression of the range. That is the puzzle for me. How the hell did the land conveyor work?"

She had just finished when a thought hit Duke. "Dennis, how far from I-10 did the car move before coming to its current location?"

Dennis sat there looking at Duke and Mary when a shocked look crossed his face. He looked back and forth between the two of them. "Duke I-10 is seven miles north of the lake."

They all three fell quiet. Duke looked at Mary. "How far did the hunting cabin move from its original location?"

"Duke, I'm not sure. We hadn't thought of that until just now when you asked."

She picked the phone up and made a call and after several minutes conversation she hung up. The look on her face told Duke something different was about to happen.

"Duke, my next in charge just advised they had done a survey and had determined the hunting cabin had been located thirteen miles north of the lake before it was moved."

"All right now we have a car sitting on a section of I-10 and this car and section of road moved nine miles south, we also have a hunting cabin moving thirteen miles and, in both cases, we can see the conveyor effect in the bottom of the lake, but no effect outside the mountain either north or south. That's not possible."

Again, they found themselves sitting there looking at each other when Duke finally stood up. "All right this is what I want done. Dennis, I want you to contact Lake One and get a survey team on the south and north sides of the mountain and try to locate any signs of actual ground movement in those areas. You know what we're looking for.

"Mary, I want you to set the same process up here for Lake Two. Make sure those people do a complete and detailed survey of those areas. If there was land movement there must be some marker or some indication it actually took place.

"I'll contact the other four lakes and get them moving on the same survey of their lakes. If all goes well, we'll have the results of those surveys done at the same time and we'll be able to compare them against one another. There is just no way some indication of land movement is not there. So, find it."

By the time they had finished their discussion it was approaching noon. All the lake surveys were underway and all they could do now was sit and wait.

They walked over to the mess tent and sat down with others of Mary's team and had lunch and generally talked about their activities around the lake so far. All they had were a lot of questions and little or no answers.

After lunch the three of them got in Mary's truck and drove up to the lake to have a look around. As they came over the rim of the lake Duke thought he saw something odd. "Mary do you have any lights aimed out on the lake or under the lake surface?"

Mary seemed a little concerned by the question. "No, we don't use any lights up here. All our activity has been carried out during the day light and we pull out before it gets dark. That is basically a safety issue. No, we have no lights up here. Why do you ask?"

Duke felt he had seen something and light was a part of what he had seen. "Well, as we came up over the rim and I got my first look at the lake, it appeared to have light generating off of its surface. I don't see it now but it sure looked that way."

Mary reacted as if she was relieved someone else had observed something and it was bothering her as well. "Could it have been the sun? I've noticed some odd reflections of the sun as it moves across the sky. As we stand here looking at the lake it is still as a table top and it has been no other way. It's almost like, a mirror and I thought it was the physical makeup of the lake causing the oddities we were seeing."

As they stood there, Duke saw the boat coming back into the launch area. The oddity was, there was no wake behind the boat, but even odder was the light reflection on the underside of the boats bow as it moved through the water. As the team brought the boat to the landing it did not cause the slightest splash or movement of the water. It just slipped through the water and the water parted and slid in behind as the boat passed.

Duke's mind was racing; he was wondering if the others had seen the same thing he was seeing. How the hell can this be, there was something definitely going on here and they needed to concentrate on making the determination as to what it was? By the time they finished their overview of the lake and the progress of their research it was time to return to the base.

Duke stood there looking out across the lake and then turned to Dennis and Mary. "I'm going to stay up here until after the sun sets. There is something going on here and I need to see it from a different perspective."

Dennis decided he would stay with Duke and Mary advised that she had a number of things that needed to be done and she would come back up an hour after sunset and pick them up. She left a couple of chairs and a radio for them along with several drinks and drove off.

Two hours later the last of the research teams had gathered and headed down the rim to the base camp. Duke watched the sun setting down behind the Rockies to the west and as the darkness rolled across the land he turned to look out across the lake.

As he turned, he noted Dennis was standing and staring out at the lake, and as his attention shifted to the lake he stopped moving as well. The lake was lit up like there was a light under the surface shining up.

The light was a soft blue color and seemed to be coming off of the surface of the water. He walked over to the edge of the water and looked down into the water and noted it was luminous all the way to the bottom. He could see the bottom as clear as if it were daylight. The whole of the lake from the bottom to the surface was luminous.

All they could do was stand there and look. It was possibly one of the most beautiful things Duke had ever seen. The light seemed to come out of the water and form a bubble over the lake itself. Duke had to touch it and when he did it felt just like, well, water.

Duke walked over to the chairs and called down to the base camp for Mary and advised her she needed to see this and to also bring a sampling kit up with her.

A few minutes later she pulled into the parking area and stopped by the chairs and sat there in the truck looking out across the lake. After a few seconds she got out of the truck and walked over to Duke and Dennis and stood there. "That is the most beautiful thing I have ever seen."

They all three stood there, it was the a life experience kind of an event. They were not prepared for what they were seeing. Mary then took the sampling kit and opened it and pulled the tubes out and started taking samples. She took a total of six tubes of water and did two samples that were taken at a depth of fifteen feet. As each tube was placed in the kit you could see the blue glow coming from them.

During this time a number of others from the base camp had ventured up to the rim to see what was going on. Several had brought video cameras with them and were in the process of recording what they were all seeing.

As Duke stood there, he realized he had missed something at Lake One in regards to what the water there was doing. This lake created such a wondrous exhibition it caused him to relate back to the other lake and the appearance of the water there. "Dennis, back at Lake One did you have any feeling

60

of grandeur or beauty in regards to the water there?"

Dennis looked over at Duke, "You mean like I'm feeling right now?"

"Yes, did that lake water have a sense of wonder to it like this one does?"

Dennis's mind was going full speed at this time trying to remember anything even so much as touching what Duke was asking about. "I hadn't thought of that, but yes it did. As the water became denser it appeared more and more translucent, I mean it had almost a pearl tone to it. Yes, in a word it was beautiful."

Duke was nodding his head by now. "Yeah, it was in fact beautiful. I was still in shock by the way it was changing and let that feature slip right over my head. This water is more dramatic but the other had a subtle and mystifying element feature to it."

Duke looked at Mary. "I think we will head out for Depression Lake Three in the morning. I need to move on and take a look at the other lakes before getting tied down to one."

Mary turned to Duke, having to work to avert her eyes from the lake. "All right, I'll notify the pilot and they should be here and ready to move on by nine or ten.

"Thanks Mary, we'll stop by on the way back and let you know what we found."

They retreated back to the base camp and went to the mess tent and found a table, sat down and started to brain storm what they had just seen. It was only nine o'clock by then and no one was even close to being tired. Everyone was too excited by what they had seen.

Duke was looking at everyone and he noted the physical mood of everyone in the tent who had been up by the lake was the same. They were all excited and happy. There was a sense of joy in their voices and actions, strange.

Was he noticing an actual physical reaction to the waters of this lake among the people working here? That started to bring up a whole new realm of questions and thoughts racing through his mind. So far, his experiences with Lakes One and Two were bringing up far more questions than answers.

He then reached across the table and touched Dennis's hand. He didn't move, he was busy watching the actions of the others and obviously enjoying what he was seeing; he never felt or noticed Duke touching his hand.

Mary had seen Duke's action and then watched Dennis as well. She then leaned toward Duke. "You're concerned by the reactions of our people who have been working around and on the lake?"

He looked at her. "Yeah, I am. They seem to be in a state of euphoria and that's all right with me. The question is will there be any residual effects from this reaction once they come down off of it?"

Mary knew what he was talking about. She had had the same feelings after her observation of her people. "Duke, I have been watching these people for three days and each day it has been the same. In the morning when they finish breakfast and head out for their job assignments, they are happy and eager to get to work. That is the way they have been since the day we came here.

"However, in the days since they have been working around the lake water, at the end of the day they are euphoric, just as you see them now. So far, I have not noted any side effects that have concerned me, but I have noted the effect as they have come in off the water or from around it.

"Right now, I don't know if I should leave things well enough alone or start carrying out physical tests and examinations of those people to ensure there's nothing abnormally dangerous taking place."

"Mary, I would suggest you carry out some examinations on those who have been around the water the most. Don't make a big thing out of it, just include it as part of the research and leave it at that.

"If you actually do come up with any adverse results then you will take the appropriate steps at the time, but until then I would not worry too much about it. I have been on the water and in it and so far, I have felt nothing that would alarm or concern me. Don't get excited until there is something to get excited about."

She sat there watching the others and then looked at Duke. "Understood, I'll let them have their time. Besides, it's good for morale overall.

"Duke, what's next? What do you think is coming? I know you've been having those feelings because I've been having them as well. There is something coming and we are currently just in the beginning of this thing that is taking place. What do you think?"

"Mary, that too is something we can't let become a major issue for us. Yes, I have those feelings and their increasing day to day. What is coming, I have not the slightest idea. All I know is, it's coming. It's relentless and there is nothing you or I or anyone else can do about it.

"My suggestion to you is to keep focused on your job and when things start to jell, I'll let you know. I'm not going to let anyone go uninformed as to what is taking place. So do your job and we'll keep tying the pieces together and try to make some sense out of them.

Chapter Five

DEPRESSION LAKE THREE

The following morning, we left Lake Two and headed north to Lake Three. At two hundred twenty-six miles it was just a short hop like the one from Lake One to Lake Two. The pilot picked us up at nine o'clock that morning and we were coming into the base camp at Depression Lake Three by eleven-fifteen.

Again, as we came into the area of Lake Three, we had the pilot make a run over the lake. As we flew across the lake, we moved on down to just a couple of hundred feet over the lake. As I looked down on the surface, I could see another boat out on the lake and sure enough there was the Farm House on the bottom directly in the center of the lake.

We had turned and headed back toward the base camp when it dawned on Duke there was something odd about the surface of the water.

65

"Dennis do you see anything odd about the surface of the lake?"

Dennis leaned over to the window and took a long look at the surface. "Yeah, there is something odd about it. Right now, I can't put my finger on it, but there is something. What the hell is it?"

Duke was nodding his head in agreement. "That's how I feel about it. I know there is something going on there, but right now I can't figure it out. I want to get up there as soon as we can after we land."

They were met by the head of the research team assigned to the lake and Duke asked they be taken directly up to the lake. The team leader agreed and they headed that way. As they drove on Duke asked. "What is your name?"

"Dave Ledbetter, I've been here from day one and I have fifteen people working under me."

"Dave, have you noted any strange anomalies about this lake, in particular in regards to the water?"

Dave was nodding his head. "That we have Duke. At first it was most difficult to come up with a good description as to what we were seeing. We finally settled on the term Vibration, because that is what the water is doing, it's vibrating."

"What do you mean by vibrating?"

"Duke, it's just that. You will see when we get there as you walk up to edge of the lake you will feel it in the ground. When you take a close look at the water you will see fine ripples in the water, so fine you have to get down close to really make them out.

"The really interesting thing is as you begin to feel the vibration you want to feel it more and people tend to want to stay by the water even if it takes them away from their duties. After maybe ten minutes by the water, you feel as if you've had the finest massage in the world. It's just the strangest thing I've ever felt."

They finally reached the rim and lakes edge. As they looked out across the lake, they could see the surface of the water looked like it was covered with a fine texture. Duke got out of the truck and walked toward the lake and as he approached the water's edge, he felt the vibration coming up through his feet.

Immediately he felt a sense of comfort moving through his body and a feeling of security and strength. It was the strangest feeling he had ever had. Duke stood at the water's edge looking down into the lake. There was something more to this than the presence of the vibration and he needed to figure it out.

What he knew was Lake Three had a beauty to it as well and it was in the vibration. Standing at the edge of the water his attention was drawn down to the water and into it. Just like the other two lakes it was clear as crystal and you could see all the way to the bottom. Except there was a difference and it was the texture of the water, the texture caused by the vibration of the water itself.

Duke turned to Dave. "Have there been any physical or psychological effects on any of your crew members?"

Dave stood there looking at the water. "As of right now there have been some adverse effects. By that I mean when you're working on the lake you have this good euphoric feeling and it results in anyone working on or by the lake wanting to stay put and feel the vibration even at the detriment to their work.

"We've managed to overcome the issue by limiting the amount of time anyone can spend on or by the lake. At first no one liked the limitations but as we learned more about the water and our reaction to it, people began to understand. As of right now this process seems to be doing the trick.

"You're telling me everyone seems to be working at their normal levels once you initiated the limitation and you could see no adverse effects on anyone once the limitation results were seen?"

"Yes, just as I said, there are no recognizable impacts on anyone's performance because of the vibration once the limitations were put into effect. We are monitoring everyone continuously to make sure nothing slips by us."

Duke was nodding his head in understanding. "Great. Now, can you tell me if the vibration is in effect all the way to the bottom of the lake and everywhere else?"

Dave had expected that question. "Yes, it is. We have found no spot on the lake where there is an absence of the vibration. In addition, the frequency of the vibration is uniform to the fourth decimal point. Everywhere we have checked it and that is probably ninety-nine percent of the lake."

"Have you noticed any impact on the shore or rim of the lake?"

Dave knew this would be a concern for Duke as well. "You know, when we first discovered the vibration this was the first concern we had, could it, being about the failure of the lake rim. We have covered the entirety of the rim both on the water side and on the open side and the lake rim shows no adverse impact at all. The rim is firm and water tight."

Dennis reached down and touched the water and when he did, he felt the vibration engulf his body. At first, he withdrew his hand and then he put it back into the water. He looked up at Duke. "You have got to feel this. I can't explain it to you but it is the most strange and wonderful feeling I have ever experienced. You have to check this out."

Duke reached down and touched the water and felt himself relaxing. It was as Dennis had said the strangest feeling yet and he wanted more of it. He withdrew his hand and stood back up. "Is this the same response you get from everyone who touches the water?"

Dave reached down and touched the water and remained there for several seconds. "Yes, it's the same response everyone who has so far. They seem to be able to pull back and walk away without any difficulty, but they do report it felt so good they wanted to stay there with their hand in the water. A few said they wanted to undress and get in the water completely. Those we have removed from the area of the water for safety sake."

That response touched Duke. "Dave, has anyone gone in the water all the way?"

"Yes and no, we have had divers down to the Farm house in special diving equipment and they report no special effects from the water." Dave was looking into the water and stroking his hand back and forth in it. "Those people are completely covered with diving suits so there is no direct contact with the water on their skin."

Duke was watching him as he stroked the water and noted how relaxed he was becoming. "Have you considered letting someone enter the water without any covering?"

Dave turned and looked up at Duke but kept his hand in the water and continued to stroke it. "No, we have not as yet. It has been considered, but so far we have not come up with anyone we feel could handle any impacts that may hit them once they enter the water."

Duke continued to press the question. "Have you considered a retrieval line attached to the person as they enter the water, one they can't remove easily without assistance?" Duke had dropped down on one knee next to Dave as he asked the question and then reached down and pulled Dave's hand from the water.

Dave looked down at Duke's hand and then pulled his hand away and stood up while still looking down into the water. "No, we have not, but I would be willing to do it myself if you think it is important."

Duke stood there looking into the lake and

then turned to Dennis. "What do you think about that?"

Dennis was shaking his head. "Duke I don't want to jeopardize someone's safety, but if it could be done it may be vital to our understanding of this whole thing."

Duke turned to Dave. "Look, if you're willing, I would be willing to do it with you, what do you think?"

Dave smiled and looked at both Duke and Dennis. "Let's do it. It needs to be done sooner or later and I'm more than willing to try it."

Duke was still watching Dave and his reaction to the idea of them entering the water. It hit Duke that Dave was still excited about having his hand in the water and the thought crossed his mind this may not be a smart move having Dave enter the water, but he wanted to see Dave's reaction to a full immersion into the lake water.

They returned to the base camp and brought all the personnel together for a discussion of their plans. To a person everyone agreed it would be something that would help in the overall understanding of what we are facing.

So, the plans were made to run the test that afternoon. Both men were prepared for the test. It actually was rather simple, they would go back to the lake, remove their clothes, have the recovery harnesses fit onto them and then they would walk into the water and lay down in it. A simple plan if there were no major hazards waiting for them in the water itself.

Duke walked over to Dennis and took hold of his left elbow and gently pulled him aside. "Dennis, I want you to watch Dave closely and have several people on his rope and ready to move. If I signal you to pull him out, I want him out in seconds. Don't be gentle with him just get him out of the water. Understand?"

"All right Duke, I can do that. Did you see something I missed?" Dennis was looking around to see if anyone had moved in close enough to hear their conversation.

Duke waited a few seconds making sure he got his idea organized. "Dennis, I was watching Dave as he was by the water with his hand in the lake and he was acting rather odd. No matter what he was doing he kept his hand in the water and kept stroking it through the water nonstop. It was as if he could not control himself."

Dennis looked at Duke. "I hadn't seen that, I guess my attention was on something else. Do you think it's a real problem?"

Duke was shaking his head. "I don't know Dennis. All I can say is it seemed odd to me and I felt I needed to remove his contact with the water. When I pulled his hand out of the water, he had the strangest look move across his face."

Duke paused a moment trying to come up with the right description concerning Dave's reaction. "He didn't like it, but there was control behind his actions and he let me move his hand and then stood as I did. When the suggestion came up about getting into the water, he jumped at it. Dennis,

72

we need to watch him."

At two o'clock that afternoon Duke and Dave walked up to the edge of the lake, dropped their robes and stepped into the water. Each took one step in and placed both feet on the bottom of the lake. They immediately felt the surge of the vibration enter their bodies.

Next, they waded out into the water until they were knee deep and then they sat down. As more water covered their bodies the more intense the vibrations became. Finally, they both laid back into the water on their backs and immediately started to float. The feeling of the vibration in their body covered them completely. Even their eyesight started to react.

Duke called out to Dennis. "Dennis, it feels like my entire body has been assimilated into the water. Everything has the vibration running through it. First thing I noticed was my mind became much sharper and clearer. Everything seems to have become more acute and sensitive."

Both men became quiet. Just then Dennis could see they were looking their bodies over when Duke came back. "Dennis, the scar on my left arm is going away."

Dennis was not sure what Duke had just said. "Duke, say that again, did you say a scar on your left arm was going away?"

There was a pause. "Yes, Dennis, that's what I said. I have a two-inch scar on my left arm just above the wrist and it is visibly going away."

Dave then came into the discussion. "I have

an appendicitis scar on my side and it is going away also."

"Dennis?"

"Yeah, Duke."

"Is this being recorded and videoed?"

"Yes, it is Duke."

"Dennis, I think you better pull us out of here. We need to talk. Yeah, get us out of here."

The team immediately pulled the two out of the water and helped them put their robes back on. "Duke, what was going on, why the need to pull you out right then?" Dave had taken hold of Duke's arm. His expression was one of mild anger

Duke stood there looking at the lake. He had a confused look on his face and he turned his head and looked straight at Dennis. "That water was changing us."

He then turned to Dave. "Dave, do you understand, the water was changing us not just the scars, but everything about us.

Dennis moved closer to Duke, "What do you mean, Duke?"

Duke turned his attention to Dennis. "It was changing us. I need to sit down and think this out. All I know is the water was changing us and it was more than just taking the scars off of our bodies. Give me a few minutes to get my thoughts organized. Oh, and don't let Dave back near the lake."

Dennis turned to Dave who had not said a word since referring to his appendicitis scar. "Dave, how do you feel?"

Dave just sat there looking out across the lake. He acted like he had not heard Dennis.

Dennis leaned down to Dave and looked him square in the face. "Dave, how are you feeling right now?"

Dave snapped his head up and directly into Dennis's face. "I heard you the first time." There was anger swelling out of him as he replied. "I'm trying to get my thoughts together so I can respond to your question, but I'm having a problem doing it. It's like my mind simply does not want to deal with anything right now. It's centered on the water and that is all it wants to deal with, the water, the water."

Duke reached out and grabbed Dennis's arm. "Get him the hell out of here and do it now. Get his eyes off the water and get him away from here." Duke looked at several of the people standing there. "Do it now!"

Several of the team members grabbed Dave and headed for the nearest truck and forced him into the truck. All this time Dave was trying his best to keep his eyes on the lake, on the water. The truck wheeled around and headed over the rim and then down to the base camp where Dave was taken to the medical tent.

Dennis helped Duke up and they walked over to the truck and got in. Dennis turned to Duke. "What the hell just happened, Duke?"

Duke had a look of fear in his eyes by this time. "Dennis, I'm not sure just yet, but the water is dangerous and we need to keep people out of it. In fact, we need to keep them from touching it." He was looking at his hands and opening and closing them in a rhythmic manner. "Get the word back to Lakes one and two they are to keep everyone from touching the water. If they have to work around it then do so with gloves. Dennis that is vital."

Dennis was already pressing the radio mic button as he responded to Duke. "All right, I'll get the order out right now and follow it up with a more detailed order as soon as we get to the base camp, anything else?"

By this time Duke was rubbing his hands together and every so often shaking them. "Yeah, I want to get dressed and then get over to medical so I can talk to Dave."

The two of them went back to the base camp and Duke got a quick shower, got dressed and they walked over to medical. When they got there Dave was sitting on the edge of a bed holding his head. Duke turned to the doctor. "How's he doing?"

The doctor turned to Duke. "He'll be all right. He has one hell of a headache right now, but it should go away shortly."

Duke continued his inquiry about Dave's condition. "Besides the headache, is he showing any other side effects?"

The doctor stood there looking at Duke and then back to Dave. "Well, I don't know if you would call them side effects, but besides his scar going away, his skin has become a little translucent, not thinner, but more transparent than it was."

Duke pulled his shirt sleeve up and sure enough his skin was as well. He stood there looking at it when the doctor took a hold of his arm and started pressing against his skin. "It's the same effect all right. The skin thickness has not changed at all, but the transparency has. See you can see the blood vessels in far greater detail.

It was seven hours before we saw the next change and the change had the skin return to its normal opacity. So, the effects of the vibration in the water were not permanent and it gave relief to both Duke and Dave. Where the skin opacity returned to normal the removal of the scars did not change, they were gone and showed no sign of returning.

The next issue was the response of Dave to the water when he could not take his eyes off the lake. That one bothered everyone and they were now ready to address it. Duke sat down beside Dave. "Dave do you recall your reaction to the lake as they were taking you out of the water?"

Dave was working hard to remember the situation almost as if he did not know he had been there. "Duke, I don't think I do, I mean I seem to remember everything that happened, but the issue does not register at all. Could you give me more details?"

Duke then started to describe what had happened at the lake side. He took great care to try and be as clear as possible on the facts and leave no room for Dave to misunderstand what he was saying. "Look, as we were lying in the lake our skin started to change in opacity, the skin was becoming transparent. It was while this was happening when you seemed to slide into a mental linkage or connection with the lake or the water itself. We could not get you to turn away from it and had to drag you to the truck and take you down off the rim and away from the lake. Do you remember anything about that?"

Dave sat there looking at Duke and then he seemed to become more alert. "Yeah, I do remember. I didn't understand what was happening. All I knew was I needed to watch the water, know what I mean. I simply had to watch the water, there was something that was going to happen there and I needed to see it."

That perked Duke's interest. It was a signal and he knew it had meaning. "What was going to happen? Dave."

Dave shook his head. "I don't know. I knew something was coming. Something I wanted to see and I had to see it no matter what happened. I still feel that something is coming I just can't put a finger on it, all I know is it's coming."

Duke and Dennis and everyone else standing around Dave looked at each other. No one knew what the hell he was talking about. "All right Dave lets back up a little bit. When did you first start feeling something was coming?"

Dave was now becoming more confused and unsure of himself. "It was when we were just entering the water, wait that's not right. No, I had the first feeling the first time I saw the lake. I had this feeling wash over me and it was like I knew something big was coming here. It really set in while we were in the water."

"Can you be more specific, just what the hell is coming?" Duke was pressing now and pressing hard. This was important and he knew Dave had to remember.

But Dave was at the end of his ability to relate what he was feeling about the lake and the water. "That's the issue Duke, I don't have the slightest idea what is coming at least not at this point in time."

Duke turned to the others standing in the tent. "Have any of you had this feeling or anything similar to it?"

A younger woman raised her hand.

"Yes, what is your name?"

"I'm Susan Dempsey, my first day on sight was to collect samples of water from around the perimeter of the lake and then run analyses tests of the water to try and breakdown its makeup and verify it is in fact water. It was while I was doing the sampling I looked across the lake and I had this almost overwhelming feeling something was just seconds away from coming over the rim. I don't know what it was to be, I just knew something was coming."

Duke stood there looking at her. "Is that all you experienced?"

She was now squirming and having a hard time holding still. "No, it was just the first time. Every time I go up on the rim, I have that same feeling. Lately it has been bothering me more than before. I know something is going to come over the top of the rim and it's starting to scare me."

It was getting late so everyone was sent to bed down and told we would continue in the morning after everyone got a good night's rest. As Duke and Dennis walked over to their tent, they started to talk about what they had seen in this location and tried to tie this place into the other two lakes.

Dennis had said little during the meeting and was still being silent when Duke asked the question. "Dennis, I think this place is much more involved than Lakes one and two. I have a feeling this lake may be a key lake in this whole mess."

Dennis was hesitant to jump to that conclusion, "I don't know it may just be a part of the overall issue with the vibration and its effect on humans." His mind was struggling with the issue and everything he had seen so far. "We're going to have to come up with some way of nailing this thing down as a separate and distinct issue and not just a reaction to the vibration itself."

He slowed down and turned toward Duke. "Well, what do you think we should be doing tomorrow then?"

Duke was deep in thought himself. "I think we need to finish our debriefing in the morning and then I think we need to take the helicopter and head to Lake Four."

Dennis was not too sure what Duke wanted to do. "You sure we should be leaving this lake this soon? Maybe we need to dig a little deeper here first?"

Duke was finally coming to a determination,

and he knew he needed to continue the overall survey before being tied down to one lake and one issue. "Dennis, I think we need to keep on our schedule and get to the other three lakes and determine what their unique anomalies are." The more he discussed it the more certain he became they needed to move on. "Once we have done all three lakes, we can schedule special projects for each lake and follow up to see if we can tie everything together."

Dennis could see what Duke was trying to do. "Yeah, as I think about it, you're right, we need to get to all six lakes and then we can address the oddities after that." With that they headed for bed and the new day to come.

The following morning everyone met at the mess tent to go over the prior day's event. Duke started the session advising everyone he had no additional adverse or odd events over the night and he felt great. The scars he had were gone and his skin had returned to normal.

Dave had the same results including the fact his fixation on the lake had gone away as well. Still Duke advised him and Susan and anyone else who had those feelings to never go to the lake on their own, to always have several people with them or close by so they could be assisted in the event the problem returned.

Duke then advised the group he and Dennis would be leaving that morning. They needed to get to the other three lakes and determine if there were any specific oddities at those locations. One thing

Duke made clear he would be checking to see if anyone at the other five lakes had the same fixation issues with their respective lakes. With that the meeting ended and Duke and Dennis headed for the helicopter and their next lake visit.

As they boarded the helicopter Duke put on his head set and made a radio call to Lakes One and Two. At both lakes he related the fixation issue to the team leaders and asked they check with their people to determine if anyone was having that type of event happen. He emphasized the necessity to identify and find anyone demonstrating those reactions and getting them away from the water permanently.

Baxter from Lake One then advised they had already ran into that issue and they had pulled several people off the lake detail and reassigned them to other duties.

As Dennis settled into his seat and put his head set on Duke reached over and touched him. "Lake One has had several events related to the fixation issue. When we get to Lake Four, I want you to put together a directive and send it to all six lakes advising them of the fixation problem and the steps they should be taking to ensure their people are safe."

"Right Duke, how forceful do you want that directive?"

"Make it indisputable Dennis. I don't want any misunderstandings on this one. I have a feeling this particular issue is going to be uniformly present at all the lakes. I also feel it could become physically dangerous to those working at or near the lake. Make it mandatory, hold nothing back.

Duke settled back in the helicopter as it lifted off and headed north. As they flew over the lake, he had a thought. "Dennis, when those people talked about the fixation feeling they said they expected something to come over the rim of the lake. Nothing was said about anything possibly coming from within the lake. If I were sitting back and looking at this thing from an outsider's position, I would have expected something coming from within the lake and not over the rim."

Dennis was looking at the lake as they flew clear of it and over the rim. "Yeah, I see what you mean, it doesn't seem rational the issue would come over into the lake, but what if they were talking about it coming over the rim from the lake?"

It was so obvious Duke felt he should have seen it. "Damn, you're right. It's not from outside the lake it's from within the lake itself. Now that make sense and it also tells me we are not even close to the end of what is going on at these lakes.

The helicopter continued on to the Depression Lake Four and their next discovery.

Chapter Six

DEPRESSION LAKE FOUR

Again, it was a two hundred twenty-six-mile flight directly north from Lake Three and as they came into the area of the lake the helicopter pilot followed the same approach pattern to the lake. As they flew around the rim and across the lake, they noted nothing strange about the water or its surface. From the air there was no indication of a specific oddity that was unique to this lake.

As they landed, a truck approached them and stopped, an older man got out and walked toward them. He introduced himself as Paul Bowman; he was the team leader for Lake Four.

Duke and Dennis introduced themselves, got into the truck and headed to the main base camp. It was approaching noon so, Paul, drove directly to the mess tent and they entered and sat down to talk over what Paul and his team may have found during their study of this lake.

Duke started the discussion. "Paul, as you may know, we are here to review the activities of your team and to try to determine if there have been any odd anomalies tied to this particular lake. As you may also know, the other three lakes we have visited had identified unique oddities at each lake and we feel there is probably one here as well."

Paul then started his briefing. "Duke, at first we could not see nor determine if there were any oddities about this lake. Except for the way it came into existence we had found nothing other than a four-mile wide five-hundred-foot-deep lake with a railroad bridge sitting dead center of the lake bottom. At the time I thought it was oddity enough."

Paul had been trying to determine if there were any anomalies in his area once he had heard of the others at the first three lakes. "Well, as we heard the news from the other three lakes south of us, we started to dig a little deeper and we did in fact find the oddity and it was one I had not expected."

Dennis pulled out his note pad. "Paul, we need to have you tell in detail what the oddity is and how you discovered it. It is important you give us everything. In two of the lower lakes, we failed to do that up front and it created problems for us."

Paul sat back and ran his hand through what hair he had left on his head. "Right, I guess its best I start at the beginning. We had been here two days when we first started to notice the oddity. Most of those two days had been spent setting up the base camp and then starting the construction of the road to the rim of the lake. We had no problems and each and every task was being carried out within schedule and with no difficulties.

"Frankly it had been one of the easiest base camp and approach projects I have ever worked with.

"We were probably about two hundred fifty feet from the rim of the lake with the road and had decided to work as late as possible. This was the third day. In the prior two days we had worked till five in the evening and called it quits, but we were so close and the going had been so easy we decided to finish it that evening so we could approach the lake the following morning.

"It was the spotter for the cat driver who had the first experience. He was working ahead of the cat, to the cat driver's right about fifteen yards and was basically just standing there as the cat finished filling a depression. The driver noted his spotter kept looking up the slope and shrugging his shoulders. A couple of time he bent over like he was trying to get something off of him. The driver stopped the cat and called the spotter over to him. 'What the hell are you doing over there anyway?'

"The spotter looked back at where he had been standing and then back at the driver. 'It's getting hot over there. I can feel the heat coming down from the rim and washing over me. Every time it does it, I swear it's getting hotter.'

"The driver then made a radio call to me and he held up the road project until I arrived at the scene. They both related what was happening and so

86

I took the spotter and we walked over to the location. We didn't even get there before I felt the effects myself. It felt like a gentle breeze coming down off the rim of the lake and it was warm. I mean the temperature of the air felt like it was twenty to thirty degree warmer than the air where we were standing.

"I had a Tech bring a thermometer to the sight and we started taking temperature readings. When we moved down the slope of the rim, about two hundred feet, the temperature there was around seventy-three degrees. As we moved up the slope it increased and when we reached where the spotter had been it was ninety-six degrees and we then discovered it was increasing as well.

"I had everyone pull back to the base camp and we decided to set things up to do a complete survey of the slope of the mountain from the base camp up to the rim itself.

That following morning a crew started out doing just that. We used the base camp as our median temperature and then started up the mountain stopping every twenty-five yards to check the temperature. From the base camp to the rim the difference in temperature was only four degrees. It was eight in the morning and the base camp temperature was at forty-six degrees, the rim was at fifty. That was not significant.

"I had the road crews get back to work and we put a monitoring crew with them as they went to work to finish the road. They finished by one o'clock we moved our entire surveying crew up onto the rim. Everything went well the rest of the afternoon.

"Water temperatures at, fourteen thirty hours was at forty-seven degrees. The lake water was clear as crystal and you could see all the way to the bottom, including the railroad bridge. It was too late to venture out onto the lake so we set up our monitoring station, took a series of water samples and when done headed back to the base camp.

"After about twenty-one hundred hours, right at sun down, one of my Techs and I went back up to the monitoring station to check the readings. It was then we noted it was getting warmer as we moved up the mountain to the rim. As we came over the top the lake was covered with a cloud or mist. We got out of the truck and walked over to the monitor and when I checked the water it was ninety-three degrees. When I checked the chart, it showed from sun up to the present the temperature had been going up continually.

"We took a number of samples and headed back down to base camp. By the time we got down to camp the temperature of our sample was at a hundred five degrees. Sun down came fifteen minutes later and we noted the sample temperature flattened out and then as the evening continued the temperature started down and continued down. By sun up it was at thirty-nine degrees and then it stopped and started back up as soon as the sun came up."

Duke had been transfixed by what Paul was telling them. "Did you notice any change in the density of the water?"

Paul started to nod his head. "Duke, we checked at the time and the water density stayed as it should be and never changed. That alone was odd in that the warmer it gets the less dense it should get. No, this stuff was acting strange and we have no answer for it."

"Paul, has anyone touched the water and if so, was there any reaction to that touch?"

Paul continued to nod his head as Duke posed questions to him. "At this time, I don't believe anyone has touched the water itself. We have been by the lake, but not in it. The only samples we took were when we first got to the lake and then the one I and the Tech took to check the temperature."

Duke finally wanted to head out for the lake. "All right Paul, I think we need to go up to the lake and try a few simple experiments."

With that Duke, Dennis, Paul and three techs headed to the lake. When they got there, they set up a table next to the lake and set out their monitors and sampling tools. Duke was ready to try a few simple tests to see if there were any results or unexpected issues.

Finally, Duke was ready to try the touch test on the water of Lake Four. It was thirteen forty-five hours and the sun was just past vertical when he stepped up to the water and bent over. He took his left hand and reached down and touched the water. It was warm to the touch, but there was something else about it. He held his hand in the water for about thirty seconds before he felt another sensation. The water was wet as it should have been but it felt like

89

velvet. It was soft and warm and he wanted to jump right into it.

Yet, there was a problem and he felt it almost at the same time he felt the texture of it. His fingernails started to soften up and he had to pull his hand back before he lost all of them. They actually turned soft and started to separate from the finger. The open air dried his hand fairly fast and the nails re-hardened and further checking found no lasting issue.

Duke looked at everyone. "No one, but no one goes in or near that water, is that understood?"

Paul was already nodding his head as Duke was talking. "Paul, we want to take one more sample of the water and I want this sample to be a fairly large amount. I want to boil it off and see if there are any crystals or other chemicals remaining of the sample."

"I agree Duke, there has got to be something in the water that is the problem."

A one-gallon container was taken and they returned to the base camp. The tech took the water to their lab tent and placed it on a burner and set the burner on high. They figured about six to ten minutes before it starts to boil off.

After fifteen minutes they checked the waters temperature and found it to be just over two hundred degrees and the water didn't even look hot. Lake Four was at five thousand one hundred- and eighty-five-feet elevation, the water should be boiling when the temperature reaches around two hundred three degrees.

The tech increased the stove temperature and then waited. The temperature passed two hundred three and rolled on past two hundred twelve and the water didn't show a single sign of getting hot, no bubbles, no rolling, nothing. At two hundred fifty the water was hot but still not boiling or releasing any steam. At two hundred seventy-five it was the same, there was no indication the water was hot except for the thermometer monitoring the temperature.

Paul got a second thermometer and put it in the water and it registered the same reading as the primary thermometer. Paul looked at Duke. "I don't understand, it should be boiling and spitting water out of the pot by now, but nothing. On top of that it's hotter than hell and could severely injure someone if it spilled on them."

Finally, Duke turned and walked outside and stood there looking up at the rim of the lake. "We have a lake full of water that increases in temperature as the day moves along. If you put your hand in the water at any time your fingernails start to soften and come off. As evening comes along and the cool of the air hits the lake a haze of fog forms, but it's not water from the lake, it's the moisture in the air forming the haze or fog.

"When we take a sample of lake water and put it on a stove and raise its temperature, the water becomes hot, but has no other reaction to the heat. It just gets hotter and hotter. That's amazing in itself."

Dennis looked at Duke and then back toward the rim of the lake. "What do you think about

sending a probe down into the lake and getting a number of temperature readings down at the bottom?"

Duke started to nod his head and then added. "I think that may help and I would do it over the bridge and all the way to the bottom at hundred-foot levels,"

The order was given and a team took the boat to the lake and launched it and headed out to the center and over the bridge. It took them a little over four hours to run the temperature scan of the lake from the surface to the bottom and then back up. The lake temperatures remained constant surface to bottom taking into consideration the time element as well. That was in itself unbelievable, yet the hard numbers showed and confirmed what they were finding.

After reviewing the hard numbers from the lake measurements Duke looked at Paul. "All right Paul, this is what I want. Dennis and I will be going on to Lakes Five and Six to finish our survey of all the lakes. On our way back we will stop off here and pick up a box of samples of the lake water. I want twelve one-quart containers of lake water and they must be sealed and protected against contamination. Can you see those are ready when we come back through?"

"Yes, we'll have them ready. Can I ask what you're planning?"

Duke nodded his head. "Paul, I will have our main lab run a number of tests on all the water and those tests will include combining the waters in as

many different orders as we can put together. I want to see the reaction between the different waters to determine if any of them are hazardous."

Dennis and Duke made their call to the helicopter for a pickup in the morning and transport to Depression Lake Five. Everyone then broke and went to the mess tent for their meal and then spent the rest of the evening talking about the overall progress of each lake team as they worked with the research of each one.

The following morning the helicopter arrived and Duke and Dennis boarded. Duke immediately got on the radio to lakes three, two and one and advised them of the need for a dozen sealed quart containers of water from each lake ready for pick up when they finish with their visit to Lake Six. But first they had to go to Lake Five.

Duke had no idea what to expect from Lake Five. If it was anything like the first four lakes it had a surprise waiting for him and he could only hope it was not something that would increase the level of danger for his teams working with the waters of the individual lakes.

He knew they were tied together in some way and if any of the lakes were an extreme danger then who knows what it would do when combined with waters from any of the other lakes or all of them, only time would tell.

He couldn't help but feel there was something far more involved. Each lake was a location all unto itself. Each one had its own identity and oddity. Yet they were tied together. That was

93

obvious due to the fact that position wise they were linked north to south. No, the six lakes were there as a unit. Within that unit they each had their own oddities from the number of people in the manmade objects at the bottom of the lake to the special properties of the lake water.

By now these two issues had taken hold of him and he knew there was something far more involved than anyone could ever think of. There was a foreboding about the lakes and their hazard to the geological crews who were working at them. He was beginning to understand and he was being drawn deeper and deeper into this issue and the feeling he had was not good.

He looked over at Dennis and could see Dennis was dealing with the same gremlins he was. At least he was not alone.

Chapter Seven

DEPRESSION LAKE FIVE

Just like clockwork the chopper arrived the next morning to take Duke and Dennis to the next lake, Lake Five. They headed out to Depression Lake Five again two hundred twenty-six miles due north of Lake Four. Again, as they approached their destination the helicopter pilot did the normal fly over of the lake and then around it giving the two a good look at the location. Again, the lake was an exact copy of the other four even down to the layout of the base camp and the road leading up to the rim.

As they landed, a truck approached the helicopter and a man got out and stood by as they exited. Duke walked up to the man and they shook hands. "You're Aaron Smith?"

"Yes, sir I am, and you're Duke and this is Dennis?"

Dennis reached out and shook Aaron's hand.

"That's right. Thank you for picking us up. May we move on to the base camp please?"

Aaron took Duke's bag and nodded his head and placed Duke's bag in the back of truck. "Yes of course. Are there any special items or issues you want us to prepare for?"

As they got into the truck Duke was looking at the lake mound and wondering what was next. "Aaron, not at this time, I think we need to just find a place to sit down and Dennis and I will fill you in on what we have found so far and what we need to address here."

They left the landing zone and headed into the base camp area. They stopped in front of their administrative tent and went in to Aaron's office and sat down. Duke finally sat back and took a few seconds to gather his thoughts and then started to brief Aaron on what was going on.

Duke looked across the desk at Aaron. "Aaron, during out visits to the other four lakes south of yours, we have discovered a number of anomalies related to those lakes. Each anomaly is different and is unique to each individual lake. I firmly believe this will be true for this lake, if you have not already discovered it.

"I need to have you go over all you and your crew have done and are doing in regards to this lake. Have you discovered anything you feel would be unique to this lake?"

By this time Duke was beginning to feel something was not right. The demeanor of Aaron was not right. He was polite but seemed to be defensive. He was listening to everything Duke was saying but seemed to be preoccupied. There was something going on here and it was not the normal process he had found at the other lakes.

The warning signs were all over Aaron and Duke was sure he was going to have to deal with a situation. The question was whether this issue was a product of the lake water, and if so then he had one hell of a problem sitting there before him.

Aaron sat there a few seconds and seemed to become a little uncomfortable in his demeanor. "Duke, I don't know if I should discuss this with you or not. I did not know you were coming until three days ago and then it was from your office and not from headquarters in Washington."

Duke looked closely at Aaron. "You do realize I am the chief director and manager of this overall project and my authority includes all six lakes?"

Duke looked over at Dennis and nodded toward Aaron. Dennis pulled out his notebook and started to write. As he did, Aaron was watching him intently.

Aaron stood firm on his response to Duke. "Well, yes, but I was not informed your authority extended to directing me and my staff in duties and directions we may or may not agree with. We are working with some sensitive issues here and we feel any knowledge anyone should have is on a need to know basis."

The storm signals were flying high and Duke took it straight on. "Aaron, let me fill you in on something here and now. I am the primary director of this project. I am the chief administrator of the entire project and that includes Lake One, Two, Three, Four, Five and Six. My authority covers the entire range of activities that takes place at all six places. All of your requests for equipment and personnel pass over my desk and under my signature. I have total responsibility for all that happens in all six locations.

"Now to come here and find one of our location managers resistant to my directions disturbs me considerably. The fact is Aaron; I approved and signed your appointment to this position and location.

"Now, if you wish to continue to question my authority and position, I will have only one option and that is to remove you from this position and this project. Do you understand me?"

Aaron took a hard swallow and looked over at Dennis. There was something going on here and both Duke and Dennis were becoming more than a little concerned. Aaron sat there looking at them and then started to say something and stopped. His mind was going at top speed and he was clearly weighing his position and cost if he continued to resist.

Duke had had enough of it and leaned forward. "Aaron, you have five seconds to get your ass straight and start working for me or you will be on the helicopter and out of here within the next five minutes after that. Hear me?"

Dennis had stood up and was walking around behind Aaron's desk when Aaron finally raised both his hands. "All right, I'm sorry but we have found an anomaly and I didn't want you coming in here and taking it away from us. We found it and we should get the credit for it."

That set Duke off and he was up and had his phone out in just seconds. He called the helicopter pilot and ordered him to have the helicopter ready in ten minutes. He was going to transport a person back to Lake One for removal from the overall research project. He turned to Aaron. "Get your bags ready and meet us in front of this tent in ten minutes. You take any longer and I'll come after you and I can assure you, you don't want that."

He then walked to the door of the office and opened it. Duke stood there holding the door looking directly at Aaron and then nodded his head toward the door. Aaron stood and walked around the desk, stopped and picked up a file and started toward the door. Dennis reached out and stopped him and then took the folder and placed it back on the desk.

Duke then walked out to the clerk's desk and told her to contact their security director and get him to Aaron's Office immediately. She nodded and made the call. Aaron had been escorted out of the office by Dennis and stood there not saying a word. His animosity toward the two men was obvious and clearly evident.

Several minutes later the director of the Lake Five facility security arrived and came into the office. Duke turned to him, "your name please."

"Adam Stewart, sir."

"Adam, do you know who I am?"

"Yes sir, you're the director of the Six Lakes Research Project."

"Do you understand my authority in regards to this location and facility?"

"Yes sir, I do."

"And, what is that?"

"You are the primary administrator of this overall project. I am to report to you any and all issues that could be of a security issue and or safety issue."

"Thank you, Adam. Now Mr. Smith here has proven himself to be most difficult and resistant to my authority over this project. I am removing him from his position and sending him off and away from this project. You will take Mr. Smith to his tent and help him pack and then escort him to the helicopter pad and see he boards and leaves. I have instructed the pilot as to what he is to do. I then want you to notify your counterpart at Lake One and he is to see that Mr. Smith is removed from the helicopter and placed in a holding location until such time I can return to Lake One and continue our discussion with him, is that understood."

"Yes sir, I do and it will be done."

Adam turned to Aaron and gestured toward the door. Aaron nodded and walked around him and toward the door. He stopped and turned toward Duke, "I really meant well in questioning your authority. I guess I'm not used to someone having authority over me, sorry." He then stood there for a few seconds looking at Duke and Dennis and turned and walked out the door.

Duke turned to Dennis and they both returned to Smith's office. "Who is the next in line of authority here?"

Dennis pulled a small notebook out of his pocket and looked through it. "Jackie Taylor, she has been here from the start and her background looks impressive."

"All right, would you have someone locate her and advise her to come to the administrator's office?"

Dennis picked up the phone and the secretary answered. "Would you call Jackie Taylor and request she come to the administrator's office as soon as possible?"

He hung up and he and Duke sat down to wait. "Duke, do you think anything really bad was going on here? I mean, do you think Aaron has taken advantage of our project for his own personal gain?"

Duke sat back looking up at the ceiling. This was the last thing he had expected during this tour of the Six Lakes and it had hit him hard. "Yes, I'm sure of it. One of the first things Miss Taylor will be asked to do is to determine what Aaron was up to and to what extent it may have compromised our project.

"I don't know, but there is something really wrong there. By the way, who ran the background check on him and what did they come up with?"

"Duke, I don't know but I sure as hell will get on that. Give me twenty minutes and I'll get back to you.

Duke nodded his head and then reached over

and opened the center drawer of Arron's desk. Sitting in the drawer was a small black book. He picked it up and opened to the first page. There he found references to several people he did not know. Below them was the name H.A.W.K. What the hell did that mean?

He slid the book across the desk to Dennis who picked it up and opened to the same page. As he looked at the page Duke saw him react. "What is it? Do you know any of those people?

"No, I don't, but I know that name and it's the name of a paramilitary organization with links to our regular military. When I was in the service this group of people was working hard to develop a relationship with our military. They were working the officers of several of our military bases across the country.

"The only reason I know this is true, I was hauled in one day and questioned about anyone from that group making contact with me, and if they had what did they ask of me. The fact was I had not been approached but the event has stuck in my mind.

"To have people from the intelligence department of the army bringing you in and questioning you tells me this outfit was a problem. If their showing an interest in the Six Lakes Project then we have something to be concerned about."

Something to be concerned about, hell everything he has seen so far there at Lake Five had been something to be concerned about. If this was going on here then to what degree was it a problem in the other five lakes.

They had already been to the first four and at no time had he noted any kind of a problem concerning outside influences with the teams working the lakes. What he would find at Lake Six was all together another issue and one he would have to take on as soon as he got there.

About twenty minutes later a young woman walked through the door. Dennis turned toward her. "Are you Miss Taylor?"

"Yes sir, I am."

Duke then stood up and turned to her offering his hand, which she took. "Miss Taylor, I'm Duke Ridgeman, I'm in charge of the overall Six Lakes Project. May I call you Jackie?"

She was looking back and forth between Duke and Dennis obviously unaware of what had just happened and what was about to happen. "Yes sir, I recognize you and yes, please call me Jackie."

Duke continued. "Jackie, Aaron Smith has been relieved of his responsibilities here at Lake Five. As a result, that leaves the position of Chief Administrator empty, would you be willing to assume those responsibilities until further notice?"

Jackie stood there looking at both men for several seconds and then cleared her throat. "Well yes, I guess I would like that. I don't understand what is going on right now. This all comes as a surprise."

Duke was nodding his head in understanding. "I understand Jackie and I will be filling you in on just what has happened and why the change at this time."

103

A small smile came across her face and she nodded back. "All right, I'll take the job."

"Good, now sit down and Dennis and I will fill you in.

After almost three hours they finished filling Jackie in and briefing her on what they were working on and where the overall project study of the lakes was taking them. "Now Jackie we need to ask you if you know of any anomalies here at the lake, was there anything that was strange and unexpected going on here?"

She looked at both of them "Why yes, there has been. Aaron didn't inform you about the issue?"

Duke flashed a quick look of anger when she mentioned Aaron's name. "No Jackie, he didn't. That resulted in his being removed from this facility and now we need to know what was going on."

Jackie leaned forward. "The fourth day we were here the discovery was made. We had completed the access road to the rim and had set up a testing station at the edge of the lake. One of the tech people had taken a number of samples of the water and he had placed one of the samples bottles on a scale on the station table. It must have been ten minutes or so before he looked at the scale and saw the reading.

"He had expected the one quart container to weigh in at its proper weight of .946 kilograms and it was not. The weight of that sample came to double that at 1.892 kilograms.

"Every container weighed had the same reading. So, we did the same in imperial quarts. One imperial quart container of regular water weighed in at 1.089 kilograms which is normal. When the one imperial quart container of lake water was weighed the weight came in at 2.178 kilograms, again twice the normal.

"Every water sample was double what the weight of water as we know it normally weighs. The water feels the same and pours the same and heats the same except it is double in weight."

That was crazy, how could that be. Duke looked at Dennis and then stood up. "Jackie, let's make a run over to your lab tent. I want to see this thing for myself."

The three of them left the tent and Jackie showed them the way to the lab tent. As they entered the tent Duke observed one table full of quart jars full of water. He walked over to the table and then looked at Jackie.

"Yes sir, those are all lake water samples taken over a period of twenty-four hours and they all weigh exactly the same no matter what time they were taken.

"We decided to let them sit and see if time caused any changes in the samples, so far it has not.

Duke took a small vial and dipped it in the container of lake water and then held it up to his nose. There were no odd or different scents to it. He put a small amount into his hand and felt it and it ran and felt just like any water outside of the four other lakes they had visited. "Has this water been tested for any poisons or other chemical contents?"

She nodded. "Yes sir, it has and it comes

back pure. In fact, it comes back purer than any water anywhere else we can find. Right out of the lake it is as pure as any sterilized water that we use. That is, in itself, a puzzle as well."

Duke repeated the results she had given them. "So, the water is pure and also weighs twice the normal weight of water?"

"That's right."

Duke picked up the phone and called Lake One. He got the administrator on the line. "Betty, Duke here, can you tell me if you ran any purification test on the lake water?"

"Yes Duke, we did and it is pure, as pure as any water we have found."

"Thanks Betty, that matches the discovery here at Lake Five. I'll talk to you later"

He then called Lakes two through four and got the same answer, pure as any water they could find. He then started to pace and think for a couple of minutes. "This means when we get to Lake Six the water there will be as pure as those of the other five lakes. The question is what will be the unique feature of that lake."

The next question to come to his mind was the one that met him when he arrived. What was with Aaron Smith and his reaction to their coming to Lake Five? That was still digging at Duke and he had no answer. None of the other team leaders had reacted this way. The question was, did it have anything to do with the lake or was it strictly Aaron's personality?

He looked at Jackie. "Do you have any idea

as to why Aaron Smith acted the way he did?"

She cleared her throat and then looked at Dennis and then back to Duke. "Yeah, we all do. He didn't really seem to know what he was doing. I was sure he was lacking in any scientific training but accepted his being here because many times an administrator does not need a working knowledge of science or whatever they are overseeing.

"Right from the beginning he was secretive and set up protocols that required all information and discoveries to be brought to him the moment they were discovered. He wanted in-depth data on everything. That file cabinet back of his desk has all we gave him."

Duke turned to Dennis. "Dennis, I think I want security to do an in-depth background check on Aaron and I want it started now."

Dennis picked up the phone and called the Chief Security Officer Tanner Marshall. Tanner was the head of security for the whole of the project. "Tanner, Dennis here. Duke needs to have a complete background done on Aaron Smith. He wants it done as soon as you can. He wants everything covered."

Tanner knew about the firing of Aaron already and was planning on taking him into custody for further investigation. "Right Dennis, I'll get my people on that right now, anything else?"

Dennis looked at Duke. "No, that's all we need now, but we need it top priority. Aaron's reaction to our coming here to Lake Five is a puzzle and we are trying to determine if it was in relationship to the lake or something about him.

"We have found a notebook here in his desk that references H.A.W.K. I think you had better get on that outfit as well. I'll have the secretary here fax a copy of it down to you.

"All right Dennis, we'll get on it and I'll call you as soon as I have anything. Oh, by the way I plan on taking Aaron into custody as soon as he gets here. There is something really wrong and we need to keep him tied down until we have cleared up everything."

Dennis raised his eye brows. "Thanks Tanner, I'll advise Duke of that as well."

"All right Dennis, let the boss know, we're on it and I would guess we should have something by morning. Is there anything else you need?"

"Nothing at this time Tanner, we'll talk later."

As Dennis hung up Duke looked at him. "You know Dennis, I've been thinking about our approach to this issue and maybe we have been too aggressive and direct in our approach to these different bases. Could it be we created the problem with Aaron ourselves?"

Dennis started to shake his head and pointed at the chair behind Aaron's desk. "No Duke, I don't think so. These people know the head of the project could drop in at any time and the rest proved that by their acceptance of us when we arrived. No, Aaron's reaction was not caused by us, I think it will be much more personal and involved than our coming to this site."

Duke sat there looking across the desk at Jackie sitting in the chair. "Yeah, you're probably right. Well, anyway we have a lot to do so let's get on with it and wait till Tanner calls back."

"Oh, one other thing, Jackie do you know if Aaron sent any messages or data out of this site over the time you've been here at Lake Five. If he has then we need to know where the information was being sent."

Jackie got up and walked over to the door and leaned out. "Anna would you know if Aaron had sent any items or papers to anyone other than the main administration offices for the Six Lake Project over the past weeks we have been on site?"

"Yes ma'am, he has been sending files out every week to some place called HAWK. I don't know what that is but he told me to just do my job and he would worry about protocol and who got what."

"Thanks Anna, would you get copies of all those files made up and bring them into us?"

Jackie walked back over to the desk and sat down. "She'll bring copies of what he sent out in a few minutes. I don't think I like what I've heard about him sending those files off base."

Duke's emotions were running wild by this time. "Jackie, H.A.W.K. is a paramilitary organization that has a questionable background. The fact Aaron was sending classified files to this group tells me they have infiltrated at the least Lake Five and possibly some of the other lakes.

"We're going to have to have everyone on

this base re-investigated to ensure none of them were with Aaron. It will be your job to brief them and advise them of the coming investigation. Will you do that?"

"Of course, I will and I would hope I'm the first one who will be re-investigated. That will give the others an understanding what is taking place is not personal toward them, but is a necessity."

"Thank you, Jackie, then we can continue with our tour.

"Dennis, will you contact Adam and advise him of what we need?"

Dennis nodded toward Duke and the three of them walked out to the road. Jackie went off to start the follow up actions Duke had requested and Duke and Dennis walked up to the rim of the lake.

As they came over the rim and saw the lake it dawned on Duke he had never stopped long enough to take a good look at the lake from the most fundamental angle, the approach. It would be a process that would take them back to the first lake and start from a whole new perspective. But first they would finish this tour before starting the second.

As he looked at the landscape before him, he noted the perspective of the lake from this approach was different, even when it was compared with approaching it in the cab of a truck. This lake gave one the impression from the shore to the center of the lake it actually bulged.

They had to stop and get low and look from left to right and back to get a clear view of the bulge.

There was no doubt about it; the lake did bulge in the center by several feet. Whether it was an optical allusion or actually was a bulge, Duke didn't know and he would have to investigate that on the second run.

They finished their final view of Lake Five and returned to the base and prepared to make their run to Lake Six the next morning.

Duke called the other four lakes and advised them of the perceived bulge issue and requested they assign a survey team to each lake so they can determine if there is a bulge there. He then made a note to advise Jackie of what they saw and for her to follow up on it. He called Lake Six and advised them of the same issue and he would expect a report when he arrived there the next morning.

Meanwhile Jackie had contacted them and advised them security had the report they needed and she would see them at the administrators office.

Duke returned to the administrative office and made a call to his primary security officer. "Tanner, this is Duke. You have a report for me?"

Tanner's voice was stressed and serious. "Yes sir, we have a preliminary report and I don't think you're going to like it. We determined Aaron is not who he said he was. In fact, the man has no degrees in the field he was working in. Basically, he's a shill.

Whether he is working for someone other than us or the government we have not determined yet, but right now I would say our activities have been compromised, the extent of the compromise we

111

cannot say as yet.

"Right now, we can't even tie him to the H.A.W.K. group, but I would bet that is where his final affiliation is tied. We'll continue digging. I have a number of friends in D.C. who I have called and their running a number of leads down for us.

Duke's face flushed and he slammed his hand down on the desk top. "Damn it anyway. Where is this guy at right now?"

"Well believe it or not he is right here on base and seems to be staying in his tent for the time being."

Duke was puzzled. "Why the hell would he want to stay there anyway?"

Tanner then advised Duke. "We're checking in on it right now. The fact is we will be holding on to him and will be bringing federal agents in to deal with him. Bottom line, he is not going anywhere now or in the near future."

Duke was nodding his head and thinking about what he was going to do when he got back to Lake One. He wanted fifteen minutes with this Aaron guy. "All right Tanner, that's great. Keep working on him and we'll be heading on up to Lake Six in the morning. If you need me, I'll be there by noon tomorrow."

"Right Duke, we'll keep you informed."

"Thanks Tanner."

Duke had not expected something as serious as this. He had this feeling deep inside his guts he had only just begun to discover what Arron had been up to and why he was there.

The last thing he needed was some group of people working on the inside of the project and answering to someone he knew nothing about. He picked up the phone and called Adam Stewart. "Yes, Adam I need to talk to you. Could you come over to the admin tent?"

"Yes sir, I'll be there in five."

Duke sat looking at Jackie and Dennis. "There's something here that is starting to eat at my guts and I don't like it.

"Jackie, I'm going to be putting you in the hot seat on the security check issue. If Aaron was able to infiltrate us at this level then there could easily be others. Do you understand?"

There was a flash of red across her face. "Yes sir, I understand and I'll stay on top of this. Damn-it anyway, that's all we need. I'll assist Adam in every way he desires. How do you want us to handle anyone else we discover?"

"Get them down to Lake One. Make sure you advise Tanner of the subject's issues and when to expect them."

Just then Adam entered the office. Duke turned to him. "Adam, I hate to drop this on you but we're beginning to think there is more to this Aaron thing we first thought.

"I'm going to want you to dig into this issue a little deeper. Namely, I want to know if there are any others at this base who are not what they claim to be. Understand?"

"Yes sir, I do. The fact is I have already started an in-depth look at everyone. After talking to

113

Tanner, we decided that would be the best way to go."

Duke looked over at Jackie and nodded his head. "Good Adam. I have talked this over with Jackie and she agrees as well. Please keep her informed.

"Oh, by the way have you checked into Jackie's background?"

Adam looked at Jackie. "Yes sir, I have and she is clear. I hope this does not create a problem between us, Jackie?"

She smiled. "Of course not, all I want is to be assured the people I have working under me are clear and loyal. If we have to do some digging then we'll do it. No, Adam I have no problem. Just do your job."

Duke was satisfied with what he was hearing and then turned to Dennis. "All right let's make the arrangement to head for Lake Six in the morning."

Chapter Eight

H.A.W.K. AWAKENS

"Damn it anyway Larry, I didn't expect Arron to screw things up this badly. You're sure they're on to our work there at Lake Five."

"Mike, I can assure you he screwed things up royally. I told you from the start not to put that little jerk in there, but you insisted.

"Not only did he snub Ridgeman, but he almost accused him of being a traitor. The dumb shithead really set us up and he's going to pay for it."

"You sure you can get to him?"

"Yeah, we have a man there at Lake One and he's already been advised to put him down."

"You can trust this man?"

"Yes Mike, I trust this man. He's been working for me for years and he has never failed me.

Arron will be dead within hours after he gets to Lake One."

"All right, let's set that aside for now. You've been in touch with the General?"

"Yeah, he called me yesterday and advised the Stryker Units have been assigned to their field training programs and will start to move out to the six locations by weeks end."

"Good, then we will be able to move on any one of the lakes any time we need to?"

"If the General is right they will be in place well before we need to worry. I asked him about each unit's team leader and he advised each unit to the man is with the program and ready to take whatever action they're assigned to."

"Larry, what about the H.A.W.K. units, where do you have those units assigned?"

"Mike, I don't want to discuss locations right now but I can assure you each unit is in a position to augment and assist the Stryker Units. We have ample people assigned to take on each lake and control it.

"All right now, we need to talk about the people at those lakes and what we are going to do with them. There is a lot of knowledge there and I would prefer we take advantage of it when we gain control."

"Mike, we have a problem there. The General wants everyone eliminated and he will be moving his own people in to take over the scientific work that needs to be done.

"I have to agree with him. It will keep us from having to have the support necessary to maintain control over all those people. No, we're better off just putting everyone down and dumping them in a mass grave."

"Larry, I don't know if I like that, but I can see the reasoning for it and will leave it to the General and his people. My main concern is gaining the control of this part of the west coast and that will depend on taking those lakes and the General taking the President out.

"Understood Mike, I can assure you everything is covered. This situation with the Six Lakes has given us the moment when we can actually see our moves paying off.

"What these lakes really mean, we don't have the slightest idea about, but just their presence has placed the government and the world in a position of preoccupation with the issue and it's leaving them open for the takeover we've been working on all these years."

"Mike, the General is still depending on you and your group coming up with the money and the people to support his moves. There are going to be a lot of people dying in DC when this thing kicks off and the General must have coast to coast support.

"If you and your group want that region for your own purposes, then you're going to have to work for it. Understand?"

"Larry, advise the General we understand and will be there when he needs us. We're committed to this action and we'll never back down."

"All right then. We have the H.A.W.K. units moving into position to support the Stryker Units and the targets are set.

"Everyone understands the lakes are killing zones and everyone is to go in prepared for the Generals people to take over.

"The issue in DC will be done within an hour of the initiation point and the General will have firm and complete control of the government at the time.

"I would say the coming coup of the United States Government is on a fast track to victory. The people of this country will eventually understand the necessity in this action and will ultimately support it.

"All right Larry, you do your thing and I and my group will be ready whenever the General moves. Oh, and be sure Arron is dealt with?'

"Will do Mike. Talk later."

Chapter Nine

DEPRESSION LAKE SIX

Again, and for the last time on this round, Duke and Dennis left Lake Five and headed out for Lake Six. They had a list of questions and concerns related to the other lakes and then there was the particular anomaly they wanted to learn about.

The pilot picked them up at just a few minutes after nine hundred hours and they were off for Lake Six. This was the last one and was probably the most difficult one for them. Their minds were swimming with questions and doubts as well. This was the big one, no not by size, but because it was the last one and they still needed to know what the special issue was.

They followed the same protocol as they flew over the lake and then finally landed. Dick Sherman was at the pad to meet them. They drove into the main base area and went to his office and he started to brief them as to what was going on.

It was the same thing all the other lakes

reported. The approach road up to the rim was not a problem and they had started taking samples as soon as they got to the lake. It was noted the lake was, again, crystal clear and the Rangers Lodge on the bottom was clearly visible.

It was then he gave them the first actual body count of those who were killed in the formation of the lake. They had sent a small submersible down and gained access into the building and took videos of what was inside. He reached over and turned the television on and started the disk player.

Duke and Dennis watched as the submersible approached the front of the lodge and then pushed against the door and it swung open. As the sub moved into the lodge the first person, they saw was the receptionist sitting at her desk. She was sitting on the chair and had both hands lying on the desk top.

Each person was located and each one was found at their post and in their normal position. It was one of the strangest things Duke had ever seen. When the disk had ended, they counted a total of six bodies in the lodge building. The big thing to Duke was they were in perfect condition.

The next thing that hit him was there were six in Lake Six and one in Lake One and four at Lake Four. This confirmed his thought there would be matching numbers in the other three lakes. Dennis made a mental note to have the other three lakes do the mini sub thing and see if they can determine the number of dead at each lake.

Duke thought back to when he first approached Lake One and had speculated on the

120

numbers of people missing. He had said there would be a total of twenty-one and that was the facts of the case. They had twenty-one down there, but the question was, did they all look like those seen here at Lake Six.

A chill ran his spine and he physically shivered from it. He looked at the other two. "I would bet the number of dead would match the lake numbers and now I know I'm right.

"This couldn't get any stranger. As I looked at those people in the Ranger Lodge it came over me they actually looked alive, but of course that's not possible."

Duke finally found himself thinking again and moved back to the issue they came for, the anomaly. "Dick, has there been any issues considered odd or out of the ordinary, something you did not expect?"

He sat there looking at Duke and then leaned back. "Yes, there is something and I think it is the oddest thing I have ever seen. It's the touch and feel of the water. I'm not too sure just how to explain it."

He then sat forward and placed his arms on the desk top. "But when you reached down and touched the water it was more than just a little strange. At first the touch was soft and appealing, but the longer you touched it the rougher and more uncomfortable it became."

He shook his head as if he couldn't believe what he was saying. "This is so hard to relate to you, but that's the best I can do. I feel like it would be best if you two would go to the lake with me and

121

experience it yourselves. So, may I invite you to lunch and then we can go to the lake?"

Duke nodded and they got up and left Dick's office. During this time Dick tried to relate to them more on the anomaly of touching the water.

After lunch they walked out to the truck to head up to the lake. As Duke approached the truck, he looked up at the mountain that formed the bowl of the lake and he stopped dead in his tracks. He found himself looking at the road built up to the summit and the fact it went around the mountain from the right to the left.

It was the exact same layout done at each of the other five lakes. He then turned and looked at the base camp and it too was laid out in the exact same way, each tent in the same location as every other base camp. It dawned on him this was the strangest of all the anomalies at all six lakes.

They entered the truck and headed for the lake. As they came over the rim of the lake Duke noted the hump in the center of the lake and the calmness of it.

Dick parked the truck; they got out and started walking toward the water. As Duke walked around the back of the truck he stopped and turned to look down on the base camp. Dennis stopped and looked as well. "Dennis, have you noticed all the base camps and roads built up the six mountains are all exactly the same?"

Dennis looked at Duke and then back to the base camp. "No, I hadn't but when I think about it, you're right. How the hell could that be? You have six lakes and six teams of scientists assigned to each of the lakes and when they arrive, they all set their camps up the same and build the road to the lake in the same location and same direction. Duke, what's going on?

They turned toward each other and Duke placed his elbow on the rail of the trucks bed. "I haven't the slightest idea, but it's something we had better take into consideration. Something like that just does not happen. Right now, I think we need to finish our look at this lake and then deal with the other issue once we're done with this project."

They both turned and walked toward the lake. Again, it was clear and clean and when they got to the edge Duke could feel the freshness coming off of the water.

Dennis bent down and put his hand in the water and held it there. "Duke it's soft and most appealing. I could leave my hand in it all day. I see no problem with my fingernails or the skin. Wait, the feeling seems to be changing like it getting harder and rougher on the skin."

Duke was watching him as he dropped down on his knees and still kept his hand in the water. Duke could actually feel him starting to panic and then he noticed that Dennis was trying to pull his hand from the water. As he pulled back his hand seemed to go deeper into the water. The more he pulled the deeper his hand went and he was starting to cry out.

Duke moved over by him and grabbed him by both shoulders and pushed him toward the water.

123

As he did Dennis' arm reversed and came out of the water. Duke then set him back on the ground and took hold of his hand and looked it over. There were no marks on it, nothing at all.

Duke kneeled in front of Dennis. "Dennis, why the hell did you do that anyway?"

Dennis looked up at Duke, still in pain. "I didn't want anything to happen to you. We really need you on this project and I felt it was better if anyone was going to get hurt that it be me."

Duke shook his head and stood up. "Damn, guy this doesn't make sense at all. We could have done preliminary tests to determine the hazards involved."

He shook his head while looking directly at Duke. "No, we would not have. You have a habit of just walking up to an issue or question and reaching right in to feel things out. You have done it at every lake and I decided you were not going to do it again."

Dennis' response set Duke back, he was right, it was his style, just dive in and see what happens and this time it almost cost Dennis. "Your right I have a bad habit of jumping right into things, but it does not mean you have to sacrifice yourself in order to protect me."

Dennis was starting to feel much better now and had stood up. "How else am I going to get you to listen and take the time to do things right, crap man, I had a strong feeling something dangerous was going to come along at one of these lakes and I was right."

Duke walked several steps away and turned. "Dennis, we have found hazards at each lake, you know that. What makes this lake any different?"

A look of bewilderment came across his face. He looked down at the ground and then back up to Duke. "Duke, I'm damned if I have an answer to that. I knew I needed to reach down and put my hand in the water and that's what I did, but now I'm not sure if I know why."

Dennis stood there shaking his head and running his hand through his hair. "You're right about the other lakes having their own hazard, so why did I do this? Duke, there is something strange going on around these lakes and now I'm certain we need to move fast.

Now we have the identical organizing of the base camps and access road. If I didn't know any better, I would think this is all being orchestrated in some way or manner.

"Remember the young lady, Susan Dempsey at Lake Three, telling us she had those feelings something was about to come over the rim of the lake she was working at. Well, I have the overwhelming feeling right now. Something is coming. I don't know when, I don't know what, and I don't know how, but I can tell you now, it's coming and we're nowhere near ready for it."

With that Duke stood up and turned to Dick. "We need to get everyone away from this lake now. Move everyone back to the main base and I need you and your lead scientists in your office as soon as possible. Let's get Dennis out of here and back to the base."

Within an hour everyone was off the rim and back at base camp. They had gone to Dick's office and were settling there. Duke looked at Dick. "May I use your phone?"

"Sure, here sit at the desk and take your time."

Duke dialed the main office at Lake One. After a couple of rings, the office manager answered, he asked for Betty Baxter. The manager asked him to hold on. About twenty seconds later Betty came on line, "Betty here."

"Hi Betty this is Duke, you got a minute?"

Betty seemed to be her up beat self at the moment. "Sure, do Duke, what can I do for you?"

Duke took a deep breath. "Betty, I need a couple of things. First of all, I need a determination as to whether you or your people have experienced any adverse effects from working around the lake? Second, I need to know if anyone of your staff has experienced any odd or unfamiliar feelings. By that I mean feeling of something coming or about to happen. Third, I need you to restrict your people from coming into direct contact with the water of the lake.

"We have talked about this before, but I am emphasizing it at this time. If anyone must touch the water of the lake, they are to do it with protection on. Betty, it is vital we separate ourselves from the water and not let it touch us.

"We have found some disturbing things in that regard and I find it necessary to enforce these

126

restrictions. I cannot emphasis the importance of not coming in contact with the water until we have a better understanding of its makeup and impact on people in general. Do you understand?"

Betty's demeanor became serious. "Yes Duke, I understand. I need to advise you in regards to issue two. We have had several of our people expressing feelings of forebodence, feelings something was coming and it was just over the rim and would be appearing in a short time. Are you telling me others at the other lakes are having the same feelings?"

That confirmed Duke's bad feelings about what was happening at the lakes. "That's exactly what I'm telling you Betty. So far we have talked with maybe half a dozen people and then Dennis started having the same feeling. Betty, I need to have you contact Tanner and have him put a security clamp down on all six lakes and do it now."

Betty then hurriedly replied. "Duke, Tanner is here right now and listening in on our conversation. He said he would get right on that lock down."

There was a sense of relief in Duke when he heard that. "Great Betty, Dennis and I will be finishing up here in a couple of hours and will head back to Lake One in the morning. We'll probably stop off at the other four lakes on our return and finish up on a few issues we need to deal with. We should be there in two to three days."

Betty was in full gear by this time. "Good, that will give us time to correlate our data and be ready to start in on the details when you get here."

Duke was impressed with her response to the situation and how fast she was working things up. "That's great Betty, see you in three days."

Betty was in full control. "Right Duke, three days. Bye."

"Bye Betty."

Duke turned to Dennis and Dick. "Now we need to address those same issues here. Dennis we will leave in the morning if you're up to it. Dick, we need to take a long hard look at everything that has been going on here from day one."

Dick turned and opened a file drawer and started pulling tapes and file folders out and setting them on his desk. "Duke everything, we have done and experienced here at Lake Six is in these files. I require all paper work and support media to be placed in this office at the end of each and every day. It keeps things centralized and works perfect for moments like this."

By this time Duke was looking for specific things he had determined would probably be taking place at this lake sometime during their research. He knew some of the specifics he was looking for and knew when he found those, other issues would follow close behind.

He had been storing thoughts and ideas from when he first saw Lake One and as a result, he was coming up with a number of ideas he needed to start confirming. Most pressing on his mind were the number of dead. He had been totally surprised when he saw the videos of the lodge at the bottom of Lake

Six and the condition and position of the six bodies. That number had jumped out at him and he related to the one body in Lake One and the four bodies in Lake Four.

Next were the individual anomalies they found at each lake. Those took a little explaining and generally were mind busting. In the back of his mind he felt, and had proven in a couple of the lakes, not only were they wonderful and complex anomalies, but there would probably be bad side effects from every anomaly as well. So far nothing matches what he thought was true and firm scientific understanding.

The substance they had been calling water was turning out to be anything but water as we knew it. This stuff was doing things that boggled the imagination. How could a substance be so many things in different places and still be what we would consider water? It had his mind swirling with thoughts, none of which gave him any logical answers to what was happening.

One thing kept coming up in his mind was a day of reckoning was coming and it was not far off. He had no idea what form it was to come in, but he knew it was coming. It then hit him he had just experienced the same concern or fear the others had been relating to him. Something was coming and it was going to be big.

By big he had no idea as to just how big it was going to be, but if it was anything near seeing six mountains and depression form in less than a half hour and then fill with a water like substance, then

129

big meant something he didn't even want to think of.

As he thought about it, he began to realize he had been having those thoughts from the beginning. Ever since he first saw Lake One, a feeling of something big coming was there. It hadn't been anything that felt threatening or ominous but it had been there and now he recognized it.

He had to think, and sitting there in the tent was not helping. He looked over at Dennis and Dick. "If you two will excuse me, I need to go for a walk and get some in-depth thinking done.

"Right now, I feel overwhelmed and I need to get out and into some clear air and give myself time to let my mind dig through all we have seen and heard over the past seven or eight days. I'll be back in a few hours."

He got up and walked toward the door, stopped and turned around. "Dennis, I think you were right about the hazards we are faced with on these lakes. I think you had better pursue those issues now and fill me in when you get done and I return."

Dennis nodded and sat back as he watched Duke walk through the door. He looked over at Dick. "That is one man who has a hell of a lot on his mind right now.

"I haven't really known him long but I can tell you he is dedicated and serious about this project. I would venture to say when he comes back through that door we will have a whole new agenda laid out for us."

Dick was nodding his head. "Yeah, I think

you're right about that."

Chapter Ten

REVELATIONS

During the seven or eight days they had been traveling from lake to lake the application of the mini subs had been taking place as a means of reaching the structures at the bottom of each lake. Duke had speculated at each structure they would find bodies, the number of bodies would depend on which lake they were found in. Lake One would have only one body while Lake Two would have two and so on for a total of twenty-one bodies in all six lakes.

It was while they were sitting in Dick Sherman's office the first call came in. Lake Four was found to have four bodies by a small tool shed at the base of the center pier for the bridge. The bodies were in perfect condition and all sitting on the ground leaning against the shed with their hands in their laps, and they appeared to be sleeping.

Over the next two days the rest of the lakes called in. Lake Two reported two bodies in the hunting shack sitting at a table across from one another. They were sitting upright with their hands on the table top and facing directly at one another. The bodies were in perfect condition.

Lake Three reported that three of the family members were reported home at the time of the lake's creation, they were found in the living room sitting on a couch side by side looking straight ahead and sitting upright with their hands in their laps. Again, they were in perfect condition.

Lake Five had five bodies in an office and sitting in various chairs and places all upright and all-in pristine condition.

After receiving the reports from each lake Duke knew the issue with the bodies was just getting started. He had a strange and sickening feeling coming over him and he could not define it or get rid of it.

Dennis saw the reaction in Duke's face. "Duke, what is it, what's bothering you?"

Duke looked at Dennis and then over at Dick. "They're not dead."

"What did you say?" Dick asked leaning over his desk. "Duke, what did you just say?"

By this time Duke's face had paled and looked clammy. He shook his head and tried to get his bearing and then stood up and walked over to the water cooler and got a drink. He finished the drink and then returned to his chair and sat down. "Dick, Dennis, I don't know how and I don't understand, but I am certain every single one of those twenty-one people are not dead."

Just then the call came in from Lake One. They had gone down and checked the car and there was a young lady sitting in the driver's seat with both her hands on the steering wheel and her face looking straight ahead, just as if she was driving. Her body was in perfect condition.

As soon as he heard that, Duke jumped up and ran out of the office and to the restroom and threw up everything that was there to come up. Dick and Dennis had followed him and waited outside the door until he was done. As Duke came out of the restroom door Dennis took him by the arm and walked him out of the tent and into the fresh air.

They all stood there listening to the breeze as it passed by them. Duke was still weak and a little shaky from his experience and wanted to let time pass before having to go back and start again. He turned to Dennis. "It was the idea of that young woman sitting down there in her car so lonely and scary I just lost it. I don't know if they are aware of what is going on, but I do know they are alive and I can't tell you how I know."

Dennis turned to Duke. "Then we will just go down there and bring them up. Maybe we can revive them and get them home."

Duke shook his head. "We can't do that. They're five hundred feet down and the decompression when we brought them up would kill them for sure. No, we have to leave them there until such time whatever is going to happen brings them back up."

That hit Dick like a bat. He literally fell backward. "What the hell do you mean, whatever is going to happen brings them back up?"

Duke turned and walked a few paces away from Dick and Dennis and then turned and looked at both of them. "Gentlemen, I am convinced something monumental is about to happen. These lakes did not just appear as the result of some freak happening of nature. No, these lakes appeared as a result of a planned and initiated action by someone or something we know little or nothing about."

"Duke, don't tell us you're talking extraterrestrials or something freaky like that?"

Duke could feel his face flush as he watched Dennis' reaction. "I don't know what the hell I'm talking about"

Duke was standing there clinching his fists. "There is something in or around those lakes that is not known to us in any way. It is real and it is dangerous to us, just how I don't know. All I can tell you is these things are happening for a reason and what that reason is I don't know, but we had better figure it out."

Duke stomped back into Dick's office and sat down at the desk and started going over the reports and test results that had been produced to that date. He was like a demon as he went through each and every paper searching for one illusive bit of information that would unlock what was going on.

Shortly Dick and Dennis entered the office and started going over papers as well. It was about

135

an hour and a half later Dennis tossed a paper down in front of Duke. "What do you think about this paper and the results of these tests it refers to?"

Duke picked it up and started reading and then held it off to one side and started leafing through a pile of papers on the left side of the desk. After several second, he grabbed a piece of paper and held it up by the one Dennis gave him. He sat back and looked at the other two. "I think we have our first stepping stone in this mystery.

Duke looked at the two pages moving his eyes from one to the other. "Dennis, I want you to get in touch with your friends in NASA and this is what I want."

Duke handed a page from his note pad to Dennis. "We will need this as soon as they can get it to us. Dennis this is a top priority issue and you need to make it clear to them. Use our status code. I need that information by tomorrow morning at the latest."

Dennis took the page and headed out the door. Duke then turned to Dick. "Dick, you and I are going back up to the lake. We will need both video and still cameras and a laser survey unit.

Dick headed off to get the needed equipment and Duke turned to the phone. He called Dick's secretary and asked her to set up a conference call with the Lead Scientists of the other five lakes.

It took her ten minutes to get everyone on line and ready. She advised Duke and he then answered the phone. "Good afternoon everyone, are we all here?"

Everyone checked in and he told them what

they needed for this meeting and waited as each got themselves prepared. Finally, everyone checked back in and they were ready. "Okay now, here is what is happening so far. We are sure of these points even though we cannot prove them at this time. First of all, these lakes are not an accident. They were put here for a purpose.

"Second, with every good issue we found there is an equally dangerous hazard to each lake. If you have not determined that, then this is your first priority after this meeting is over.

"Third, the people at the bottom of the lakes are not dead." Duke could hear everyone gasping. "Listen up people, I know that comment is a little startling, but we have come to this conclusion after looking at several of the bodies close up. By now they should have shown decomposition, but they are not. In addition, their coloration is perfect. And, the texture of their skin is perfect.

"For those of you who have your photos from the mini sub, all you have to do is take a close look and review the videos to understand why we're saying this. Now this does not mean we can go down and get them. They are five hundred feet down and the decompression in bringing them up would kill them for sure. No, we leave them and see what happens.

"Fourth, we have NASA working on an aerial view of the six lakes at this time. When they are done, we will get copies of those views to you, both the ones of your individual lake and the overall view of all six lakes. Be prepared to take a critical look at these views, I think they will tell us a rather interesting story, any questions?"

"Duke, this is Jackie, we're not too sure just how to take what you have told us. Is it possible to fill us in a little more on what brought you to these conclusions?"

Duke was nodding his head and felt good they were taking this seriously. "Yes Jackie, that is just what I'm about to do. Just about three hours ago Dick Sherman and I went up on the rim of Lake Six and took a series of still photos and video shots.

"We took a laser surveying instrument with us to run a couple of experiments on the lake. As I had told you before, there's a bulge in the center of each lake and the bulge is around three feet high when compared to the edge of the lakes. We thought this bulge was constant, but we have determined it is changing and I would advise each of you to run the same test on your respective lakes to confirm what I am about to say.

"The bulge is increasing. When we ran a survey of the bulge today it was three feet higher than the last survey. It is my recommendation you survey the bulge each day and try to do it at the same time.

"Now here is the kicker, the edge of the lake should be dropping as the bulge is increasing. But it is not, it is remaining at the exact same level. Next, the bottom of the lake is bulging as well. That bulge is exactly the same as the surface bulge.

"People, the bottom of the lake is deforming and it is showing on the surface of the lake, the surface is an exact copy of the contour of the bottom of the lake and the structures at the bottom of the lake are riding the bulge upward.

"Now I don't understand and I don't know just how it will take place but I'm willing to bet the lake bottom is going to continue to deform and raise up to the surface. I don't know what the water is going to do and I don't know how long it is going to take. I just know it is happening and it is not going to stop.

"Those of you who have had those feelings of something coming over the rim of the lake are right on. The problem is it is not something coming from outside into the lake, it is the lake itself coming over the top of the rim. If our current measurements and the NASA survey prove to be right on, then the lake water will be displaced from the lake as the structure and whatever is under it come to the top of the rim."

There was absolute dead silence on the other end of the line. No one was saying a thing. They were all waiting for someone else to start. Duke decided to sit and wait until someone stepped forward and asked the first question.

Finally, Betty spoke up. "Duke what test or surveys is NASA running for us?"

"Betty, they are doing a series of scans in different wave lengths and then they will do a number of deep earth penetrations."

"Duke, what do you expect to find or discover?"

"Betty, we are looking for an object. It is

139

either one object under each lake or one that is of such massive size it is under all six lakes."

Paul spoke up. "Duke, the present locations of our base camp must now be considered unsafe as well?"

"Yes Paul, that's right. If the lakes go over the top of the rims, anything on the face of the mountains and at the base is in jeopardy. My recommendation is you move the base camps out and away from the base of the mountains and if possible onto areas that are elevated. I would not stay in the valleys from now on.

"And by the way, you didn't know it but each and every one of the six base camps and roads at the six lakes are identical in makeup and location. Every team set their respective sites up in exactly the same way and same places in respect to the mountains and lakes.

It fell quiet again. "Duke, Paul here, what if you're wrong?"

"That Paul will be the end of my career. But I feel so confident in what I'm saying I doubt very much I have to worry about my career.

"Now what is even more important than my future is what lies under the bottom of these lakes. That is going to be the prize and I would venture to say you and I will be seeing something never experienced in all the history of the world and for that I am willing to chuck my career."

They were beginning to understand why Duke felt there was something under the lake and it was pushing up the bottoms of the lakes. The key to it all was the NASA scans and those were thought to be just hours away. Duke then advised everyone as soon as the data came in from NASA he would call another meeting and make the data available to everyone.

He then called the meeting to an end and the wait was on. It was almost ten hours later when they got the call from NASA and the scans were sent to them. Duke could hardly wait to see the results and called the staff of Lake Six together so everyone could see.

The first shots that came up were light wave shots and they indicated something was under the lake. This was followed with heat shots and then soundings. When all was put together there were massive objects under the bottom center of each lake, right below the manmade object sitting on the bottom.

As the NASA data continued to come in, the actual size of the objects under the lakes became more detailed. All six objects are exactly the same in outline and size. They appear to be round and just under the manmade structures at the bottom of the lake. A second rounded area appears to be deeper into the ground. One thing about these things is they are huge, massive objects.

They were stunned by what they were seeing. There was no way this could be true. These objects, or should we call them machines were sitting in a line from Mexico to Canada were off set from the center of the continental United States. Then, to realize, they were buried more than five hundred feet under the surface of the land was even more unbelievable.

Duke looked over at Dennis and Dick and they were just as shocked as he was.

Dick stood up and leaned over the desk. "This is unbelievable. Duke, Dennis, I cannot believe this is real. There must have been something wrong with their monitoring system or their scanning system."

Duke was shaking his head. "No, they advise they rechecked everything and what we are seeing are real objects under each of the lakes."

Dick began to grasp the situation. "Okay, if they are real objects then what is their purpose in being there? Next, when were they put there? And, finally what is the purpose of each lake and the substances that are in them?"

Duke looked over a Dick and shook his head. "Those Dick, are the bottom-line questions we need to ask. The problem is we have no way of answering those questions. But I can tell you this, those objects are pushing upward. We can see the bulge in the center of each lake and that bulge is growing. We also know the bottom of each lake is a perfect copy of a bulge on the lake surface. No, something is happening and all we can do is sit and wait."

They sat there looking at the data and photos on the screen waiting for something to come. Dennis finally shifted himself in his chair and leaned toward Duke. "Duke, is it possible those things will actually push themselves all the way up to the top of the rim and displace all the water with its odd characteristics out onto the land?"

That question startled Dick and he looked over at Duke to hear his answer. Duke had discussed issue with the individual lake administrators, but he had not thought about the anomalies of each lake being released onto the land around the mountain that was confining them.

He looked back at both of them and saw the fear and concern in their eyes. "I think if those objects do in fact push themselves all the way up to the rim of the lakes, we will have a flood of those waters over the land around the mountains. I have no idea what impact will be and especially when waters from the adjoining lakes come in contact. I just can't answer that question and I don't know how we would keep it from happening.

"However, I can tell you what I want, and that is a monitoring system around each lake. I want the level of the water's edge monitored round the clock. I also want a monitor placed in the middle of each lake to measure the bulge as it develops.

I'm afraid at this time we are in a waiting game and all we can do is monitor the lakes and respond to whatever happens. Meanwhile, I think I'm going to have Lake One analyze all the water samples and try to combine them to see if they can determine any adverse reaction if and when the waters come in contact."

Dennis and Dick agreed with the idea and Duke then called Betty at Lake One to get her started on the tests. When Betty came on the line, Duke advised her as to what their plans were and then laid out what he wanted. "Betty, we sent to your lab samples of each of the other five lakes. What we want you to do is run some test by combining the waters of say Lake One and Lake Two, then Lake Two and Lake Three and so on. What we need to know is if anything happens when we combine those waters.

"Please be careful, we have no idea as to what may happen when you do that, so take all the necessary precautions, got that?"

"Sure, thing Duke. I'll make sure everyone understands the danger involved. We will probably work with less than a gram of sample in order to keep any adverse reactions at a minimum."

"Good, let me know if anything odd happens, in fact let me know one way or the other. Oh, and Betty, we need the results yesterday."

Things were beginning to heat up now and it appeared they were on a time schedule, the length of which they had no idea. If the bottom of the lakes were actually coming up then it meant the manmade objects were coming up as well and so were the people.

Just the thought of it made Duke nervous. What would those people be like when they came to the surface? It was possible they would have severe psychological problems they would have to deal with. Just the trauma of the event would be enough, but the period of time they had spent at the bottom of the lakes would increase their trauma, is if they remembered it.

Duke turned to Dick. "Dick if we are right

144

and those buildings are coming up with the bottom, somewhere along the line those people down there will surface as well. Now if they are alive, and I'm sure they are, then when they come too or wake up or whatever, they may well be facing some serious psychological issue. Do you agree?"

Dick sat there looking at the ceiling of the tent and then at Duke. "Yeah, I think you're right about that. My problem is I don't have any experts on site who can deal with those issues."

It dawned on Duke it was the same for the other five lakes. "All right we need to see we have people here who can deal with those issues. Dennis, get someone on that job right away. I want specialist at each lake before those buildings get to the surface."

Dennis was nodding his head and writing down notes. He got up and headed for the door, stopped and turned. "You're sure we will need these people?"

"Dennis, I don't know, but in the event we do I would suggest we have them here anyway. If I were one of those people down there and I suddenly find myself being flooded and some unknown time later I find I was all right I think I would need help.

"No, you get those people to each lake and do it as fast as you can."

Dennis nodded his head and went out the door. Duke turned to Dick. "I think we're in one hell of a situation here and eighty percent of what I'm doing lacks scientific support. But I can tell you this, something is coming and it is going to be something we had better try to be ready for.

"As I sit here and look at those scan pictures, I know whatever those things are they were not put there by mankind. If they were not put there by mankind, then who the hell did and when did they do it?"

Chapter Eleven

A COUNTER FORCE BUILDS

It was around midnight when the phone in Mike's apartment started to ring. He had been working on the plans for the coming events. As he reached for the phone, he noted the name on the incoming call registry. It was Larry.

"Hi Larry, what's up?"

"Mike, you better get down to the command center as soon as you can. Things are starting to happen at the lakes and it's getting crazier than hell."

"What the hell are you talking about Larry?"

"Mike, not on the phone, head on down to the center and do it now. I'll be there waiting for you, also."

"Yeah, go ahead."

"The General is involved as well and is waiting for you to get here. Things are moving fast and you better get moving as well."

Twenty minutes later Mike was walking through the door into the subterranean command center after using his entry key and password to get through security. He looked over at the map wall and saw the six lakes sitting there with flashing red circles around each one.

Just then Larry walked up to him. "Things have started to happen at the lakes. Ridgeman had called for some special scans by NASA and they show an object under the bottom of each lake and those objects are pushing themselves up toward the surface.

"We have learned the people in the structures at the lake bottoms are not believed to be dead, but are in fact alive and in some type of a suspension. Mike, our person in NASA insists whatever these things are they are big and they are something that is beyond any known technology.

"The General is currently waiting for you to come on line with him. He's pissed off and I don't think you want to keep him waiting."

Mike walked into the office and sat down at his desk and reached over and pushed the phone button. "Hi General Halverson, what can I do for you?"

"Mike, you can tell me what the hell is going on out there. My staff and I have been getting a number of briefings on something happening at the lakes. Haven't you and your people been on top of this thing?"

"General, I just got the information myself and we've not had time to study the data we have

148

received. But if things are going as this tells us, then nothing is really happening at this time.

"General, we have time to make our plans and start to move our people to the places they need to be in order to deal with this issue."

"Mike, I don't think you understand the gravity of this situation. If those are actually machines coming to the surface then we need to know what their purpose is and how we can control them. If need be, I want to take possession of those machines as soon as they surface."

"Hold everything General, I don't think you want to do that right now. We need to wait and see what they are and try to determine what they are here for.

"May I suggest I send my units in, they can set up observation posts and monitor what is going on and what the machines look like once they breach the surface of the lakes?

"General, I think your Stryker Units need to stay put and not venture into the lake area until we have more information on what is going on. Have them in the ready in the event we need them, but keep them out of the game. If you move too soon and too fast, it's going to give away our game plan and probably get us killed.

"All right Mike, I agree with what you're saying. I just don't want this thing to get out of control. By the way, has the little pig Arron been taken care of yet?"

"No sir, he is still in isolation at Lake One. Our man is watching him and has been told to do

149

him the moment the opportunity affords itself. I think the movement of those machines will help in that respect.

"As I understand it, as the machines move up, they are bulging the lake surface and the research teams working the lakes have determined they will have to move to safety soon. While they are making that move, we will deal with Arron."

"Sounds good to me Mike. All right, I'll leave the Six Lake thing to you and concentrate on the moves here in DC. I think this whole Six Lake thing will help us here as well. If all goes right, within a week we will have carried out the coup and reinstituted our constitution as it was meant to be.

"Good luck and keep me informed as to what is going on and when you'll need the Stryker Units."

"All right General Halverson, we'll do that, and good luck. Mike out."

He pushed the phone button and sat back in his chair. Things were starting to move now and over the next week to two weeks he and his partners would be seeing the development of a new nation on the west coast of the United States. A nation dedicated to fulfilling the demand for drugs and other illicit commodities across the world.

He was looking at becoming one of, if not the richest men in the world. He had gambled everything and now the final stage had been set and thing were going to happen and happen fast. In this game the winner would be the ones who were the fastest and the boldest.

Chapter Twelve

THE RISING

It was two days later when the call came in from Betty. "Yes, Betty, how's it going down there?"

"Duke, I really don't know. I guess it depends on how you react to the information I'm about to pass on to you."

Duke felt an emptiness enter his body as she spoke. "You mean the results of the tests I asked for?"

Duke was sitting at his desk and setting a stack of papers off to one side and pulling a pad over in front of him in order to get ready to receive the findings.

"That's right." She sounded a little subdued and edgy. "The tests were run on every sample we had in the order you suggested." She hesitated at that point.

Duke was waiting to hear the results and was getting a little impatient with her. "Okay Betty, give it to me straight. Take your time so I can get this all down as you give it to me." He sat there waiting.

Finally, Betty cleared her throat. "Duke, there was nothing. When the samples were put together, they all reverted to water, nothing more."

There was dead silence at Duke's end and she sat there waiting for what she had said to sink in and then waiting for his reaction. "Betty, I think you need to explain these results to me." There was a sense of disbelief and surprise in his voice.

Betty cleared her throat again. "Duke, we combined those samples in every way possible including combining all six samples and when we did, we could see the reaction between the samples and when the reactions ended the samples all proved to be water. Just clear perfectly pure water and nothing else."

Duke sat there silently doodling on his note pad and letting the test results slip through his mind. He had not expected this result and it had him in a quandary at the moment. He thought, so if the lakes do overflow the rims and the waters meet and combine, it will simply be water and nothing else.

Then he thought, but until the waters from each individual lake come in contact with waters from any of the other lakes, those waters will still have the anomaly present and active. So, they still need to be out of the way.

Duke then got back to Betty. "Betty, are you still there?"

"Yes Duke, I'm here."

Duke was busy making notes on a note pad

as he talked to Betty. "Betty, I need you to do one more test for me. I need a contact test between two or more of the samples. I want you to place an amount of sample, from any one of the six lakes, in one spot, and then place a similar amount of another sample from one of the other five lakes next to it so that they just come in contact at only one point, and then see what happens."

Betty paused as she noted what Duke wanted. "Duke, standby while we get those samples and determine what happens."

Duke sat there waiting and continued writing on his note pad. He then turned a page and started to draw a picture and then made a notation under the drawing. It was maybe fifteen minutes before Betty came back to him.

"Duke you there?"

"Yes Betty, I'm here."

Her voice sounded a little excited and stressed as well. "Duke, it was violent as hell. When the two samples came together, they reacted. It was like an acid hitting a piece of meat. It sizzled and there was what appeared to be smoke or steam coming from where the two samples met. Once it started they came together rapidly and violently. It only took about twenty seconds and it was all over. What was left was pure water nothing else."

Duke sat there nodding his head and then he leaned forward. "Betty, we need your team to follow up on this. We want every test you can do with that stuff. I want samples from every lake to be joined with samples from every other lake to see if the

153

reaction is the same. The last test is to be samples of all six lakes coming together at the same time and the results recorded."

Betty was quiet for several seconds. "All right Duke, we'll get on it right now and as soon as we're done, I'll get back to you. I need to let you know we already joined all the samples together from all six lakes and the results were the same, just pure water and no violent reaction."

"Yeah Betty, I know, but we have missed something and so I want more tests run. Those lakes have different water qualities and there is a reason for it and I want to know why.

"Thanks Betty, and by the way, it makes no difference what the time is when you get back to us. We'll be waiting. There is no way I can sleep right now."

Duke was more alive right at that moment than he had been for years. They were on the verge of something that would make the greatest change in the earth's makeup has ever happened. He was sure of that.

It was around three hundred hours when the phone rang. Duke answered and Betty was there. She sounded tired but excited as well. "Duke, is that you?"

Duke's demeanor sparked and he sat up. "Yes Betty, it's me, what do you have?"

Betty then started to talk and then stopped and you could hear her shuffling papers around on her desk. "Duke, you were right, everything came out pure water. But there is something else you need

154

to know. There were after effects we had not expected.

"Duke, when we combined all the samples, we saw the same reactions. Everything was reacting just as the individual tests and double up tests results except, at the end of the final test we had pure water and there in the middle of the pure water was an object.

"God Duke, it was alive and it was growing. That thing was growing and we had to do something so we got it into a container and sealed it. At that moment it stopped growing but it is still alive. Well, let me put it this way, it appeared to be alive.

"Duke, it came from the joining of all the samples."

Duke sat there listening to Betty. He could tell she was scared as well and a little overwhelmed. This was a veteran scientist and she was stressed to the maximum. "Betty, describe the object to me?"

There was a pause again and then she came back. "Duke, it was round like a small ball, and it's transparent and that is it. There is nothing else to describe about it. It is transparent and looks like water and is round."

Duke tried to calm her. "Betty, you all right now?"

She came back. "Yes Duke, I'm doing fine it was just so unexpected and chilling as well. As I sit here and think about it, when we joined all the samples together there was a violent reaction just like all the other except it appears all the anomalies separated from the water and joined together and we ended up with this object and a bunch of pure water.

"Also, we found the amount of sample waters we used made a difference. It was then when this thing appeared. It took a certain volume of sample to get this reaction. Other than that, I'm at a loss to explain it."

Duke sat there and then said to himself. "Everything not water joined together and formed an object."

He looked over at Dennis who had been sitting there all this time waiting things out. "Dennis, do you get what she just said?"

He was shaking his head like he was trying to shake a bunch of cobwebs from his mind. "It doesn't make sense at all. How the hell could anything, let alone something alive, come out of the anomalies? But even more strange, how did the anomalies separate from the water?"

They both sat there looking at each other and then Betty came back, "Duke, you still there?"

Duke leaned toward the speaker phone. "Yes Betty, we're still here. We're trying to determine what our next move should be."

"Duke, we have been discussing what happened when the object formed and everyone here is in agreement, they felt a sense of fear, then comfort and then a feeling they were not in danger. Right now, we all feel the same way." There was calmness in Betty's voice as she related the information to us.

Duke looked at Dennis and then sat back a moment. "Betty, you're telling me you are no longer afraid of the object as you were when you first witnessed its creation and actions?"

"Duke, that is correct. We are certain this thing is not a threat to us. I don't know how we know that, but we are sure it is safe and will not harm us."

Again, Duke could hear a calmness from Betty and he didn't like it one bit.

He stood up and walked across the office and then back to the speaker phone. "Betty, Dennis and I will be heading back there as soon as we can get the helicopter on line and out of here. Listen to me do not touch that object or the container it is in no matter what. Do you understand me?"

There was a long pause. "I understand Duke, and everyone else has been sent to their tents and will remain away from the labs until you get here."

"All right Betty, we're on our way. We will have to stop at some of the other lakes to fuel up but we'll be there by late tomorrow. You get to bed and get some rest and we'll see you then."

Betty came back. "Will do Duke, and please take it easy."

"Bye Betty."

"Bye Duke."

Duke looked at Dennis. "I don't like this one bit. Get the helicopter on line now and let's get going. I think we're too late. Damn, I hope we're not too late."

In twenty minutes, the helicopter was ready and they were taking off. Just then Dennis reached out and touched Duke. "Duke, what do you mean by 'being too late'?"

There was a hurt look on Duke's face and he started to shake his head. "Dennis, did you notice the change in Betty's demeanor over the course of all the phone calls and conversations?"

Dennis sat there a few seconds and then started to nod his head. "Yeah, I did. She seemed to becoming softer and easier."

Duke was nodding his head as well. "That's right and I have a feeling she has fallen under the influence of the object. Dennis, I think this thing is more than alive, it is taking her over and maybe the rest of her research team."

They arrived at Lake One late the following afternoon. Duke and Dennis went directly to Betty's office and as they entered the main administrative tent, they found the receptionist sitting at her desk with her arms on the desk top looking straight ahead and not moving.

Duke walked over to her and bent over and looked into her face and eyes. She was alive, but not moving and she was not responsive to his voice or his touch. He looked at Dennis and then motioned him to the door to Betty's office. They both entered the office to find Betty in the same position sitting behind her desk and with her arms on the desk top.

On her desk top and between her arms was a glass container with its lid lying beside it. The container was empty, but Duke was sure he knew what had been in it. He stepped back from the desk and turned to Dennis and motioned him out of the office and out of the tent.

When they got outside the tent Duke looked around the Lake One facility. He noted all the tents had been moved about half a mile from their original location to an area that was elevated about an equal elevation as that of the lake rim. Dennis walked up beside him. "Duke, I don't see or hear anyone around, do you?"

Duke was straining to hear the people who should be there and also looking around the compound. "No Dennis, I don't hear anything, I don't think anyone is here and if they are, I don't think they can respond anyway."

Duke reached back and took hold of Dennis' right elbow and started walking toward the security office. As they approached the tent where Tanner Marshall would be, he could hear something coming from inside the tent. They got to the entrance and stopped and listened to the sound coming from the tent. It was someone humming.

Duke and Dennis looked at each other and then Duke reached out and pulled the entrance flap back and stepped into the tent. There was no one inside the main entrance area but they could still hear the humming coming from the office of the security officer.

Duke walked over to the door, turned sideways and then put his ear to the door. The humming was definitely coming from within the office and was continuous. Oh, so gently Duke pushed to door open and looked in. Tanner was sitting at his desk with his head back on the back of the chair and looking up at the ceiling at about a forty-five-degree angle. He was quietly humming.

Duke stayed put and adjusted his sight and looked up where Tanners eyes were looking and there on the ceiling of the tent was a clear round object pressed up against the ceiling. As he looked at this thing, he noted there was a small black dot on the side facing Tanner and it seemed to be fixated on him.

Just then he noticed the right hand of Tanner move and his index finger lifted off the desk top and he wagged at Duke. Tanner was clearly in control of his situation and was in a standoff with this thing, whatever it was. Duke stayed put and then reached back and grabbed Dennis and pulled him up close to him.

"Get us a metal container with a lid we can secure and lock, got me?

Dennis couldn't see what was going on but he knew something bad was in the making. He nodded and took off looking for a container that fit Duke's description.

He ran back to the helicopter and told the pilot to kill the motor and stay put, not to leave the helicopter no matter what. He then reached in and grabbed the utility box from the helicopter opened it up and dumped everything out. He then took off running for the security tent.

When he got to the tent Duke was still at the door looking in. When he got up by Duke, he handed the box to him and then readied himself for whatever was to follow.

Duke closed the door and backed away from

160

it and then turned to Dennis. "There is a clear colorless object up against the ceiling of the office and it appears to be watching Tanner. I think it's the object from the jar in Betty's office and if the jar did not hold it then we need something else that can."

Dennis nodded his head and started looking around the office. "That box won't hold it so we need a second container to put that box in, one we can seal."

Duke was nodding his head in agreement and at that moment spotted a number of heavy-duty black plastic bags over on a shelf by the front door. Get two of those and empty them and bring them here. We can put the box in them and seal the plastic."

After a few minutes they were ready. Duke moved back to the door and looked in. Tanner was still there watching the ball of whatever and humming. Duke looked at Dennis. "Listen, that thing does not appear to move fast and it gives us the advantage.

"Do not let it touch you, got me. I think we're all right as long as we don't come into contact with it. Now, take the broom and when we get in there I'll hold the box under it and you knock it loose. We'll have just seconds to close the box lock it and get it into a bag and seal it. You ready?"

Dennis nodded his head and moved into position. Duke counted down and both entered the office through the door. Dennis went for the thing with vengeance. Seldom do first time efforts prove to be successful and in this case it did. Duke got the box under the thing and Dennis hit it at almost the same moment and down it came. The thing barely started to move when they got to it.

Duke slammed the box lid closed and Dennis grabbed a bag and they stuffed the box into the bag and twisted the bag and taped it off. They then took a second plastic bag and put the first bag into it and then they sealed it with Dennis' lighter.

Duke stepped back breathing hard and turned to Tanner, "you all right?"

Tanner sat there looking at the two of them. "Am I glad to see you two. I don't know how much longer I was going to be able to hold out."

"Tanner, what the hell happened here?"

Tanner stood up and walked around the desk and then turned and went out the door and out of the tent into the open air. Duke and Dennis were right behind him. Once outside Tanner turned to Duke. "Duke, I'm not quite sure just what the hell happened. The first thing I knew I heard a panic outside here and when I went out everyone was running from their tents and up into the hills over there. They just kept going. I've never seen anything like it.

"I grabbed one woman, Lois I think, and asked her what was going on. She was scared to hell. All she could say was it was out and it killed Betty. I let her go and headed for Betty's office and when I went through the door, I found Mary sitting at her desk trying to talk and then she brought her arms up, set them on the desk, then looked straight ahead and stopped moving.

"I pushed on into the office and Betty was sitting there at her desk and this thing was on her face. She was fighting as hard as she could but it forced her mouth open and I could see through it and it released a small part of it into her mouth and then backed down off of her and onto her desk top. It stood there watching her as she continued to struggle and then she brought her arms up and placed them on the desk top and then just froze with her mouth open just like Mary's."

Duke and Dennis stood there looking at Tanner. Duke reached out and put his hand on Tanner shoulder. "Tanner, are you able to continue on with us?"

Tanner turned toward the two of them and nodded. "Yeah, I'm ready but I need to do something. I'll meet you back here in this spot in fifteen minutes and I'll wait here until you two come back for me."

Duke nodded and then pulled Dennis with him and they returned to the helicopter and lifted off. He ordered the pilot to make a run over the hills to the west of the main camp and see if they could locate any of the people who had gone in that direction. It only took them ten minutes to find the people. They had all gone up onto a high ridge and were sitting there waiting for whatever to happen.

They then returned to the base camp and found Tanner waiting for them. Tanner entered the helicopter and Duke gave the go ahead for the pilot to take off. Duke had the pilot return to the ridge area set down about a quarter of a mile south of the

163

research team.

Duke, Dennis and Tanner exited the helicopter and walked over to the people; most were milling around still appearing to be scared silly. As they walked up to them several approached and started asking questions. Duke quieted them down and had everyone gather around and sit down.

After they all were present, he started to talk to them. "The first question I have of you is this. Was anyone of you touched by the creature?"

Everyone started looking around at each other and gradually started to shake their heads no.

"Good, now we have captured the thing and have sealed it into a metal box and then put the box is double wrapped and sealed plastic bags, it will not get out."

He again watched, everyone and that seemed to calm them some. "Now we found both Mary and Betty in the administration tent and they have both been attacked by the creature and are not able to assist us."

Just then a hand went up.

Duke looked at the young lady. "Yes, what do you need?"

"My name is Joann. I just want to know if they are dead."

Duke thought for a few seconds. "Joann, I'm not sure at this point. I did not have enough time when we were in the tent to make that determination, but we will do it upon our return to the camp. Off the top of my head, I don't think so. The way they were sitting and the manner in which they took those positions is not normal for someone who is dying. No, I think they're alive, I just don't know anything more beyond that."

Everyone started to look around and talk among themselves. Duke raised his hand and quieted them. "Now listen. I believe we have taken care of any threat down there in the camp. The one thing we must remember is never to combine those water samples again. Do you understand?"

Everyone started nodding again.

"All right let's get off of this ridge and back to our jobs. We have a hell of a lot to do between now and when whatever is supposed to happen does in fact happen."

With that everyone got up and started back for the camp. Duke walked over to one of the medical teams who had formed and asked which one was the leader. One of them stepped forward. "What is your name please?"

The Doctor advised Duke that he was Doctor Michael Long. "Okay Michael, I need you and one of your senior doctors to come with me to the helicopter, we're going back to the base and take a close look at Mary and Betty. Can you do that?"

The doctor looked at Duke and nodded. He then stepped over to one of the other team members and took him aside and they both came back to Duke. "We're ready to go. We have our gear with us so we will be able to go directly to the ladies and do what needs to be done."

They all boarded the helicopter and headed back to the base camp. When they landed the two doctors, Duke, Dennis and Tanner went over to the administration tent and found Mary and Betty in exactly the same position they had been in before. "Gentlemen, we believe the thing deposited something into their mouths. That's why they have their mouths open, so be careful around those areas."

Both doctors nodded and approached Mary. The first thing they did was check for a heartbeat. Michael checked for a heartbeat and stood up and looked over at Duke. "She has a regular heartbeat. She's not dead at all."

Duke and Dennis moved in closer. "Doctor, can you see anything in her mouth or throat?"

Michael bent over and looked into her mouth and then stood right back up and backed off. He looked over at Duke and then turned and walked over to the wall.

Duke followed him. "Michael, what is it? What did you see in her mouth?"

The doctor turned, his face was white gray in color and he was shaking all over. "Sir, there is a chunk of stuff in her mouth just at the back and in front of the esophagus. It is pressing against the tongue and soft palate and forming to the shape of the area and blocking any access through the mouth. In effect she can breathe but cannot swallow or eat."

Duke stood there looking at him and giving him time to compose himself. "Can you tell me anything else about her condition?"

"She is breathing well and she has a strong heartbeat. I noted her skin is soft and pliable. Her eyes are bright but I doubt if she is actually seeing anything right now. She does not respond to any of the stimuli I introduced which tells me her central nervous system is either shut down or drugged."

Duke could hardly believe what the doctor was saying. "Doctor, can we remove that object from her throat?"

Michael was starting to recover from the initial shock of the situation and looked at Duke. "I don't think so. The object has conformed itself to match Mary's throat perfectly and I have a feeling it has made some form of contact with her brain as well due to the lack of any central nervous system reaction.

I would say she is being held in some sort of suspended animation and is probably all right other than the fact she is basically comatose. Right now, I would say we should leave her and Betty just as they are until we have a chance to run a number of tests."

Duke stood there looking at the doctors. He didn't like the idea of just leaving those two women as they were, but he also needed to follow the advice of the doctors, the women's lives depended on it.

Reluctantly Duke agreed and then ordered the tent off limits to anyone except those given permission by Duke, personally. "Okay, I want a guard on this tent Tanner, and make it a twenty-four-hour guard."

"I'll have people on it in ten minutes."

Then Duke remembered. "Tanner, whatever happened to Aaron Smith?"

Tanner turned and shrugged his shoulders. Gees I forgot all about him. I don't have any idea where he is at. We had him confined to his tent under guard and then when things broke loose, I don't know where he went or who he is with."

Tanner started walking toward a tent. "Tanner, is that his tent right there?"

Tanner looked back. "Yes, I think we need to take a look just in case he's still there."

As they entered the tent, he was laying there on his cot with metal rod sticking out of his chest. Duke walked around Tanner and over to the body and looked down at him. He then looked over at Tanner. "We have someone in this camp who is working with those who put this guy here. The one way to make sure no information slips out is to kill the possible source of information. Aaron had to go."

Dennis looked at Tanner. "Who was on guard duty at the time the panic started?"

Tanner reached into his pocket and pulled out a notebook and opened it to the last page. "It was Kyle. He just took duty an hour before the panic hit and after that I never saw him. In fact, I did not see him on the ridge either."

Tanner ran to the tent door and stepped out and looked over by the security tent. Kyle's car was gone. "He must have left during the panic and before he did, he probably killed Aaron. I'll see the rod is removed carefully so we can check it for prints and DNA."

They all three stood there looking around the area outside the tent. There were several cigarette butts on the ground and Tanner got busy collecting them. He also pulled his radio and called his security people to the tent.

In less than ten minutes the other three security personnel were standing there with them. Tanner asked if any of them had seen Kyle leave in his car. None had. He then asked the man who Kyle relieved what took place when Kyle arrived.

The man stood there a minute and then took a deep breath. "I didn't wait for him to get here. My time was up and he was late and I had several things I needed to do so I skipped out about five minutes early."

Duke looked at Tanner and raised both his hands about chest high and shrugged his shoulders and turned and walked about four paces away and looked up at the lake rim.

Tanner's face was red, he had been embarrassed by this revelation and he knew somewhere along the line he would have to make an accounting of his organization and its discipline. He turned to the man. "I don't want to talk to you about this now. Please leave and I'll call you later. Oh, and I want you to know I'm more than just a little disappointed in you."

Just then Duke started running. He was running like hell itself was after him. He ran over to the rim road and started up toward the lake. Dennis saw him take off and went after him. He thought Duke had gone crazy and felt he needed to stay with him. Tanner went for his truck after telling the remaining two guards to keep the tent secure.

About half way up the rim road Tanner

169

caught up with Dennis and Duke and took them in the back of his truck. Duke was yelling. "Get to the lake now, it's happening now."

As they topped the rim of the lake the water was churning and bulging higher than the rim of the mountain the lake was in. Tanner stopped the truck and Duke jumped out and ran to the edge of the lake. He stood there looking down into the lake and turned and screamed back at Dennis and Tanner. "The car, the car it's coming up. Tanner, call the other lakes now and find out if their structures are coming off the bottom of their lakes."

It was happening. With everything else going on it was happening, the structures and car were rising, coming to the surface and he knew who or whatever was behind this thing was coming too.

Whatever was happening it had a schedule and whether they were ready for it or not it was coming. Duke figured they had less than an hour before the car breeched the surface of the lake. What happened after that he had no idea? They were in a waiting game and the lake was going to do as the lake wanted and they could only stand by and watch.

Dennis moved up by him. "Duke, don't you think that we should get down off of this rim. As the bulge continues to grow the water is going to have to go somewhere and we're standing right where it will be going."

Duke started to turn and walk back to the truck when he stopped and looked at Dennis and Tanner. "I don't think so."

Dennis looked at him. "Duke, what are you

talking about?"

"Dennis, I don't think the lake is going to overflow. I don't know how I know but I know. Somehow all that water is going to remain in the basin."

Chapter Thirteen

HIGH ALERT

The team sitting up in the hills to the west were watching the Lake One camp when the people started running from the camp and up onto the ridge overlooking the main facilities. The team sat there looking at one another. "What the hell was that all about anyway?"

They continued to watch when they noted there was one person standing outside of a tent just to the west of what they knew to be the administration tent. The man was one of the security members. He was pacing back and forth smoking a cigarette. After a few more minutes he stopped, dropped and stepped on the cigarette and then turned and walked away.

About five minutes later another security man arrived and took up the observation position. It was then the people all started to run out of the camp and up onto the ridge. It was then when the guard went into the tent and after about five minute came

172

back out and walked over to a truck, got in and drove off.

It was within twenty minutes after the guard left when a helicopter landed and the two men exited it, leaving the pilot in the craft, and walked over to the admin tent. They went inside and then came out a short time later. Both appeared to be disturbed by something. They then walked over to the security tent and entered. It was several minutes later one of the men came running out of the tent out to the helicopter and retrieved a box and ran back to the tent.

About ten minutes afterward three men left the tent and walked over to the tent where the security guards had been working and entered the tent. Another ten minutes and one of them came out and stood there looking at the ground. He pulled out his radio and three more men showed up.

Just minutes later another security man walked up and there was a discussion. One of the four men turned and walked away from the group and stood there looking at the mountain. Suddenly he started to run toward the mountain and up the rim road. A second man started after him and then a third ran to a truck and took off after the other two.

Half way up the rim road the truck picked the other two up and they went up to the lake. It was then when the observation post saw the lake start churning. Something was happening and one of the team picked up their satellite phone and made the call.

"Sir, lookout post two, in the last three minutes the lake has started to churn and really bulge. A number of the scientists have gone to the lake and are currently standing by and watching whatever is happening.

"From our vantage point we can see the top of the water as it bulges above the rim. Sir, there is no overflow. The water is just bulging up."

"Thank you, Mark, keep watching and recording what is happening. We feel this is the time we've been waiting for."

"Yes Sir."

Mike reached over and picked up the phone and pushed the dial button. He sat back, a mass of thoughts racing through his head. 'The lake is bulging yet there is no overflow. Strange, I'm not sure what to think of that.'

He was so deep in thought he had not heard the phone being answered at the other end. "Is someone there, this is General Halverson's office?

Mike jerked himself back to the call. "Oh yes, I'm sorry things are just a little bit busy here right now. This is Mike Herald, is General Halverson available. Please advise him this is a Smack One Priority."

The line went dead and he sat there waiting for the General to come on line. "Yeah, Mike what's going on?"

"General, the lakes have started their activity. The bulges are currently active and can be seen above the rim of the craters. General there is no overflowing of the lakes. We have observed a number of people up by the lakes observing what is taking place."

"Mike, do you have any idea as to what is happening within the lakes?"

"No General, we don't, but I would bet something is coming to the surface. Sir, it's the only thing that could be happening, if the water is not overflowing then there must be something else happening and I would bet it's something coming up in the lake."

"All right Mike, that sounds reasonable to me and my staff. There had to be a reason for those mountains and now we're about to find out. Keep your people on this and I want to know exactly what is going on as soon as it happens.

"Mike, it's vital our information is up-to-date and accurate. Let your people know and keep the information flowing to me. We're going to set up an open line from you to this location. Put someone on the line and keep them there and keep them relaying the information as it comes in."

"Will do General, I'll have it up and running within five minutes after this call. Is there anything else you will need?"

"No Mike, right now I need the line active and after that everything will follow our plans, understand?"

"Understand General, we're ready and will implement our plan now."

"Good Mike, off for now."

"Good luck General."

Six calls were made to the observation point in the next five minutes and the primary plan went into effect. The information and video data started to flow as the observation teams moved into high gear.

As the plan of action moved into full operation the Stryker Units and H.A.W.K. Teams started to move into their pre-determined location and set up for the takeover move that was coming.

Chapter Fourteen

RE-EARTH HAS BEGUN

Duke stood there watching the water as it bulged higher and higher. The first thing he noticed was the shoreline was not coming up as he had anticipated. What was happening the water was forming a dome over the area of the lake and yes he could see the car coming up. It was almost half way up by the time he had reached the shore of the lake.

Just then Dennis came running up beside him and grabbed his arm. "Let's get the hell out of here before we get washed off the mountain."

Duke jerked his arm away from Dennis and looked at him. "Dennis, take a look at the shoreline. It's not rising at all; the water is just doming up. I don't think there is going to be an overflow."

Dennis stopped and looked at the shoreline and then over at Tanner who had run up and stopped right at the water and was looking the whole lake over. "Damn, what the hell is going on here anyway?"

Tanner looked over at both Dennis and Duke. "Duke, you were right. This whole place is a planned and carefully built system and it will probably not overflow the rim. The question I have is what happens when the car comes to the surface?"

Duke had turned and walked away from the shore and pulled out his phone. He called the base communications officer and asked he set up a party line with the other five lakes. That took about five minutes and he came back and advised he had the head of each lake on the line. "All right everyone, report in as to what is happening at your locations, Lake Two, you first."

Lake Two advised the lake was bulging and the hunting cabin was coming up. Lakes Three through Six reported the same situation. Their starting time correlated with that of Lake One and everything Lake One had been doing the other five were doing as well. As far as Duke could tell they were in perfect sync.

Just then Tanner's phone rang, "Yeah, Tanner here." He stood there listening and then looking over at Duke. He hung up and walked over to Duke. "Both Betty and Mary are coming out of whatever it was they were in. The blocks in their mouths are turning to water and draining out. Both seem to be in perfect condition."

Duke stood there trying to grasp what he had just been told. "They're all right?"

Tanner started nodding his head. "Yeah Duke, they said both women were in perfect shape. They have not been able to question them yet, but they appear to be all right."

All Duke could do was stand there thinking the situation over when Dennis called out. "Duke, the car it's coming to the surface."

They all turned toward the lake and watched as the top of the car came into view. It didn't pop into view it came up at the same rate it had been coming all this time. It took another ten minutes before the surface of the old I-10 came into view and then everything stopped.

Duke walked over to the shore of the lake and looked down into it. There it was a machine of some kind had pushed the bottom of the lake up to the top. It was just feet down and was about fifty feet in from the shore or so. The lake water had run down the side of the machine between the shore and the machine to where, he was not sure.

He looked up and could see the top of the water bulge was well above his head. It had to be twenty-five to thirty feet above his head and it was holding its position and form. He backed up onto the rim until he was at the top of the rim and at the same exact elevation as the water bulge.

All three were standing there along with half a dozen technicians. Just then the driver's door of the car opened and they could see movement in the car itself. Duke grabbed his phone and made the party call to the other lakes. "Are you seeing activity around your respective structures?"

Each and every one of the other lakes responded in the affirmative. Duke was getting ready to ask another question when he saw a head appear above the roof of the car and the head then moved toward the back and a young lady came around the rear of the car and walked over to the edge of the section of I-10. She stood there looking at them and appeared to be in complete control of herself.

The problem was the car was about two miles away on the top of the water bulge and they were watching her with binoculars. Even at that they had a fair view of her, enough to identify she was a woman and she was not in a panic.

Maybe thirty minutes passed as Duke talked to the other lakes, and the others standing there were talking among themselves. Then they noticed a disturbance on the surface of the lake in front of the young woman. It calmed and she stepped off the roadway and onto the water.

The word coming from the other lakes was the people in those structures were doing the same thing and they all appeared to be calm and in control of themselves.

After stepping onto the water, the woman remained still and she started to move toward the boat launch area where Duke and everyone else were standing. Her progression was about of a person walking at a normal gate except her legs were not moving. Whatever was transporting her did it smoothly, acting more like an escalator than anything else.

It took almost half an hour for her to come from the car at the center of the lake to the shoreline. Even when coming down the side of the bulge she maintained the same speed and her balance never

180

faltered. It looked like she was just standing on a street corner and hadn't a care in the world.

Others started to move toward her as she came within fifty meters of the shoreline. Duke called out, "Everyone stay back. I don't want anyone touching her at this time. Just let her come to us and we will wait and see what follows."

Everyone pulled back and waited. It wouldn't be a long wait. The woman continued on to the shore and as she came up to it the flat area, she was standing on stopped moving and she stepped off onto the ground and stood there.

This was the first time they were able to get a good look at her and she was absolutely beautiful. Her skin was smooth as silk with an unbelievable luster to it. Her hair was a soft blond color and appeared to be as soft as the color itself. Physically she looked to be perfect in every way. Her height to weight ratio looked to be perfect. Her arms and legs were well proportioned and appeared to be perfectly muscled.

Her breasts were absolutely perfect and fit her body as did her waist and hips. In a word, this individual was so perfect Duke would venture to say there was not another like her in the whole of the world, except for those coming out of the other lakes.

Just then a truck pulled up and Betty and Mary got out and walked over to and past Duke and down to the woman, then stepped sideways and moved into a position alongside the woman on both sides.

181

Duke had not expected that maneuver and he wondered if the same was happening at the other lakes. He made a quick call and the answer was no, the people who had just come up were remaining together and they too were perfect human specimens.

Meanwhile the section of old I-10 and the car were driven off the top of the bulge away from where Duke and the others were at, and it all appeared to sink on the far side of the lake. At the same time, the bulges started to lower, as they stood there, the bulge slid off into the sides of the lake and the machine underneath then rose to the top and sat there.

Dennis leaned over to Duke. "Where the hell do, we go from here?"

Duke stood there watching this impossible happen. "I have not the slightest idea at this point. I think we're here as spectators and nothing else. I don't know of one thing we could do to cause this thing to happen any other way.

"Right now, I believe this thing is not a threat to humans. If it had been, we would have been gone a long time ago. No, whatever this thing is, it may darn well need humans to achieve whatever it is trying to achieve. But right now, I have no idea what is happening or what is to come after this."

Up to this day we had been progressing well in starting to determine what the six lakes were all about. We had identified there were twenty-one victims in the bottoms of the lakes and in each lake, there were the same number of people per the lake number. That seemed odd, when we named the lakes we just happened to start at the south end of the line and moved north. Yet, the name of the lakes correlated with the number of people captured in each lake.

Then we discovered the anomalies associated with the water in each of the six lakes. In our zeal to learn something or anything about the water we started to run test involving the mixing of the waters together and this resulted in two of our people being attacked and eventually put with the other twenty-one victims bringing the count to twenty-three. The only difference was the two ladies at Lake One had not changed physically in any way.

We managed to capture the thing that got the two women at Lake One and sealed it in plastic, but we had no idea what it was, or if it was still alive, if it had been alive in the first place. Bottom line it had cost us Betty and Mary. Then we found Aaron Smith dead after we found and returned everyone back to the base camp at Lake One. This ended up with one of the security officers leaving the area and the odds were good he was the one responsible for Aaron's death. Other than that, it's been a rather uneventful day.

As Duke continue to mull the situation over in his mind, a humming sound came from the machine sitting in the middle of the lake. At first it was a low-level hum and then it started to increase in volume and the frequency level of the hum. As the frequency increased Dennis noticed the lake water around the edge of the machine started to vibrate and as everyone moved in to take a look it seemed to flash over and turned solid.

When the lake water turned solid it locked the machine into its position in the lake. Even in the solid state it was clear as air.

Things were happening one after the other and no one had time to stop and speculate as to what was going on. We were all in a catch-up situation and had no way of knowing what was coming next.

Just as Duke had the thought the hum changed to a loud grinding sound, well not exactly grinding, but moved up to a high frequency squeal. He turned and looked back at the young woman and then Betty and Mary. He started walking toward them and that's when Betty and Mary stepped forward and placed themselves between Duke and the young woman.

Betty raised her hand. "Duke you cannot go near or touch this being. If you attempt to touch her you will die instantly. Do you understand me?"

Duke stopped and looked back at Tanner and Dennis and then turned back to Betty. "Betty, what the hell is going on here? Can't someone give us something to help us understand what is happening?"

Betty stood there looking directly at Duke and then seemed to refocus her eyes and stepped toward him. "Duke, this situation is something beyond anything you can say or do. What is going to happen is going to happen no matter what you say or try to do. The young lady was selected at the moment the event initiated. She has been reformed

184

and made to be perfect in every physical way as well as being mentally far more advanced over us than we are over the simplest of insects. Duke, they will protect her with everything and anything they need to ensure her welfare during this process and the same goes for the other twenty."

Duke had come to a complete stop and was clearly confused over what Betty was telling him. "Betty, I don't understand. What are they, whoever they are, what are they doing here and what are these six mountains all about?"

Betty smiled and turned to face the young lady for a few seconds and then turned back to Duke. "Duke, you are the primary person with the responsibility in researching these mountains and coming up with some form of answer as to why they are here and what is going on.

"We can only tell you what is about to happen had been going on for no less than twenty million years and it will continue to its climax over the next six months." Duke was looking at her like she was some kind of weirdo yet he knew he needed to listen.

"Duke, they are here to carry out a re-terraforming of the earth. It has been over twenty million years from the last re-terraforming process and it is time for the next. They advise no one will die from this action, but we must be prepared and be patient as the process takes place."

Duke stood there, not believing what she had just said yet knowing full well what she had said was true. Damn, what the hell was going on here? He turned to Betty. "Who the hell are they?"

She stood there as if she was listening for something. "Right now, that's not for you to know."

Duke was becoming more impatient with Betty. "What the hell does that mean anyway?"

"That my dear Duke is all you're going to get. They mean what they say and right now you don't need to know." She was most adamant this time and by her tone he had little to argue with or for.

Just then Mary stepped forward and took Duke by the upper arm and turned him and walked him to the edge of the lake. She then pointed down. "Duke you need to look down there and tell me what you see."

Duke looked into the water and it seemed to have cleared up even more and then he could see. They appeared to be arms coming out of the side of the machine and pressing up against the side of the lake walls that made up the mountain. He looked at them and then back to Mary with a quizzical look in his eyes.

Mary nodded her head. "Duke this is the start of the process that is going to take place on earth over the next few months, everyone on earth needs to know about this and needs to prepare for the process."

She stood there waiting for him to respond and when he didn't, she continued. "Duke, those arms are going to continue to increase the pressure on the walls of these mountains. What you don't know is the shaft of the mountain goes deep into the earth and as the pressure increases the tectonic plate known as the North American Plate will start to split along the line of the six mountains. This plate will completely split and separate from the other plates to the south of this location. When it starts, the oceans will surge into the opening and the split will increase.

"The process is designed so once the North American Plate starts then the several other larger plates located around the world will start their splits in the areas of their natural locations of weakness. A total of six plates, including this one, will be split in half. During the process those six plates will be moved apart by as much as fifty miles at the farthest and only eight miles at the least."

Mary waited for this to sink in and then she turned to Betty and the young woman and then back to Duke. "Duke, at the same time this young lady plus the other twenty who were at the bottom of the lakes will oversee the progression of these continental splits and work with the human race to ensure we move our people out of the way as the actions takes place.

"Once started it will progress rapidly as the splits drive deeper into each plate the waters will angrily rush in to fill the voids.

"Now listen carefully, this process is not meant to be hazardous to the population of earth. However, just the fact there is such a cataclysmic action taking place, if the people of earth are not made aware of what is happening and what they must do while this is going on, then there will be vast numbers of people lost. It is yours and our obligation to carry out the directives of these beings and do it quickly and without hesitation. Do you understand?"

It was crazy, but Duke understood. "How long do we have to prepare for our part in this thing?"

Mary turned back to Betty and the girl and then back to Duke. "You and your teams have forty-eight hours to prepare and then you will start to receive the directives you will be required to carry out."

"Where are we to go in order to do these duties?"

Mary turned back to Betty and the girl again and then turned back to Duke. "You are where they want you to be. You have all the facilities you will need and this is the safest place to be while the process is going on. You are expected to remain here during the full implementation and completion of this action."

That struck home and Duke turned to everyone. "All right everyone let's head back to the base camp."

He then turned to Betty. "What are we to do with you two and her?" Pointing at the girl and then at Betty and Mary.

Betty smiled. "We'll take care of her; you just go and get prepared to do your job and we'll keep you informed as to any of hers or their needs."

Duke's mind was screaming with questions and concerns. He was totally unprepared for what

188

had just happened and now he found himself in a position where he would be working for whomever or whatever beings were doing this.

It did explain the mountains and their coming into existence so fast and in such a unique and geometrical layout. But he had not expected this to be a machine designed to reshape the face of the Earth and to do it with little or no harm to the people of Earth as long as we did as we were told and did it quickly.

There was a hell of a lot of organizing that needed to be done and so the first order he gave was for all directors of the other five lakes to come to Lake One for briefing and coordination meetings. They had to be there within twelve hours and no later. His next problem was trying to determine the purpose of the people from the lakes and what they were doing. The real puzzle was the issue of the number of Lake People for each lake.

He could readily see the one woman from Lake One, but why two for Lake Two and so on. What would six Lake People at Lake Six do or what did it mean? This was the real pressing issue for him. They now had twenty-one Lake People. Not knowing what to do with them was clearly the question, that's if he had any say in what would be done with them.

Maybe he was fixated too much on the Lake People. Maybe it was the responsibility of the beings who were carrying out this re-terraforming process to take care of them. There was so much we needed to know and so far, little had been provided to us.

He knew this, if they were to coordinate the actions for the movement of people around the world in order to avoid the hazards related to this thing, they needed information now and not forty-eight hours from now.

Duke could feel his frustration building as he watched everyone moving down off the lake rim. He looked back across the lake and noted the machine was actually coming up out of the lake some more. There was no doubt about it, it was one hell of a big machine and anyone who had the ability to build something that big, let alone six of them, he had better prepare himself for working with them and not against them.

Still, he had the issue with Aaron Smith and the rogue security officer Kyle on his mind. Those were just two people, there had to be others and how they fit into this mess he had no idea. He had a deep down feeling things were not going to be that smooth.

Smith was tied into some group, thought to be this H.A.W.K. outfit, and what their interest was in the Six Lakes Project could only be speculated at this time. He knew this much; they were up to no good and it meant trouble for him and everyone else working the project.

It wouldn't take long for him to learn the answer to those questions. It came walking through his office door just at that moment, right on time, right on cue.

Chapter Fifteen

H.A.W.K. AND STRYKER MOVE

Mike had been sitting there thinking over the plans they were about to put into effect when the outpost phone lit up like a spotlight. He reached over and pushed the answer button.

"Yeah Mark, what have you got?"

"Sir, there are people coming out of the lake."

Mike sat up and leaned forward. "Mark, slow down and tell me what you're seeing."

"Sir, the manmade things at the bottom of the lakes have come to the surface and as each one appears there are people coming out of them and moving across the water to the shore. We count twenty-one at this time."

Mike sat back trying to grasp what he had just heard. He thought to himself, 'I thought they were all dead.' "Mark, are they human or something else?"

"Sir, based on our information at this time they are the people who had been trapped in the structures at the time the mountains and lakes formed.

"At Lake One, two others have come up to the rim and walked over to the single woman who came from the car in the lake. They seemed to have some kind of a confrontation with the head of the project.

"Once it was over everyone headed back down to the base camp and the two women from the base camp and the one from the car are going down in a separate truck and away from all the others."

What the hell was going on anyway? Mike had just started to deal with the information he had been given when Mark came back on line.

"Base, Mark here."

"Yes Mark."

"Base, the car has been moved north on the lake and then sunk. Sir, there is a huge machine coming though the surface of the lake. Sir, it filled the entire lake except for a small ribbon of water around it. That ribbon is about fifty feet wide.

"Hold on, wait, the ribbon of water has now solidified and appears to have locked the machine into place.

"Sir, what do want us to do?"

"Easy Mark, I want you to continue to monitor what is going on and keep the information coming. I need to contact the operations team and determine what the overall plan is. You stand by."

"Will do."

Mike sat back, a damn machine, but one four miles across. God, what the hell is going on here anyway?

He then turned to the command phone and pushed the button.

"General Halverson's Office."

"I need to speak to the General stat."

"Yes Sir, one moment."

"Mike, what's going on?"

"General, all hell has busted loose here. The bottoms of the lakes have come to the surface along with the objects trapped down there. Once they cleared the surface the people in those structures came out, moved across the lakes and walked on shore.

"General, after that the structures were then moved to the north side of each lake and sunk there. Then a machine surfaced in each lake and they are huge. The water at the edges of the machines has solidified, locking the machines into place.

"At this point everyone, including the Lake People, have gone down to the base camps."

"All right Mike; it's time to set Plan Two into effect. That will move the Stryker Units into striking position. I'll be called into the White House Situation Room and once there I'm sure the President will be in contact with Mr. Ridgeman and we will get the details as to what has taken place.

"Mike, everything is moving along just fine. Be patient, we're on top of this. We don't have long to wait now.

"I need to have you contact your H.A.W.K. teams and inform them of the Stryker Unit's movements. We will need those teams to come in from the west and prepare for action."

"Have that General. I'll get them moving to their jump off points. We should have everyone in place within the next twelve hours."

"Mike make sure they coincide with the Stryker Units movement's just as we have planned it."

"Mike, we just got the call from the President so I'll be moving over to that location. My second will be here for anything you need to report. He can then relay it to me as I need it."

"All right General. We'll get things moving from this end."

"Good work Mike, we'll talk later."

Mike hung up, then got up and walked into the communications room. "Terry, would you advise the H.A.W.K. Teams to move into their planned jump off positions at this time. They have twelve hours to get there and set up for their next move."

"Yes sir, I'll advise the teams now."

Mike stood there watching the people start to initiate the planned move in the communications center. He had one more job that needed to be done and he was not eager to get into this activity.

He needed to let the cartels know what was going on. They have proven to be difficult to talk to and work with. No one trusts anyone else and everyone is continually vying for a position of domination and control. They all could see the advantage of their own nation on the west coast. It was just that every one of the cartel leaders wanted to be the permanent president of the new country.

The General had assured him everything would work out all right. The cartel leaders were not going to be a problem, he would see to that. Mike trusted the General. After all he has not missed on one thing while setting up this plan. Still, he was dealing with these South American cartel leaders and they cared nothing about friendships, partners, or anything else. They would kill anyone and everyone to gain their ultimate control. He was certain this would end in a blood bath.

He returned to his office, sat down, picked up the phone and dialed the number. The phone rang six times before someone answered. 'That was normal. They were probably fighting over who would answer the phone.'

"Who is this?"

Mike sat there a moment. "It's Mike. Who is this?"

"Ah Mike my man. We've been waiting for your call. What's going on?'

"Again, who is this? Don't play games here. Follow the proper protocol."

"Yeah, Mike its Afredo."

"Thank you Afredo. Now who else is there?"

"Mike, we're all here and have been waiting to hear some news as to what is going on. We thought you had forgotten us, what's happening? Why have you not contacted us sooner?"

"Afredo, things have been crazy here but they have been moving along. My job now is to advise you of the current status of the situation. Right now, we do not need any action on your part. We just want you to know all is moving just as we had planned."

Mike continued to cover the details of the situation for the cartel leaders. After an hour he sat back. "Are there any more questions?"

He could hear the exchange of comments in the background. "Mike, we're happy with everything you have told us. What we want to know now is have you told us everything?"

That was normal for these people. You could never give them enough to eliminate their doubts and distrust. They could never be satisfied and in the end, he knew they would have to deal with these guys one way or another.

"Alfredo, I have given you everything I have given to the General. All we can do now is sit back and wait for the next move to take place. Right now, we're in a reactionary mode and this means we wait and we respond as each point of need comes about. Understand?"

Again, there was the background activity and then Alfredo came back. "OK Mike, we'll be waiting. We just have one little issue you need to understand Mike. If anyone does anything we see as a threat to us we'll kill the whole lot of you. You can't stop us Mike and you know it."

"Damn it, Alfredo, those threats are not needed. You know damn well we have as much to lose in this thing as anyone else. If you don't start to control your attitude, it's only going to make matters much more difficult, hear me."

"Mike, we know what you're saying and we agree, but we also want you to understand our position. We don't take failure well. If we fail someone is going to pay and it's not going to be us."

"All right Alfredo, you've made yourself clear on the matter. Is there anything else you need?"

"No Mike, we'll just sit here and wait for you to get back to us. Good luck my friend."

Alfredo hung up and Mike sat back in his chair. Damn those people simply screw things up every time they open their mouths. Well, the General has the answer for them and I'll just put up with them for the time being.

Chapter Sixteen

TECTONIC OVERLOAD

Duke had returned to his office and was sitting there trying to come up with a rational understanding of what had just happened. When they left the lake, Mary and Betty had taken the Lake Woman in their rig and brought her back to the main administration tent. They had taken her to Betty's office and closed and locked the door.

Duke had called all the administrators from the other five lakes to an organizational meeting there at Lake One for later that afternoon. He also learned the other lake administrators had been ordered, by Betty, to bring their respective Lake People to Lake One as well.

The orders had been specific. The Lake People were to be transported in their own aircraft with only the pilot and co-pilot on board. No one was to touch any of the Lake People and if anyone did either by accident of on purpose they would die. No questions, no excuses, they would die. Once they landed at Lake One, the pilots and co-pilots were to leave the aircraft and stand clear while the Lake People were picked up by Betty and returned to the administration tent.

It was clear there would be no discussion about these orders. They were to be carried out to the letter and if not, then people would pay with their lives. Both Betty and Mary had made it clear. In addition, if any attempt was made to divert the Lake People to some place other than the administration tent at Lake One, every crew member of the aircraft transporting the Lake People would die and be ejected from the aircraft and the Lake People would finish the trip on their own.

These orders had no sooner been given and were in the process of being carried out when there was a knock-on Duke's office door. He called out for whomever it was to come in. There was a pause and then the door opened and in walked Betty with the Lake Woman right behind her. They both walked up to Duke's desk and Betty stepped aside and back behind the Lake Woman.

Duke sat there looking at this young lady waiting for whatever was to follow. She was looking around his office and taking everything in, which she was doing in detail. Finally, her eyes settled back on Duke. "You're in charge here?"

It almost knocked him out of his chair. Her voice though soft and melodious, carried with it a level of authority rivaling anything he had ever heard or met before. "Yes, my name is Duke Ridgeman."

199

She stood there looking right at him and then turned and walked around to the left side of his desk, from her perspective, until she was standing directly in front of Duke. She then held out her hand. "My name is LeAnn Larson, Mr. Ridgeman. May I call you Duke?"

Duke was standing up by this time and reaching out to shake her hand as she presented it to him. "My pleasure, Miss. Larsen, now can you tell me what this is all about?"

She withdrew her hand and turned and walked back around to the front of his desk and turned facing Duke. "Duke, over the next six months there is going to be a lot going on across the face of the earth. It will be my job, along with the other twenty selected people, to oversee the process of the re-terraforming of Earth. Now there are two things you must know.

"The first is the re-terraforming will take place and cannot be stopped or interfered with. You will need to notify all worldwide governments this is happening and there is nothing they can do about it. If they attempt to interfere in anyway, it will result in complete and total annihilation of that governing body.

"The second thing will be you sir, will help us in every way we request during this process. That will go for any individual or government we make a request to. The purpose is to reduce the possibility of any one on Earth being killed by the subsequent movement of the oceans during this process and the splitting of the land mass they may live on.

Please understand we do not wish any harm to anyone. The problem is, it is time for Earth's re-terraforming and it must take place. If it does not happen then the resulting pressures within the Earth itself will cause cataclysmic Earth movement and as a result many cities and many people will be lost.

This is common among the many planets across the universe. They are active at all times and if the active process is not controlled then the planet can and will tear itself apart. If this happens then you know full well what it will mean to the beings living on this or any other planet.

Next, I am here to advise you this is not an invasion or an attempt to take over control of this planet. Our purpose is solely to oversee the re-terraforming of the planet and once done to assist in any way in those areas where undue damage took place. Once all is complete, we will leave this world not to return until the next procedure is needed. That would be in another twenty million years' time.

Duke was almost beside himself. He was sure what he had witnessed so far was in fact, as she had stated. The problem was he was not prepared for it to go this way. What had started out as a mystery was now real and he preferred the mystery.

Finally, he was able to compose himself. "I am really confused about what is happening here, but I also realize what is happening is real and for a reason. My staff and I are prepared to assist you in whatever way you need."

LeAnn smiled a soft and reassuring smile at Duke. "Duke, as the next weeks and months pass you will come to know and understand what is happening. I can only assure you this needs to be done and it will mean the continued existence of your planet and your peoples.

"The pressures building up within this planet must be relieved. If they are not then this planet will come apart and everyone will be lost. All that will be left is a debris belt around the sun in this location.

"In time the debris will rejoin and form a new planet and the Earth will begin a new beginning. We would prefer it not happen this way. We prefer to let your civilization survive and have a chance of advancing to its highest level of existence."

It was at this moment Tanner entered the office and advised Duke the flights with the other Lake People were on their final approach to the Lake One field. Duke thanked Tanner and then looked over at LeAnn. She smiled and turned to Betty and Mary and nodded her head. Betty and Mary turned and left the office and tent and headed for the air field.

LeAnn turned back toward Duke and a strange look came across her face, she looked off toward her left and after several second returned her gaze back to Duke. "There is a group of beings coming toward this base and they are not friendly. They are going to try and take control of the aircraft as they land and then take control of my companions. They will not succeed.

"Duke you are to call the head of your government leader now and advise this being all which I tell you to say to him."

Duke started to say something and then stopped and picked up the phone. He had a direct line to the President and he knew full well this was the moment when he had to talk directly to the Commander in Chief. As he waited for the line to be answered he looked at LeAnn. "What am I to tell him?"

She redirected her attention to him. "When he comes on line you are to advise him as to what is taking place. Advise him all the data he will need will be sent to his Incident Command Center at the White House. You are to advise him the main job of this government is to inform all other governments directly involved in this process, of the nature of the event taking place and what they are to do in order to avoid any undue loss of life in their respective countries."

She had finished when the President came on the line. "Mr. Ridgeman, what can I do for you?"

Duke took a deep breath and began. "Mr. President, there has been a significant event happing here at the Six Lakes site and I need to let you know what has happened and what is going to happen.

"Sir, I will need your complete and uninterrupted attention on this. I know you're busy, but this situation is so vital everything else must be set aside. I think once I start you will understand."

There was a pause on the other side. "All right Mr. Ridgeman, fill me in."

Duke took a second breath and then started to fill the President in on what was going on. He had to give the president credit for letting Duke finish his presentation and not interrupting him. Finally, after Duke had finished the briefing, the President cleared this throat. "That doesn't give me many options Duke. In fact, it gives me no options at all. You're sure this is happening and will happen?"

Duke found he needed to be direct and forceful in his response. "Mr. President, I personally witnessed the rise and initiation of the machine in the lake and have confirmed the same results in the other five lakes. This is a machine and it is big and it is non-stoppable. Sir I feel certain we must cooperate and do everything we are advised to do in order to make sure no one is killed.

"Sir, I'm standing here and I can hear and feel the machine working. It is deep and it is powerful and there is nothing we can do about it. That thing is going to split the continental United States into two pieces. The separation will be anywhere from eight to fifty miles wide. In addition, Canada and Mexico will experience the same split as it progresses from these lakes north and south."

Again, there was a pause and then the President came back. "Duke we are in the command center now and all the data promised is coming in at this time and our scientists are in agreement with everything you have said so far. We have also received the directives on what we need to do to notify our people and the other world governments who will be impacted by this event.

"However, there are some problems. A number of the other governments we are to contact are hostile to us and will probably reject any attempt on our part to contact them. Are there any suggestions?"

Duke looked over at LeAnn, she was standing there looking at Duke but saying nothing. Finally, she reached over and touched the phone speaker. "Sir, it is not our problem if the governments of this world cannot communicate or work with one another. That is your problem.

"But let me tell you this. You are expected to carry out each and every action assigned to you. Do not come to us with trivial matters that are solely solvable by the people of this world. We have given you the information you need to avoid loss of life on this world when the re-terraforming takes place.

"If one government will not speak to or take the information being offered them in regards to this event, then it is that government and none other who will be responsible for any loss of life. We consider your actions as childish and without merit. Carry out your obligations and let the leaders of the other governing bodies carry out theirs. If they reject the process then they will pay the price for their stupidity."

Everything fell deadly quiet at that moment. LeAnn stood there looking right at Duke and he sat there waiting for the President of the United States to respond to the dressing down he had just been given.

Duke heard him sigh before he started to talk. "I guess I had that coming. Young lady, I agree with what you have said and I can assure you we will do everything we can to fulfill each and every task you give us. All we can do is try and that, I can assure you, we will do.

"I have assigned people to each task and we are now in the process of carrying out those directives. I don't know if it will do any good, but we will try and we will persevere.

"Duke, is there anything you will need over the course of this process?"

Duke looked at LeAnn and she nodded for him to continue. "Sir, there is one issue that is in process here at this time. The other twenty Lake People are being transported to this location at this time. In fact, they are in their final approach. We have also discovered there is a force coming into this area with the express purpose of taking over this site for what reason we are not sure of at this time.

"That force is heading for the landing field and we think they are going to try and take the other Lake People prisoners when they land. LeAnn has assured me it will not happen. We think this force is related to a security issue we just discovered. I had removed the administrator of Lake Five and sent him back to the Lake One base for further processing.

"During the panic that took place as the lake machines came to life, this administrator was murdered, we believe by the security officer who was on duty guarding him. That guard then left the area and we believe he had returned to whomever he was working for. We have discovered this particular administrator was tied to H.A.W.K. and it is this group who is currently approaching the base. We think it is this group who is trying to move in and take control of the Lake People. LeAnn has advised me they will fail and while attempting to take the Lake People they will be killed to the person."

The President sat there listening to Duke. "All right Duke, I will need the name of the administrator who was killed and the name of the security officer involved. We will pursue this issue from this end and make sure you have no other interruptions from here on out. Is there anything else?"

Duke looked at LeAnn and she shook her head no and Duke advised the President. "Sir, that is it right now, we will be setting up our activities with the Lake People and will keep a continuous flow of data and activity reports to your command center from here on out."

The President seemed to be a little more relaxed at that time. "Thank you, Duke. You keep it up and we'll keep in touch." He stopped. "Oh Duke, you're doing a great job and we totally trust you. I want you to know no one will replace you and if anyone questions your authority or tries to tell you that you are no longer in charge, I can assure you whoever says, it is not true. You're there for as long as you wish and that is final."

"Thank You Mr. President. I can assure you I will strive to carry this duty out to the end and successfully."

With these final comments the conversation was ended and Duke then turned to LeAnn. "What is happening with the force approaching the airfield?"

She stood there a second and then smiled. "That force no longer exists."

It was that simple and matter of fact. Duke had no idea what was meant by "no longer exists," and frankly he didn't want to know.

It was twenty minutes later when the other twenty Lake People arrived at the base camp. At that time everyone went to the main meeting tent to find out what was going to happen and when it was going to happen.

As Duke entered the tent, Betty walked up to him and asked that he step back outside for a few minutes. Duke looked at her, then nodded and turned and walked outside. She took a few steps beyond him and turned facing him. "Duke, I need to fill you in on what took place out at the field when the planes landed."

As Duke looked at her, he saw she was her old self she was before the attack by the clear ball thing. Her expression was calm and she was in complete control of herself.

She continued with her information. "As you know there was an unknown force coming into the base area from the southeast. They arrived at the same time as the planes were taxing to the drop off point. They came down the runaway and surrounded the planes and advised the pilots to open up and they would be taking the Lake People off the planes.

"It turns out the pilots were with the attack force and they opened the planes and several force members boarded the planes with weapons. They no sooner got into the planes when they were hit by something I could not see or hear. Whatever it was it crushed them to death before they could fire a shot.

"Then three Lake People from each plane left their respective planes and positioned themselves at three equal points facing the forces surrounding the planes. Duke, it was so fast not a shot was fired. They killed every single member of the attack force including the pilots. They then all left the planes and came directly here to the base." Betty turned away from Duke and stood there watching two trucks approach the base camp.

Duke stood there waiting as the trucks rolled to a stop, and within seconds people started jumping out of the back of the trucks. They all entered the meeting tent and moved over to where LeAnn was waiting for them. Duke and Betty had followed the group into the tent. By this time everyone had assembled in the tent and Duke stood up front and started the meeting.

It took several seconds for everyone to calm down. The Lake People remained standing. "All right people, as you can see, we have a number of visitors. I need you to slow down and listen carefully to what LeAnn is going to tell you. Everything she will say is important and will in fact happen."

With that LeAnn walked out from among the Lake People and turned toward those present.

"Thank you for coming and being on time. We of the Lakes welcome you at this time and hope you will take an active part in the process that is coming.

"This afternoon the machines in the Six

Lakes were activated and started the process of re-terraforming your planet Earth. You must understand that this process is necessary if the beings of Earth are going to survive. If this re-terraforming process is not carried out, then the Earth will, on its own, tear itself apart. This is not something we do just because we can; it is a process we do on a periodic basis to ensure the survival of the planet and those living on it.

"We travel throughout the universe maintaining many planets that have continental shifts in existence. Without our intervention most of these planets would not survive and all those living on them would be lost.

"Though the system is automatic, there are a number of needs that must be fulfilled by you and those living here. Those needs have mostly to do with the welfare of those who live here. Some will be required to move out of the way of the splitting of the continents. If we are successful in getting people moved out of the way then the process could be completed without any loss of life."

As LeAnn talked, she was watching the people in the audience to try and get a measure on what their reactions were to her being there. It was obvious there was a lot of questioning and distrust amongst those present. Over the past few hours so much had taken place the people were still confused and finding it hard to trust the Lake People and their purpose.

As Duke sat there watching he could tell there was a lot of animosity amongst those present.

He knew one thing; he had to get these people under control and moving in the same direction if they even hoped the process that was coming would be successful.

In his own mind all he could see was this crazy unbelievable event coming straight at him. The problem was he had no way of controlling or redirecting it. This whole system had been set up millions of years ago by beings who are so far beyond this current world they had everything covered and he had no options.

Finally, he could see no other way. He stood up walked up beside LeAnn and got everybody's attention. "Listen up everyone, I know it is hard for you to understand what is going on here, but I need to let you know right now there is nothing we can do to change what is about to happen.

There is a splitting of this continent that is going to take place; in fact, it's in process right now. It is our job to try and make sure no one living in this part of this nation is killed or seriously injured during this process.

"I have been in touch with the president and he has assured me the government of the United States will do everything in its power to work with the Lake People to ensure all peoples of this Earth are made safe during the re-terraforming. Our primary job is to keep the president informed of everything that is taking place here at the Six Lakes.

"As things develop it will be our job to monitor and inform the government as to what is happening and its time frame. If we fail to carry out this task, a lot of people are going to pay for our failure.

"Know this, we are going to do everything and anything LeAnn and the other Lake People direct us to do. This has nothing to do with what we believe, what our feelings are, or what our fears are. It has everything to do with the welfare and safety of the people of this nation and across the Earth.

"Understand this; you have been given the opportunity to be in a unique situation at a perfect time for an event beyond anything this earth has ever seen. My advice to you is to take that opportunity seriously and apply yourselves."

All Duke could do was stand there and wait. It was a decision that had to be made by each and every individual at the meeting. They would both see the issue and join or they would walk away and refuse to take part. One thing was certain, this thing was going to happen, was already in the process and nothing anyone could do or say would change the reality of this event. He knew whether these people came on board or not, everything was wired and was going to progress to its ultimate end.

There have been few times in the history of mankind when an event was so outlandish and dangerous everyone came together and set their ideological, social or religious beliefs aside for the good of all. This was one of those times and if mankind could not achieve that level of cooperation then there was no hope for the world and in time, we would kill ourselves off.

Duke hoped what he and LeAnn had said

would have an impression on all those there. So much needed to be done and if just one person refused it would place an added load on everyone else. No, he needed everyone to come on board.

Chapter Seventeen

BATTLE EARTH STARTS

Mike received word the people who had come from the structures at the bottom of the lakes had been summoned to Lake One. In addition, the administrators for each lake had been called to a meeting at Lake One. Separate planes had been sent to each lake to pick up the people from the lakes and the administrators.

Mike saw the opportunity immediately and picked up the phone. "Hello is Dave Pullman around there?"

"Yeah, he is whose calling?"

"Tell him it's Mike.

Several seconds later Dave came on the line. "Hi Mike, what's up?"

"Dave, we have a situation I need you to move on right now. We have information the Lake People are going to board two planes and go to Lake

One. I need to have you put our own pilots on those two planes and then get our Team to Lake One to intercept and meet up with the pilots and the planes they're flying. Can you do that?"

"Yeah Mike, we can. We've been sitting here waiting for the chance to get into action and this is right down our alley. How do you want them?"

"Dave, I want them alive, every one of them. Got me?"

"Sure Mike, we can do that, anything else?"

"Dave, if you can pull this off it will be all we need. Those people hold the knowledge of the workings of those machines in the lakes and we need that knowledge. Once we have them, we have the machines and all the technology they are carrying."

"All right Mike, I'll get on this right now. We'll have it nailed down before the end of the day. Where do you want me to take those people once I have them?"

"Once you have control, you will load them back on the planes and the pilots will bring them here to our main base. Oh, there's one other thing."

"What's that?"

"There appears to be a leader there as well. If you can find that person and include her it will give us total control."

"All right Mike, we'll go for the whole game on this."

Mike ended the contact and sat back to wait out the actions by Dave and his team. He figured it would be about twenty-four hours before the Lake People left the last of the lakes and headed for the

Lake One field. All he could do now was sit and wait and be ready for Dave's report and the arrival of the planes with their captives.

He reached over and pressed the phone button and sat back, "General Halverson's office."

"Is the General available, this is Mike Sandburg?"

Seconds later the General came on line. "Yes Mike, what have you got?"

"General, we have determined the Lake People are moving down to the Lake One base and will be flying out sometime in the next twenty-four hours. I have made arrangements for the pilots to be some of our people and when they land at Lake One, we will take over the plane and move the people over to our base here on the coast."

The General sat there a moment and then cleared his throat. "Mike, I don't know if that's advisable. We have no idea as to the capabilities of these people. Remember they are tied in with an alien force that is way beyond our technological level."

"I know General, but we need some leverage right now and this is our best opportunity to gain that leverage. If you really feel we should pull back we will, but I think this is the right move at the right time."

Mike could hear the general talking to someone in the background. It sounded like there was an argument taking place when the general finally said. "No, I think he's right and that's what we're going to do."

"Mike, that's a go, I think you're on to something and we need to move when the opportunity shows itself.

"However, I don't want one of your teams taking that action. I'll assign a Stryker Unit to carry out the action. Is this understood?"

"Yes, general it is. I'll pull our people off of it."

It was twenty hours later when the phone rang, as Mike picked up, it was the observation team. "Yes Mark, what have you got?"

"Mike, it was a disaster. The entire Stryker Unit was wiped out including the pilots. They got the planes stopped just as they planned and team members entered each plane. Seconds later the bodies of all those on the plane came out the door and landed on the tarmac. Moments later three Lake People came out of each plane and took up positions facing the Stryker Unit and then they wiped them out."

Mike was stunned by what he had just heard. "Mark, you said they were wiped out to the man?"

"Yeah, Mike, to the man. I didn't see any weapons just the team members falling over and that was it. Everyone is gone and the Lake People left the planes and went on into the base camp.

"Mike, I've never seen anything like it. Our people didn't stand a chance."

"All right Mark, stay put, your task is to maintain our observation of what is going on in the base. I'll advise the others of the situation."

"Understood boss, we'll keep the data flowing and maintain our current position."

Mike was beginning to think maybe they were involved in something they shouldn't be. If those people have that kind of power, then they didn't stand a chance. He reached over and hit the phone button, "General Halverson, please."

"Yes Mike, what have you got?"

"General, I've got a disaster here. We lost the entire Stryker Team at the Lake One airfield. That includes the pilots. General, there were no weapons visible but they knocked the whole team down in seconds."

There was silence on the other end. This time there was no background activity. He could hear the General breathing. "All right Mike, we have that. We'll get back to you shortly."

The phone went dead and Mike hung up his receiver and sat back. This had not been expected and it changed everything.

He got up and walked out of the office and out into the field in back of the building. All he wanted now was some fresh air and a little peace and quiet. Everything had changed in that one action and now he wasn't sure they were going to be able to pull this thing off.

Chapter Eighteen

CRACK HEARD ROUND THE WORLD

It took maybe fifteen minutes for everyone to finally realize they had little or no choice. After they had come to that conclusion the meeting continued and things started to smooth out. LeAnn and the other Lake People started to provide the quantity and level of data needed for our people to determine the levels of impact to be expect during the split. It was now our job to make those final determinations and then to notify the president of our findings and to give to him our recommendations.

Right then Duke had no idea as to what the real time frame was for this event. He finally walked over to LeAnn and asked if he could have some time with her in private. She looked at him, nodded her head and agreed. He then invited her back to his office where they could sit down and clarify a few things.

It was twenty minutes later when they entered Duke's office. Duke turned to LeAnn.

"LeAnn, I need to know the exact time when this split is going to start. Then I need to know the duration of this activity from beginning to its end.

"In addition, I need to know which of the major continents are going to have splits as well. I also have to know if there is going to be any cataclysmic reaction when the oceans flow into those cracks and have access to the mantle."

LeAnn stood there looking at him, not saying a word. He could tell there was something going on but he had no idea what it was. It was maybe five minutes before LeAnn looked straight at him and began to speak. "Duke, the questions you have asked are acceptable and do in fact need to be answered. I will address each one as you have presented them to me.

"In regards to when the activity starts, the actual split will begin in ninety-two hours after the initial rise initiation of the machines in all of the Six Lakes. Once the machines have come to the surface, they activate their pressure arms and initiate the forces needed to start the crack. The split will start at the center lakes which are Lakes Three and Four. The crack will start at the south and north side of each of the two lakes and then spread across the open space between them, all two hundred twenty-six miles. Once the crack is formed the crack will then start its run North and South at the rate of approximately four hundred ninety miles an hour.

"Once the crack reaches Lakes One and Six it will then progress both to the south and to the north at the same speed into Mexico and Canada.

When the crack reaches the northern coast of Canada it will continue on to the Asian continent, having completed the separation of the North American continent. To the south the crack will continue on South through Mexico till it reaches the Pacific Ocean, at which point the entirety of the North American continent will have been split. The initial splitting will last for approximately thirty-eight hours.

"There will then be approximately a six-hour period before the next continental split starts. That split will start on the West Coast of the South American continent at the border of Peru and Chile and progress eastward to the eastern most point of the South American continent at Recife, Brazil. The split will take approximately six hours.

"There will be another ten to twelve hours before the third continent starts it split. That will be the continent of Africa. The location of the African split will be directly east of the end of the South American continent split. That would be at the borders between Nigeria and Cameroon. The African split will then progress across to the furthest eastern point of the continent. That will be a point just north of Hordio, Somalia. The split will take approximately ten to twelve hours.

At the end of the African split the next and final continent will be the Asian continent. There will be approximately fifteen hours before this split starts. The split will start at the most eastern point of the Indian nation at Tripura, India and move directly north and across the Asian continent to the Ozero

221

Taymyr Region of Russia. That split will take approximately eight hours.

"Once the split starts here in the North American continent it will take approximately ninety-two hours for the split to be completed. After this is done the splits will began to separate those continents that are involved over the next thirty-three hours. The separation between the split parts will range from eight miles to fifty miles and those areas will be filled by the oceans.

"Now the question as to any interaction between the ocean waters and the mantle of the earth is not a problem. The process is designed to give the mantle enough time to cool in the exposed areas before the sea waters reach them. In addition, there will be considerable amount of material sliding into the bottom and over the mantle as the splits widen. Between the two actions the mantle will have cooled and will be protected by a covering of land materials.

"The real hazard will come with the entry of the sea waters into the cracks. Because of the magnitude of the split there will be a lot of loose material that will crumble and slide into the cracks once the ocean waters hit those weak areas. That is why, during the life of the split, all humanity must be moved at least a hundred miles minimum from the identified split locations.

"We will provide the exact coordinates of each split as to where it starts and where it stops. The system is designed to try and avoid any high population areas. Please understand this system was

222

developed, designed and implanted as a program and it was turned on over half a billion years ago.

"Every attempt was made to try and carry out an analysis of population disbursement across the face of your world by this time. That is why it is absolutely vital in the next ninety-two hours you identify each and every one of those areas that are designated as cracks start and crack ending points, and remove any high population numbers from those areas."

When she finished, all he could do was stand there and look at her. He was numbed by the level of complexity and detail she just laid out for him. Just then Dennis came to the door. "Duke, we have started to receive an extremely large amount of data on our computer data screens. We don't know where it's coming from but it's detailed and extremely complex. Right now, it appears to be pinpointing a number of areas across the world where cracks are going to be implemented.

"My question is what information is LeAnn going to give us in order for us to identify and plan evacuation procedures for those hazard areas we need to advise?"

Duke turned to Dennis. "Dennis, that's the information LeAnn has promised us, you need to pull your team together and go over all of the data and then forward it to the president's command center. Advise the president that is the information they will need to carry out the evacuation of the hazard areas as a split takes place. Make sure they have a clear understanding of the time frame.

"We have ninety-two hours before the split starts, and once started it will be another ninety-two hours to the end of the split. That gives us a hundred eighty-four hours from now until the end of the split and we have to have everyone clear by the time the split actually starts. Understand the split location when it starts is dead center of the Six Lakes, at lakes three and four.

"From that point on, the crack will continue to advance through its entire planned path. This means we must be ready here in the United States in the first ninety-two hours to start the monitoring of the splits as they move along their projected paths through each continent. Once the monitoring starts it must continue from then on as the event progresses to the time when the splits join south of the Asian continent.

"With the completion of the split, it will then take another ninety-two hours for the waters to fill the cracks and for the ground along the cracks to stabilize. When we reach stabilization, it will have been a total of two hundred seventy-six hours. At that point the machines will rebury themselves a process designed to take a total of twenty-four hours. In the end the entire event will take three hundred hours' time and the machine will be fully buried and out of anyone's access."

Dennis finished taking his notes, looked at Duke, nodded his head and left. Duke then turned to LeAnn. "Have we everything we need to ensure we have the ability to move everyone in time?"

LeAnn smiled and looked at Duke, nodding her head. "Duke, you have done well. If all the governments cooperate in carrying out their part of this project there will be no loss of life. If any government refuses to cooperate, that government will be held solely responsible for their failure to think of their people first."

What LeAnn said touched Duke. He looked at her. "LeAnn, that sounds like a threat to me. If a government fails to respond to these warnings and take action to ensure the safety of their people, will it result in any form of action against them?"

LeAnn stood there, not saying a word, looking Duke straight in the eyes. She then turned and walked over to the door of his office, looked back at him and with her right hand, gestured he follow her. Something was up and Duke had an inner feeling he did not like what was about to be revealed to him. Yet he still had to follow her and prepare himself for what was to come.

They walked out of the main administrative tent and over to one of the trucks parked nearby, LeAnn pointed to the driver's side of the truck and looked at Duke, opened the passenger door and got in. Duke walked around to the driver's side, got in and started the truck. "Duke, take us up to the rim."

Duke put the truck in gear and pulled away from the parking spot. As he drove the road up to the rim, LeAnn sat there looking straight ahead and saying nothing. As they drove over the top of the rim Duke saw for the first time the magnitude of the machine operating there in the lake. All the water or what they thought was water, and had been in the lake was now gone. In its place was a massive machine four miles across and almost a quarter mile high. When it actually reached its final position, he had no idea, they had not been monitoring the lake basin since the attack on the Lake People earlier in the day.

As Duke brought the truck to a stop and opened the door, all he could do was look at the machine and its size, he was mesmerized by it. He returned his attention to LeAnn, watching her as she walked around the front of truck and turned looking back at him, raising her left hand and signaling him to follow. He had nothing else he could do but to follow her. He knew he had to find out everything he could about this process in order for his teams to effectively keep the government informed about what was going on.

As he walked up beside her, she turned and started walking towards the machine. When they got to the edge of the lake basin, they found a metal bridge crossing the gap between the land and the machine. It was about fifty feet across. She walked out onto the bridge and as she did a door on the machine opened. He followed her as they approached the door and pass-through into the machine.

As Duke entered the machine, he was not prepared for what he was about to see. Not only was it a machine, but it was a machine of such magnitude, of such advanced engineering, his mined could barely grasp the magnitude of this creation. He was stunned by the size, the design, and complexity. There was nothing like it anywhere on the earth. LeAnn turned to him and watched as he struggled to take in the view in front of him.

"Duke, this machine was built and placed here on this Earth over half a billion years ago. The beings who built this machine did so in order to give planet Earth a chance to survive. The beings who created this machine have been in existence for over three and a half billion years. They have conquered the aspects of spaceflight anywhere in the universe. They still exist, but are not physically present here on this Earth. The reason for that is they desire not to influence the development of the beings of this planet or any other planet, for that matter.

"Understand they clearly know what's going on and what the people of this planet are doing to assist them in this re-terraforming of this world. They have little patience for those who resist or for their own reasons deny their assistance in this process. As a result, any and every governing body or peoples, who resist, deny or act in any manner designed to interfere in the welfare of their peoples, will be punished. Duke, this is not an idle threat, this is an absolute action that will be taken regardless of the logic or reasons behind those governments failure."

LeAnn turned and started walking further towards the center of the machine. Basically, all one could see was floor and ceiling and then less than fifty yards in front of them a door. From their point of entry, the wall started ten feet to the right and left of the exterior entry door and was horseshoe shaped. At the center of the horseshoe shaped wall was the second door. As they approached that door it slid open to the right and LeAnn walked through followed by Duke.

Duke found himself standing in a room approximately a hundred fifty by a hundred fifty. The walls all appeared to be made of metal but radiated a soft cool light. The floor felt firm but yet it was like someone was standing on a very thick pile carpet. The ceiling was approximately ten feet high and was black in color. There was one large table situated dead center of the room. The table itself was square and approximately twenty-five by twenty-five feet. Around the table were thirty chairs, each one built with armrests and high backed.

LeAnn walked around to the far side of the table and took a seat in the center chair. She raised her left hand and invited Duke to sit in the chair to her left. Duke obliged and once he had sat down a large area of the table in front of him lit up. Duke found himself looking at a large globe of the world rising out of the center of the table floating to a position that was about thirty inches above the table. Each continent, each government, each population center, each river, each mountain range, each border, were clearly marked and so labeled. The globe was rotating at the exact speed of the earth's rotation.

LeAnn ran her right hand across the face of a screen directly in front of her. With that movement of her hand the screen globe changed showing a view of the North American continent and the Six Lakes positioned across the United States.

She then turned to Duke. "Duke this is the overall command center for the operation of this machine. From here we will oversee the split as it takes place. There is ample room for others of your teams to sit at this table. From those positions they will be able to monitor the split and so inform your government and the other governments who are going through the split process.

Please understand this is not a gift of a machine to you or the people of this planet. This is a machine once the process is completed will re-bury itself deep into the earth and set itself up for the next maintenance split that will need to be done twenty million years from now.

"You and your people will be given access to this facility only during the process of the split. Do not attempt to take, locate, find, or in any way try to take any of this technology out of this machine. If anyone does or attempts to they will be punished, immediately without any recourse. You of this planet are not ready nor will you be for many millions of years to have this kind of technology in your hands. There are no exceptions to this requirement. Any attempt to take any technology out of this facility will not be tolerated."

Duke sat there looking at LeAnn. He could hardly believe what she was saying. The fact was he could hardly believe where he was. He knew without a doubt everything she had said was real and would be carried out if they violated the trust being placed

229

in their hands. "LeAnn, I understand what you are relating to me and I can only say we will honor those requirements to the letter.

"However, I cannot speak for everyone who may come into this facility. It is my hope I as an individual will not be held responsible for the actions some other individual may take or attempt. Am I clear on that?"

LeAnn sat there looking at Duke and a smile came across her face. "Duke, it is clear you are a little worried about this whole situation. Let me assure you each and every individual will be held responsible for their own actions. However, you need to understand as the head of this organization you must take every action possible to ensure your personnel act responsibly, ethically and properly while in this facility. No, there will be no direct action against you personally for someone else's irresponsible actions, unless you yourself are that irresponsible being."

That left little for Duke to be concerned about. He knew the ground rules and it was his job to make sure all of his personnel understood those ground rules before they entered this facility. With that they got up and walked out of the room and out of the machine to the truck, and headed back to the base.

When they reached the base camp, LeAnn move off to be with the other Lake People and Duke went looking for Dennis. He found him in the administrative offices. They went into Duke's office and sat down. Dennis sat there waiting for Duke to start the conversation. Finally, Duke leaned forward and put his elbows on the desk top and ran his hands through his hair.

He looked at Dennis. "My friend, we have one hell of a job ahead of us and I'm not quite sure just how we're going to do it. I just came back from a short trip to the machine in Lake One. Dennis, she actually took me into the machine and into a control or command room. That will be the location where we will work with LeAnn and the other Lake People in overseeing the re-terraforming.

"However, there is a problem. While in the command center she laid out a number of rules for me, and I can tell you here and now it's not going to be easy. Dennis, there are a series of punishments that could result for world governments refusing or failing to carry out the tasks they are being assigned.

"In addition, when we go into the machine, any attempt by anyone of us to remove, take possession of, or steal, any technology from the machine will result in direct action by the Lake People. I do not know what action would be taken, but after the incident at the airfield, I fear it would be serious and probably deadly.

"So, between the two of us and the other supervisors, it will be our responsibility to instill in our people it is hands off no matter what they think or desire."

Dennis sat there looking at Duke as he explained the situation. He had little doubt as to the seriousness of the situation and he acknowledged that by nodding his head. He then sat back. "Duke, when are we going to move into the machine and what is our time frame for this coming event?"

"The entire time involved in the process will be three hundred hours from when it starts to the end. The actual process will start about ninety-two hours from the initial movement of the machines from beneath the earth to their current position.

The split will actually start between Lakes three and four and then move north and south through Canada and Mexico. From there it will move down to South America and cut the continent in half and then from the eastern coast of South America it will move over to Africa and hit between Nigeria and Cameroon and end at Hordio, Somalia. Then it will move to Tripura, India and go north to the Ozero Taymyr region of the Asian continent.

"It will take ninety-two hours for the entire crack to form and complete. After that the waters from the oceans will be filling in the cracks as it progresses around the world. My fear of any volcanic activity has been answered as well and it shouldn't be a problem. Our main job is to keep the data moving to the office of the president and each governing body around the world.

"The president's office will work to get all the cooperation possible from those governments the crack will be passing through. I will be sending them the information on the negative actions by the Lake People if any governing body refuses or fails to comply with the direct action ordered. I hope it will bring everyone around and clear the way for full cooperation during this process."

Dennis sat there and Duke could see something else was bothering him. Duke waited for Dennis to bring up whatever it was digging at him. Finally, Dennis stood up and walked to the wall map and then turned and walked back to the desk. He stood there, his mind going miles an hour while trying to determine just how to bring up what needed to be said.

Finally, he placed both hands on the desk and leaned toward Duke. "Duke, I have Tanner waiting outside. He has something he needs to go over with you and I can assure you when you hear him you will not like it."

Duke knew Dennis was bothered but now he was not too sure he wanted this thing to go any further. Finally, he nodded. "All right Dennis you can bring him in. We might as well get this over with now."

Dennis walked to the door and opened it, leaned through and called to Tanner. A few seconds later Tanner came through the door, over to the desk, and sat down in one of the chairs. Dennis followed him to the desk and took the other chair. The look on Tanner's face told a story Duke immediately didn't like.

Duke looked over at Dennis and then back to Tanner. "What's up Tanner? I can just about guess it has something to do with the airfield incident, right?"

Tanner looked over at Dennis and adjusted himself nervously in the chair and then started to nod his head. "Duke, there's much more to that situation than we had thought possible. I really don't know how to start this thing so I'll just jump into it. If I am not coming through to you clearly, let me know and I'll start over."

Tanner paused for a few seconds to give Duke the opportunity to interject a comment or ask a question. None came so he continued. "Yesterday, when it had been decided to bring the other twenty Lake People to Lake One, I contacted our normal air transport company and ordered two twin engine planes to make the pickup. Because we had done security background checks on the company when we first started this project, I felt the added checks were not needed. What I didn't know was a group of individuals had been watching our activities from the moment we were dispatched to this location and they were highly interested in the people from the lakes.

"That group had decided it would highjack the two planes and take the Lake People. What they planned on after that we don't know as yet, but we do know they were being backed by a lot of money from outside the United States.

"In the process of getting the two planes to the lake locations, they managed to have crews who were working for them assigned the duties. From then on, the pilots and the ground assault group were coordinating their activities so they would all meet at the airfield at the same time.

"When the planes landed, they taxied to a location away from the normal departure spot and met the ground force that was coming in. At this point you know what happened. The Lake People killed the entire assault group including the pilots.

"Once we had the Lake People here at the base, my men and I then went back and started to investigate the assault group. Duke it's really bad. I don't know any other way to put it."

Tanner paused again and Duke then leaned toward him. "Tanner, you're doing a great job, so just continue and tell it as it happened. Take your time and get everything straight."

Tanner nodded his head and continued. "We expected to find a group of home grown anti-governmental radicals, a H.A.W.K. team, and what we found was a first line military unit. It was a Shock Assault Unit out of the 843rd Stryker Group from, Washington State. Duke, it was our own military and I haven't the slightest idea what the hell they were trying to do or were up to. Right now, I don't know just what the hell we should do.

"This I do know; those people don't go anywhere unless they mean business. I don't know where to go or who to talk to. I thought about calling Fort Lewis and then thought better of it. I have no idea how far up the line this thing runs and I could end up talking to the prime command of this whole action.

"The next question is whether this was a single attempt or whether they are planning further actions against us. Duke, I'm at a standstill and don't know what the hell I should do next."

The shock of what Tanner had just told him hit Duke several seconds after Tanner had stopped talking. He could feel his face flush and hands start to shake. He looked over at Dennis who was sitting there just as shocked and disoriented as Duke.

Duke looked back at Tanner and cleared his throat. "All right Tanner, you've done the right thing so far. Now we need to take a look at our options and plan our next move. But first I need to ask, have there been any assault groups targeting the other five lakes?"

Tanner looked at Dennis and then back to Duke. "At this time, we have no indications of assault groups in the areas of the other five lakes. The problem is we are not set up to deal with that type of action. Knowing these people, they could hit us from any direction and that includes overhead as well."

Just then Dennis cleared his throat. "What about NASA? Could we get them to do a satellite scan of the lakes to see if there is any activity going on around them?"

Duke listened to Dennis and then started to shake his head. "No, I don't think we want any other governmental organization involved in this."

"Duke, how about the president, shouldn't we be calling him now and briefing him on what has been happening?"

"Yes, I think we have to do that, but not right now. No, we need to find out more about this and then once we have it all tied down, we can inform the president."

The three of them sat there trying to come up with a viable next move when there was a knock on the door. Dennis got up and walked over to the door and opened it. Standing there was LeAnn and she had a look on her face that told Dennis to step aside and let her in.

LeAnn walked through the door and over to the desk and stood there looking at Duke. "There is a problem Duke, and I think you know what I'm talking about don't you?

This was all he needed, but he also knew she would have to be involved and so he nodded his head. "LeAnn, I have just been briefed on the situation and we're trying to come up with some answers." He looked over at Dennis, "Get her a chair please and then sit down. We've got a lot of work to do."

Once everyone was sitting Duke looked straight at LeAnn. "I hope you don't think I was going to keep this from you? I was just receiving the information myself and we were trying to determine just what steps we needed to take to counter this mess. Do you understand me?"

LeAnn was nodding her head. "Duke, I know what you were doing and I agree with what you have done so far. The problem is you need to move on this and move now. That is why I'm here, we can give you all the information you will need to deal with any outside interference with our project. The question is, should you expect your government to deal with it or should we deal with it?"

Duke was looking her straight in the eyes when she said that and he noted the seriousness of her comment and demeanor. "By you dealing with it, what do you mean?"

She sat there a few seconds. "We can scan the regions around the lakes, and if we find any forces we discern as being hostile toward us, we will take the appropriate actions necessary to eliminate those hostile forces."

Aw, man, that's all he needed now. A full-blown battle, right dead center of the continental United States and to top it off it would be with our own military. In effect, it would be an alien vs. American Military confrontation and he was sure the military would come out second best.

He didn't have an answer. If he said no then she would probably take the action anyway. If he said yes, he would be responsible for a full-blown confrontation between his country and this alien force who was ready to respond if and when they were assaulted.

Finally, he reached over and picked up the phone and looked at LeAnn. "I need to call the president and brief him on what is happening, is that all right?"

She looked at him and nodded her head.

He dialed the number and several seconds later a female voice answered the phone. "Hello, this is Duke Ridgeman could I please talk to the president, it's important?"

There was another pause and he came on the line. "Yes Duke, what can I do for you?"

Duke; that was the first time he had ever used his first name.

Duke took a deep breath. "Sir, we've had a serious situation develop here. This base has come under attack by a military force. The force was repelled with total loss of the personnel of the attacking unit."

The president was listening. "Duke, would you say that again, I'm putting you on a speaker so the others here can hear you. Please continue."

"Sir, at about ten hundred hours this morning two planes were sent to pick up the other twenty Lake People and return them to this base. As the planes landed, the pilots taxied past the departure and reception gate on to the far end of the field, meeting up with an armed force that numbered forty people, fully armed.

"Their intentions were the removal and kidnapping of the Lake People. As it turned out, the pilots were a part of this overall group. Once the planes stopped, they opened the doors and three armed men entered each plane with the purpose of removing the Lake People and taking them away. What happened next has shocked us to the core sir.

"The Lake People responded and killed the men who boarded the planes and the pilots as well. They then exited the planes, three of them from each plane, and confronted the rest of the armed unit. At that point the Lake People defended themselves and killed every single member of the assault team who had met the planes.

"After the Lake People moved on to the Lake One base. Our security unit went to the scene and started an investigation of the people who had tried

239

to take the Lake People." Duke paused at that point to see if the president had any questions.

"Continue Duke; please give me the rest of it."

"Sir, our investigation determined the assault group was a Shock Assault Group out of the 843rd Stryker Unit from Washington State. Sir, they were our own military.

"In addition, LeAnn knows everything that has taken place and she is ready to deal with any military or non-military action that may be directed at the Six Lakes. Sir, she advises if they take action it will mean the total annihilation of any forces who attempt to take control of any of the lakes. I felt I needed to contact you and advise you as to what is happening.

"Sir, if this was an actual approved assault on this base, we need to know because it is in direct violation of the conditions set down by the aliens. On the other hand, if this is a non-approved action then you have a real problem on your hands."

There was a long pause. During that time Duke could hear people in the background talking and some were getting heated. Then he heard what sounded like a fight and it was followed by gun fire. Duke looked over at the other three and felt the blood rush out of his face. "God, what the hell is happening there anyway?"

Finally, things went quiet. After several seconds a voice came on the line. "Mr. Ridgeman, this is General Halverson. The president is currently unable to come on line and so I will be acting in his

240

place. You will take into custody this Ms. LeAnn and hold her for the military police who will be arriving at your base in about three hours. Do you understand?"

Duke realized he may have just witnessed the coup of the United States Government. He looked at Tanner, then Dennis and then LeAnn. They were all just sitting there, and then LeAnn stood up and leaned across the desk. "General Halverson, I hope you have not done something foolish in regards to your president and the government of this country.

"If you have taken over governmental control then I must advise you will never be able to take the Six Lakes at any time no matter what the size of your military. Second, if it proves you have taken control of the government this base will start a series of preemptive strikes against your military bases both in this country and across the world. When we are done you will be completely void of any military capabilities of any kind.

"I can assure you in a world such as this, your nation will not survive long once your military dominance has been neutralized. You have one hour to place yourself under arrest and that of your Joint Chiefs of Staff and return the control of this government back to the president and civilian control. Do you understand?"

There was dead silence. The tension in the office was off the scale as it was at the president's command center. LeAnn sat back down and folded her arms across her chest and started to wait. She said nothing else and sat there looking straight at

241

Duke. Her face was expressionless and her eyes never blinked. It was as if she had left and gone someplace else. Duke started to say something when he felt the need to remain silent. It almost overwhelmed him. In the next hour the showdown will take place.

Meanwhile, in the president's command center in Washington D.C., the president had received the call from Duke and listened to the briefing concerning the 843rd Stryker Unit. He set the phone down and turned to the members of his Emergency Advisory Team. He advised them of the situation at the Six Lakes Project and the attempted kidnapping of the Lake People and the resulting destruction of the attack unit.

As he was presenting this information, General Halverson listened to the briefing and once the president was finished, he stood and looked at the rest of the Team. "Mr. President, it appears things have gotten out of hand at the Six Lakes Project. Mr. Ridgeman appears to have lost control and that means the entire project is in jeopardy. It is my recommendation we take that facility over and transfer the control and operation of this project over to the military. We have the people and means of running this kind of a program with a far better level of control and organization.

"As far as this so-called assault they claim has taken place, I don't believe it. They have targeted and accused the most advanced and dedicated command in our military and I can tell you here and now it just did not happen. If there were those who tried to kidnap the Lake People then they were probably a mercenary force from south of the border."

"General Halverson, if Duke Ridgeman says this force was from the 843rd then it was from the 843rd. The question is what were they doing in the area carrying out this kind of an action anyway?"

The room went quiet when the staff assistant to General Halverson stood and pulled an automatic from his briefcase. The rest of those present started to stand and the President started for the door to the meeting room. The General looked at his assistant. "Kill him and anyone else that tries to leave this room."

The assistant then shot the president, killing him instantly and then shot two others who were moving with the president. He ordered everyone else to sit and place their hands on the table top and remain still.

At the same time a second assistant to the General had moved around the table to the door and secured it from anyone entering or trying to exit the room.

The General then walked to the head of the table and picked up the phone. "Mr. Ridgeman this is General Halverson."

The action plan of the military had been initiated with the taking of the president. Military units were moving in and taking into custody the Vice President, Secretary of State, Majority Leader of the Senate and House, and the Secretary of War. The major policy makers for the United States

Government were now in their custody and the overthrow of the Government was into full motion.

Things had just gone off the wall; the re-terraforming was on schedule and would not be delayed. Duke had just witnessed an alien presence lay down a mandate that could be the end of this country as we knew it. He was looking at Dennis and Tanner and then focused back on LeAnn. "I don't know what to say right now, but I understand your position on this. All it takes is a few greedy men and they can destroy hundreds of years of progress and growth. It's obvious to me they see a load of technology they want and they're willing to destroy this country to get it.

"LeAnn, I don't want this to happen. I now find myself looking to you for guidance in this and what you can do to help us with this situation."

Duke sat there looking right at LeAnn, waiting for something positive to happen. Over the last hour little to nothing had been positive and he was starting to feel everything was hopeless as well. His problem was what LeAnn and her contingency was capable of doing and just how far would they go in carrying out the defense of the Six Lakes Project.

Chapter Nineteen

CIVIL WAR

When the phone rang Mike knew instinctively he didn't like the sound of it and surely didn't want to answer it. He let it ring half a dozen times and then reached over and picked up the receiver, "Sandburg here."

"Mike, General Halverson here. I called to let you know the takeover has started. The President is dead and the top positions of the government have been taken into custody and that includes the Joint Chief of Staff at the Pentagon.

"Mike, you can start to move your H.A.W.K. Teams into the Six Lakes regions and set up for takeover. I am having the remainder of our Stryker Units moving in from the east. We will have all six lakes between us and then we can start the move to take over the machines. Are there any questions?"

"General, this is totally unexpected. Yeah, I knew we ultimately planned on taking over the government, I just didn't anticipate it happening this soon."

"Mike, when we have to move, we have to move. The situation here in Washington changed and that required our taking action sooner than later."

"All right General, if that's the way you want it. I'll contact our Teams. I will also contact the support teams from south of the border. They can start moving north and preparing to place the civil authorities on the west coast under arrest."

"That's fine Mike. Everything is time critical now and we need to move fast and positively. One thing, make sure you maintain control of those people from the south. I don't like their attitude and I don't want this to turn into a killing fest for them."

"Understood General, I have talked with them and they understand the consequences if they over play their part in this. General, I'll need your full support in this area. Those people cannot be trusted, but right now we need them."

"All right Mike; oh, there is one other thing. One of the aliens goes by the name LeAnn. I want her located and identified and then shipped off to DC, no questions asked. She is to be isolated and delivered here within twenty-four hours of locating her. And Mike, I don't want any marks on her either."

"I understand General. We know she's in the Lake One Base Camp and she should be easy to identify and take into custody."

"Fine Mike, go get her and let's get this thing over with."

Meanwhile new orders and directives were being sent to all military bases and locations across the world. Every unit was being advised of their new command structure and they were expected to maintain their defense of the nation. Additional information as to the state of the government would be following within forty-eight hours.

Chapter Twenty

THE SHOWDOWN

It was almost an hour later when LeAnn seemed to come back. She looked at Duke. "Has General Halverson called back yet?"

Duke was a little startled by her coming back but regained his composure in short order. "No, we have heard nothing as yet. Do you want me to call them back?"

She sat there a moment and then nodded her head. "Yes, please do, but first I must warn you. No matter what is happening between General Halverson and me, you must not try to interrupt what is taking place between us or make any comments that could create any confusion. We do not have time to waste playing who has control. Do you understand?"

"Yes, but I'm not sure we should become too demanding of the General at this time, he controls a lot of power and people."

She was watching Duke closely and once he finished, she said. "Duke, you must trust me. Believe me when I tell you the General does not and could never have the level of power he would need to overcome this base or any action I may take against him. If he thinks so, he has a serious lesson to learn. Now will you trust me or must I take other steps to make sure my negotiation with the General are not compromised?"

Duke knew an ultimatum when he heard one and he preferred to be present during the coming faceoff between the General and LeAnn. "LeAnn, I do trust you. You have given me no reason not to in the past and I don't believe you would in this situation. No, I would rather remain here and be available to you for anything you may want. Besides, I really do want to see that General taken down a couple of pegs."

LeAnn smiled and turned her attention to Dennis and Tanner. "Do I have the same commitment from the two of you?"

Both men nodded their heads and looked to Duke and again nodded their heads.

LeAnn then turned back to Duke. "All right you can call the General."

Duke reached over and opened the phone line and pushed the auto-dial button for the president's command center in Washington DC. There was a pause and then the phone started to ring. It was answered and a voice other than the Generals came on the line.

At the Command Base the Communications Sergeant was tending the radio and phone line system in the command center. Just then the hot phone from the Six Lakes Project rang. He looked around the room and then at the Lieutenant in charge. "Answer the phone and give them the message the General told you to give when they called, understand?

The Sergeant nodded and answered the phone, "Command Center."

LeAnn leaned forward. "General Halverson, please?"

The person who had answered the phone responded. "I'm sorry the General is not available at this time. If this is Ms. LeAnn I am to tell you to go to hell." Then the phone line went dead.

LeAnn sat back and looked at the phone and then a smile came across her face. She closed her eyes "Duke, turn on the national news now please."

Duke looked at her, turned his chair around and flipped the power switch on the radio to on. That particular radio was always on the national news channel. He then turned to her, "Now what?"

She raised her right hand for him to wait and then closed her eyes. She opened them and sat there waiting. Ten minutes later the word came in the Pentagon had collapsed and was completely destroyed. On the scene reports advised there was no plane or other devices that hit the building, it just pancaked.

At the Command Center the General was going over maneuver plans with his command staff when the Communications Sergeant turned to him, "Sir?"

The General looked up. "What is it Sergeant?"

"Sir, we just got word that the Pentagon has collapsed. Sir, it is totally destroyed with all personnel lost."

The General stood up and walked around the table to the Sergeant and leaned over him. "Son, you had better not be playing any games with me, what was that you said?"

"Sir, I have just been advised the Pentagon has been destroyed and there are no, I repeat, no survivors."

The General slammed his fist into the table top and grabbed the hot line phone to the Six Lakes Project.

Less than five minutes later the phone rang. Duke reached over and hit the answer button. "What the hell did you just do you idiot?"

Duke looked at LeAnn and shrugged his shoulders. "General, this is LeAnn. I told you what you were to do in one hour. You choose not to respond to me and rejected my call when I called you back for your answer. That was taken as your answer and so I gave you an object lesson. Now are you ready to put the president back on line and place yourself under arrest?"

The General looked around the room at his staff and then stopped and steadied himself. "Lady, you can go to hell. We have removed the president and we are now coming to take you out and take over that base facility."

Duke was looking at LeAnn and shaking his head as the General was talking. He was watching her and her expression never changed in any way. She closed her eyes for a second and then opened them.

Just then there was a scream and you could hear people running around and yelling at one another. Duke leaned forward and yelled into the speaker phone. "What's going on there? Will someone please answer me, what just happened?"

The General had been standing there waiting for some response when he got this god awful look on his face. He dropped the phone and reached up and grabbed his neck. At the same time his head started to turn and twist until his face was facing the opposite direction. He then fell to the floor dead.

They could hear someone yell at the others to calm down and return to their positions and stay put. After several minutes a new voice came on line. "Mr. Ridgeman, this is General Howard. General Halverson just died. His head was twisted a hundred eighty degrees, breaking his spine. I think maybe we need to slow things down and talk this thing out."

LeAnn then raised her right hand and signaled Duke away from the phone. "General Howard, this is LeAnn. What happened to General Halverson was not anything major from our perspective. It was an easy matter to locate him, identify him, and then execute him. The same will be true for anyone else who defies my directive, is that understood?"

You could feel the weight of the tension at the White House Command Center. There were people moving around in the facility and after several more minutes a voice came on line. General Howard had pulled his assistant over to the table and wrote a note on a piece of paper, "Lieutenant you are the president."

The General's Lieutenant picked up the phone as the General wrote out what he wanted said. "LeAnn, this is the vice-president. I am now taking over as the president. At this time the commanders of our military who have instituted this rebellion have surrendered and are now in our custody. It may take us a couple of hours to get things back in order here, but we are ready to start working with you again."

The Lieutenant stood by the table waiting for a response from LeAnn. General Howard handed him more notes to read off of the pad. The General was standing there watching and listening to the exchange between his Lieutenant and LeAnn.

"LeAnn, a team had entered the Command Center and removed General Halverson's body and the bodies of the others who had been killed in the takeover."

As the Lieutenant was speaking to LeAnn, General Howard had started to send out the directives to the active Stryker teams directing them to start their assaults on the Six Lakes Project. The order given was no one would be taken alive. It was an all-out annihilation order.

"Mr. President, this is LeAnn and I have two questions. First who are you? Second has the military forces who were directed toward this base been ordered to stand down or are they still on the move."

Duke looked over at Dennis and Tanner and a look of confusion shot across his face. He couldn't understand why she was asking that question when she had the ability of making that determination herself. LeAnn sensed his thoughts and looked over at him and shook her head and motioned him to relax with her hands. It was then Duke knew there was more behind that question than he had anticipated.

The voice of the Vice-President came back on line. "Yes LeAnn, this is the Vice-President and I have been duly sworn in and have now taken control of the Government. I can advise you all military units have been ordered to stand down and return to their bases of operations."

LeAnn was as calm and cold as anything Duke had ever seen. She sat there a moment. "Thank you. But I need you to understand, Mr. Vice President; I know you are not the Vice President and all you have said in the last comment was a lie. I don't understand why you people think you can bluff and lie your way through this situation, but you persist. I give you credit for that anyway.

"I have now determined you, General Howard along with General Halverson, have in fact killed the president of this nation and his staff. They have been replaced by members of your staff and you are still moving troops and equipment into the areas of the Six Lakes. Before I take any other actions against you personally, I have decided to give you another object lesson in the art of war.

"The entire military element you have sent to attack this base and the other five lakes will now be destroyed down to the last person and piece of equipment. Remember General Howard, you are the ones who set this thing up and now I am going to finish is.

"The 843rd Stryker Force is now terminated. The 623rd bomber squadron is now terminated. The 477th Airborne division is terminated. General, I have saved the last act for you and your staff there in the command center. Starting with the most junior personnel and up to you, each will be terminated. The fact is General we don't need you to carry out the needs of the world during the re-terraforming of this planet. Goodbye General."

At the command center a secretary had picked up a number of forms and was carrying them to the back of the room when she stopped and started to scream. At that moment her body flew across the room against the wall.

Everyone headed for the door all at once except the General and his team. As the people piled up at the door it wouldn't open. Then one by one people were pulled from the group and hurled to the opposite end of the room.

This continued until the General was the last one present and then he felt himself being levitated and turned onto his back. At the moment his body was twisted and thrown to the other end of the room. In less than a minute it was over.

Horrific screams were heard as bodies were flung against the door leading into the room, until there was no one left alive and the phone line went silent.

In less than five minutes it was over and LeAnn reached over and hit the disconnect button. She then turned to Duke. "Now let's get to work and give the people of this planet a chance to survive this process."

Duke sat there looking at her and wondering just what the hell happened there anyway. Finally, he had to ask. "LeAnn, what just took place at the Washington Command Center?"

She had stood up and started toward the door when Duke had asked the question. She stopped and turned toward him. "Duke, those people had taken over the center and in the process they killed the president and his whole staff who was working in the center. There was no one there who was going to assist us in this process and so they needed to be eliminated. To the person they were all killed. And the Center is now out of the process. We will have to run it from here."

She turned and walked out the door with Duke, Dennis and Tanner right behind her. Duke didn't quite know what he should do. He had just witnessed what appeared to have been the killing of a number of people in the Washington Command Center, something he could not prove other than being advised by LeAnn she had just overseen that very thing.

He finally caught up with her. "LeAnn, where are we going?"

She didn't change her stride, "Duke we are moving to the control base in the machine and will continue the monitoring and controlling of the process from there until it's done."

She stopped in the middle of the yard between the tents that made up the main base camp of Lake One. She raised her right hand and stood there waiting. Within thirty seconds the rest of the Lake People started coming out of the tents and gathering around her. Not a word was spoken and then groups of three started breaking away from the main group and heading toward the trucks. Duke stepped forward. "LeAnn, where are they going?"

She turned to Duke and raised her right hand giving him a sign to stand by for a few minutes. After the last of the groups had formed and walked away, she turned to Duke. "I have assigned the different groups to go to the other five lakes and take over the command centers in each of the machines. Your personnel there will be screened to make sure there are none there who were or are working for those trying to take over this system. Once that is done, they will move into the machines and start their activities in overseeing the operation of the machines.

"We will now move into the control room on Lake One and prepare for the actual start of the split. We have less than ten hours before it starts. Once that happens, we cannot leave the control room until the process is complete, a hundred eighty-four hours from the start of the process."

Duke understood but still had questions of concern. "What if there are still groups out there who are working for the military and trying to take over this facility, what do we do about them?"

She turned to him. "Oh Duke, you are such a funny being. Of course, there are those out there who will still be trying to take this and the other five facilities over, but they will never succeed. We know who they are and we know where they are. If they make a move against even one of the lakes, the whole of their organization will be destroyed down to the last living being. We are making sure at this time they know that and have been warned. From then on it's their decision."

Duke was looking at Dennis and Tanner and shrugging his shoulders as LeAnn spoke. "Guys, I don't think we have any more control over what is happening until this whole thing is over, so stay close and be ready to react whenever she gives us an order. I really think we have to go along with them if for no other reason than the safety of the people in the areas of the split."

Both Dennis and Tanner nodded their heads and kept moving along with Duke and LeAnn. As they approached the machine and the access bridge over to the main entry door, LeAnn came to a stop and turned to the three of them. She motioned for them to step aside and as they did a group of Lake People moved by them and into the machine. Behind them came members of their scientific research team who had been assigned to Lake One. As they filed by, LeAnn was watching each one.

Suddenly she reached out and took the arm of a young woman approaching the bridge and pulled her aside. She looked at the girl. "Foolish child, you know you can't get by me or any of the others. Why did you even try?"

The girl stood there looking at LeAnn and then at Duke and the other two. She looked down at LeAnn's hand on her arm and then swung her free hand at LeAnn's head. The blow never landed and the girl landed on her back in the dirt. She lay there looking up at LeAnn saying nothing. She then went stiff and collapsed on the ground, obviously dead.

Several people in the line of base personnel saw the activity and broke out of the line and ran away. LeAnn watched them as they neared the top of the rim and then swung her arm around toward them and every one of the five who were running went down and stayed motionless.

With the last of the base personnel in the machine, LeAnn turned and walked across the bridge followed by Duke and the other two. A screening of the personnel at the camp had just taken place and those found to be part of the forces trying to take the base were eliminated. The same process was going on at the other five lakes.

By the time everyone at all the lakes had taken their places in the machine control rooms, the start time for the actual splitting of the earth was approaching. There were only minutes left and no one had any idea just what was going to happen and how they would come out of this thing once it was over. It was now a time of trust and that trust was going to be the difference between their survival or life's end.

Never in the history of the world had an event of this magnitude been recorded. Yes, LeAnn had told Duke there had been a re-terraforming before, but he knew nothing of it. Science had been able to track the movement of the many tectonic plates around the world, but nothing told them of an artificial process being present.

They were about to experience an event designed to protect this planet from a self-destructive process and in doing that save the entire Earth population from a catastrophic loss of life.

Chapter Twenty-One

TIME TO RE-THINK

The information was coming into his control room in a steady stream and he didn't like any of it. All military units within striking distance of the six lakes had been destroyed down to the last man. The General and his staff at the Washington Command Center had all been killed.

Mike was left with none of his allies either back east or around the six lakes area. He was stunned and knew if anything positive was going to come from this it would have to be through his teams. Right then he didn't think they could do anything.

He picked up the phone and called the cartel base to the south in Mexico. The phone rang a number of times and finally someone answered. "Yeah, who's this?"

"Is Alfredo there, this is Mike."

There was a pause, "Just a minute, we'll get him."

It took several minutes and then. "Yes, Mike my friend, what's going on?"

"Alfredo?"

"Yes Mike."

"Alfredo, I have called to fill you in on what is going on here. All the military units who were deployed have been destroyed. Not a single individual survived.

"Also, General Halverson and his entire staff have been killed. The coup has collapsed and we no longer have any military support.

"During the event the Pentagon had also been destroyed."

There was a long pause before Alfredo replied. "Mike, you're telling me all of your military support has been destroyed?"

"Yeah Alfredo, that is exactly what I am telling you, we have absolutely no back up and if we continue this game we are totally on our own."

Again, it fell quiet on the other end. Then he could hear people in the background moving around and talking to one another. "Mike, it appears we're not going to be able to fulfill our part of the agreement we made with you and your General Halverson.

"We are of the opinion this General Halverson has screwed up this entire project and has left us in a most undesirable situation.

"Mike, we don't need that and we will not commit our resources to a failed action such as this.

We feel we are better off following our own course and separating ourselves from anything going on up there.

"You take care of yourself, Mike. Maybe I'll see you one day in the future. But for the time being I wouldn't venture down into this part of the world any time soon. I doubt if you would survive.

"Good day, my friend."

That's just great. The cartels had pulled out once they saw the balance of power had shifted. That left H.A.W.K. all by itself.

Mike hung up and sat back. After several minutes he pulled out the call list and dialed the phone. He hadn't talked to the other leaders of H.A.W.K. for more than six months and now he needed to fill them in. He didn't like, it but he had to keep them informed.

He hated the bitter taste of defeat; it didn't settle right with him. They had underestimated the aliens and left them vulnerable to a direct attack from that force. So far, the general had taken the lead in dealing with the aliens. He felt he was probably safe from anyone knowing who he was and where he was.

Yet, he still had that desire, the drive to pursue their goals and still try and take control of the technology sitting there at Six Lakes. He knew they didn't have a chance in hell of taking the aliens out, but maybe they could still benefit from the experience. All they needed was one simple piece of alien technology and they could convert that into more money than they had ever dreamed of.

263

"Is Mr. Harper there, please?"

"Yes, he is. May I tell him whose calling?"

"Mike Sandburg."

The young woman on the other end put him on hold and went about advising Mr. Harper, Mr. Sandburg was on the phone.

Harper looked up from his work bench and nodded his head. He picked up a rag and walked around the bench toward his office area. Once inside he sat down and reached over and picked up the phone. "Hi Mike, how's it going?"

"Not good Harper. Not good at all."

"All right what's up?'

"We just lost the entire military contingency to our plans."

"What do you mean? That's impossible?"

"No, the entire contingency was wiped out by the aliens including the command leaders in DC; they're all gone."

After having said that, the other end of the line went quiet. At first Mike thought Harper had hung up but he could hear him breathing and so sat still listening and waiting. Every few seconds Harper would make a grunting sound.

Finally, after several minutes Harper responded. "You're sure of this Mike, there's no doubt about it?"

"No doubt Harper, it appears the leader of the aliens, this LeAnn, single handedly wipeout the command unit in DC and literally tore everyone from the General on down to pieces.

"She then went after the Stryker Units and their support unit and killed everyone. She did this from the base camp without even approaching the military units.

"To ensure any further involvement would be stopped she also destroyed the Pentagon."

"Damn, I hadn't planned on that. Anything else you want to tell me?"

"Yeah Harper, the cartels down south just pulled out as well. They want nothing to do with any of this anymore."

"So, you're telling me we're on our own on this thing, that is, if we decide to continue?"

"Harper, that's about it, we have no back up of any kind. If we move on this it's all by ourselves. There is one bright spot in this though, if we're successful then we own it all ourselves."

"Glad to hear there is some benefit to this thing if we continue. What's your take on us going it alone?"

"Harper, I don't think we should. It's time to pull out and re-evaluate our situation for future action."

Again, there was a long pause as Harper considered what Mike had just said. After several minutes Harper asked, "Have you talked to any of the others?"

"No, you're the first I've called."

"Really, all right I want you to call the others and get their feelings on this and when you've done than call me back and we'll decide our next move at that time."

265

"Will do Harper, give me two to three hours and I'll call you back and let you know what the others want and think."

"That's good with me Mike. I'll be waiting for you to call back."

He was afraid of this. He knew this was going to be a game of up-man-ship between all those involved. He needed to call ten other people and set to work making the calls and getting the needed information from them.

He knew all these men well, but in this case, he felt their reactions and decisions were unknown. He needed to make the calls.

Chapter Twenty-Two

A NEW WORLD COMETH

The last, almost four days, had been so confusing and disaster filled Duke was not sure if he wanted to be there or not. He and his team at Lake One have found themselves, missing six members, and now sitting inside the Lake One machine and preparing for a splitting of the Earth that would change everything they knew about their world.

Here on planet Earth, there was an alien machine preparing to re-configure the face of the earth from a maintenance perspective. If what had been told him was true, the work about to take place needed to be done or else the world as he knew it would be torn apart and strewn across space forming a new debris field of rock and ice around the sun.

Confused and scared he and the rest of his team were cooperating with LeAnn as she and the rest of her Lake People oversaw the activities of the splitting and the process of keeping the worlds governments informed of what was happening and when they needed to be clear of the split regions. The next ninety-two hours would be the most difficult to work through. If successful, then the world had twenty million years before any other maintenance needed to be carried out again.

In ninety-two hours, he would know if they had been duped or everything LeAnn had told him was true. One thing he did know there was nothing he could do about it anyway. This thing was going to happen whether good or bad for the Earth.

It then dawned on him he and his team were in the control room of the machine doing the splitting and when the split took place the oceans of the world would come rushing into the void, filling it with them still sitting there in the split.

He looked over at LeAnn and she turned and walked over to him. "Yes Duke, we will be here when the water comes. Don't worry it will not damage the machine nor will anyone here be injured. When the time comes the machine will disengage from the walls of the crack and will at that time float on the sea. We will move to the shore and leave the machine and move to high ground.

That will be the end of the second ninety-two hours and the third and final phase will then start. That phase will be the stabilization of the land masses shore lines and then the re-burying of the machine until the next maintenance phase twenty million years from now. All is moving along just fine.

It was then Duke felt a change in the machines stability. He could feel a vibration starting deep inside the machine. A number of screens on the far wall started to light up and everyone turned their attention to the screens. There were four screens and each one was showing one side view of the machine on the outside. They were looking down into the earth or lake basin. There were two huge shafts coming out the east and west side of the machine and engaged the walls of the land mass on either side of the machine.

To the north and south two more shafts came into view and these both had a sharp chisel like end engaging the walls and started to bury themselves into the walls. At the same time the east and west shafts started to press against the wall. It was a massive maneuver and they could feel it moving through the whole of the machine. How the hell could one or even six machines these sizes actually start a cracking of the Earth's crust let alone cause it to crack all the way around the Earth causing the formation of several new continents?

It was maybe thirty minutes into the initial process when they felt and heard a deepening in the sound and feel of the machine. It was like it had gone into ultra-compound low gear and the push had started in earnest. What was unexpected was the defining crash or pop when the first initial crack formed between the lakes. As it turned out, it happened in a series of pops starting between lakes three and four and then spreading to each subsequent lakes north and south of those two.

The sound had to have been heard around the world and at the time the machines seemed to move into an upper gear. The push was on in earnest now and it would not stop until all the prior mentioned continents had cracked and started their separation.

An unknown of this magnitude was more than a little unsettling to Duke. He moved over by LeAnn and looked at her, for the first time she reached over and stroked the back of his right hand. "It's fine Duke. Everything is moving as it should be. The Earth is safe and will be safe for many years to come."

Duke had not expected this level of sincerity in this woman who had just in the past six to eight hours killed more people than any serial killer had done in the worst one's lifetime. He was confused by this being, yet knew she was clearly a child of this world occupied by a being from some alien society. It then crossed his mind as to whether she would return to herself, or be lost in the process of this huge program.

The telemetry from the locations along the line of the splitting was coming in and everything appeared to be working out fine, according to LeAnn and the other Lake People. For the most part, the governments in the path of the split had done well in getting their people clear of the split areas. As with anything this big, there were probably those people who didn't listen or were too curious and, in that way, may have lost their lives. But, for the most part it was going well.

There was a long way to go in the next ninety-two hours and Duke and his people had settled in as well. They had done a good job in moving all the necessities that would be needed into the machine and then placing the equipment left outside in areas where they would be safe. The Lake People had worked with them to ensure everything had been left in the right places for when they finished the split and exited the machines.

It was at this time the word came in that a large military contingency had been spotted moving on Lake Five from the west. By now there was no threat to the machines, everyone had been sealed into the machines and for all intent and purposes the machines were impregnable. Still the observations were such they could see this military group was setting up in a position for when the machines finally completed the task and moved to the shore to let the occupants out.

Within hours the other lakes started to report similar military units showing up at those locations. It was clear the confrontation with the government was nowhere near over. The question that still needed to be answered was whether these military units were actual representatives of the decisions made by the government or were they rebel units, H.A.W.K., who were operating on their own.

They did not know what the central government in Washington DC looked like, had they followed the constitution or were there factions fighting over control of the government. Nothing had been heard and so it was totally unknown to them.

Duke, Dennis and Tanner had been talking when LeAnn came over to them. She looked at the three of them. "Is there anything I can do for you?"

Duke looked at the others. "LeAnn, we want to try and determine what is going on with the government. Is there any way we could get access to phones or radios so we can try and make that determination?

"We have ninety-two hours before this phase of the process is over and we would like to use that time to try and find out what is going on and see if we can influence any decisions that may have been made to try and take these machines over when the process is finished."

She looked at Duke and then nodded her head. "Yes, we can provide you with that access. However, I must advise you it makes no difference whether they gain access to the machines when this process is over or not. The machines will bury themselves at that time and if there is anyone on board they will go with the machines. They cannot access the technology involved in these machines and if they take the machine over, it will still bury itself. You might tell them that."

Duke nodded his head and followed LeAnn to the far side of the room where there was a second smaller room. They walked into this room and found several desks with communications equipment. Funny, it was all current day equipment. She had anticipated his wanting to make contact.

Duke and the other two set to work trying to make sense out of what was going on outside at the base and at the capital as well. The first call was made to the command center. The person who answered the phone sounded like he was in a state of shock. "Who is this?"

There was a pause. "This is Sergeant Davis, who is this?"

This is Duke Ridgeman at the Six Lake base. I need to talk to someone in charge at the command center."

The Sergeant said nothing at first. "Sir, there is no one in charge at this location. Currently everyone who was in this center is dead. Who they were killed by we are not sure, but we do know they are all dead."

"What about the president, is he alive?"

"No sir, we found him and his staff in the back hallway. All had been shot at close range."

Duke was shocked, even though he knew they were in fact dead. He was sitting there with Dennis and Tanner trying to cope with what was happening across his country. "Sergeant are you with the rebellion or loyal to the president?"

He could hear the sergeant saying something to someone else in the center and then he came on line again. "Sir we are part of the Presidents Secret Service. At this time the Vice President has been sworn in as the President and is now working on bringing the elements who have rebelled to lay down their arms and return to their bases.

"We are also trying to get the communications center back up and on line so we can become part of the process you're dealing with."

273

There was a pause and then I could hear more people in the background talking and finally the sergeant came back on line. "Sir, I have been trying to keep you on line while we finish moving everyone into the center. Please stand by for the President."

Duke acknowledged and waited for the President. Meanwhile he was working with Dennis and Tanner trying to bring all the information on their status on line and ready to report to the president. They had just finished doing that when the sergeant came back.

He sounded a little winded. "Sir, the President is on the line."

Duke turned his attention back to the phone. "Mr. President, are you there, sir?"

"Yes Mr. Ridgeman, I'm here and we have finally gotten everything back under control. Mr. Ridgeman, can you give me a briefing as to where things are right now?"

Duke turned to his monitor and positioned himself for the long haul. "Sir, we are just now entering the actual splitting phase of the event. I will fill you in on all the activity we have been involved in up to this point and then lay out the procedure we will be following during the actual split.

But first I need to advise you there are military units outside all six of the lake machines. There is no way for them to gain entry while we're in the splitting process. Once the split is done we will then leave the machine and expect the military units to try and take control of the machines at that time.

"The lead Lake Person, LeAnn, has advised me no matter what the military unit does, the machines will bury themselves and if there is anyone in them those people will go down with the machine.

There is no access to any of the technology in these machines. They were designed that way over half a billion years ago and they will stay that way. That's the current situation with this problem. I am now ready to start the briefing for you on the progress of this project."

Duke continued the briefing over the next three hours. As he came to the end of the briefing, he asked the president if there was anything he needed to cover in more detail. The response from the president was that he did not need anything more. He and his staff would start the contacts with the other countries and provide them the support they may need during this time.

It was then Duke heard a loud bang and then the whole of the machine started to shake. I was like a 7.0 earth quake had just hit except it kept going. He returned to the president. "Sir, we are currently in the process of an earthquake. I'm not sure what this means but it's a big one and it's a long one."

Just then LeAnn came in the room and approached them. "What you are feeling is the initial crack of the earth crust between lakes three and four. It will last for another five minutes and then subside. From then on the crack will start to move north and south and gain speed. This is normal and not something to be concerned about."

Duke returned to the president. "Sir, I have just been advised the earthquake we are experiencing is expected and will subside shortly. It was caused by the initial cracking of the crust between lakes three and four. The process is on its way now and will last for the next ninety-two hours. This is phase two, of the three phases."

The president acknowledged him and then advised they would get to their tasks and would contact him later. It was then they felt the crack slide past their machine and the feeling of the machine accelerated. There was nothing that could stop it; it would have to take its course and finish.

The fact was Duke felt a great sigh of relief leave his body as he hung up the phone and sat back letting time take its course. He looked over at Dennis and Tanner and they were in the same position.

After several minutes Duke started to smile and that broke the ice as the three of them clearly relaxed. It was then Betty and Mary came into the room with three meals and placed them in front of each of them. "LeAnn wants me to tell the three of you to eat."

Duke looked at Betty. "Thanks Betty, I think we all need a good meal."

Chapter Twenty-Three

EARTH RE-AWAKENS

Telemetry was flowing into the command center of Lake Machine One at an ever-increasing rate. LeAnn reported the crack had started its run north and south and would meet up at a midway point somewhere in the Indian Ocean. Where before she had given them the route of the crack, she had not given them how the crack would run. It was now clear the crack would run its course in both the north and southerly directions until they met on the opposite side of the world.

Whole continents were being divided as were countries. The result of that issue was still concerning every central government. Would they remain one nation or would there be new nations forming due to the divide between them. Not only was that a concern, but countries who had an active revolution taking place and now faced with the split could see their nation separated and a new country develop. Truly there was going to be a significant upheaval in the social and political makeup of the world.

Duke and his team could only sit and wait. The crack was on its way and there was nothing for them to do but sit there and hope everything worked out. LeAnn approached Duke and sat down at the desk. She was looking at the monitor on the wall and then turned to him. "The process is now on its way and it cannot be stopped. It must run its course. We must now get ready for the aftermath of the split. As the oceans flow into the cracks there will be a lot of violent reaction. Most of that violence will be confined within the crack areas.

"However, there is another problem and that is when the cracks reach the oceans. The impact of the crack hitting them at the speed it will be moving will cause tidal effects around the world. We need to send out a notification to all coastal governments to evacuate coast lines and prepare for tsunami situations."

Duke looked at her. "LeAnn, why didn't you tell us of this earlier? How can we move the huge number of peoples from the coastal regions in such short a time?"

She looked at him in that non-committal manner. "Duke, first things first, the preparation of each nation for the split came first. Now they must act on this next issue and they do have time. Our systems are sending them the time schedule of each and every tsunami that will result from this split. They will have ample time to move people as needed. This is not a lapse in our planning; it's the next step those facing it must take. They do have time."

Duke picked up the phone and hailed the Presidents Command Center. He informed them of the new issue and advised the data concerning those areas that would be impacted by tsunamis was being sent to them there. The notifications would make it on time in order to avoid loss of life. The president was a little shocked by the timing of the news, but felt they would have ample time to notify and move people.

As Duke sat there watching the monitors, he felt another earthquake start and then settle down. He then heard a sound that was almost impossible to describe to you. All he could say is it sounded like something that was moving extremely fast and carrying a considerable amount of power behind it. LeAnn looked over at him and smiled. "It's the crack coming at us. It's picking up speed now and will pass under us at about three hundred fifty miles per hour and still accelerating.

Just then he felt something pass under him and at the same time he saw his pencil and paper lift off the table top. The next thing he knew he was airborne. It was not violent, it was, no that can't be, weightlessness. It lasted about ten seconds and then he felt himself drop back into the chair and the paper and pencil fall back to the table top. He looked around the room. Some people had been standing and were able to land on their feet when it passed and others lost their balance and fell to the floor. No one was hurt.

The surprise in his face told LeAnn what he was going to ask her before he said it. "Yes, that was a lack of gravity at that moment. It is expected and it tells us everything is moving as it should be."

Duke got his senses back. "Will it be that way all the way around the world?"

She shook her head. "No that is an effect that only happens when the crack moves under the machine. It's normal and should not be a concern. I could explain it in more detail but your science is not far enough along to be able to make anything out of what I told you."

That felt good, she as much as said we were too primitive to understand what she would be telling us. Fact was, she was right.

It was then when a call came in from the Presidents Command Center. Duke answered the phone and the president's secretary was on the line. "Mr. Ridgeman, the President asked me to advise you there are military unit's approaching each of the six lakes at this time. They are rogue units working for a west coast based private concern. They are going to try and shut the machines down. We have warned them they cannot do that and it was highly dangerous for them to be in the area. They feel they can and have a right to protect their interests.

Duke looked over at LeAnn and she nodded her head. She then turned to the monitor and brought up the external cameras on each of the six lake machines. They were right. There were military trained units outside each machine. Duke would estimate each unit had a minimum of forty personnel and they looked well-armed. LeAnn watched them with interest for several minutes and then turned to him. "If they remain in those places when the oceans start to enter the crack they will die where they stand. Do you think you can convince them to pull back say twenty-five miles or so?"

Duke looked at her like she was a nut or something. "LeAnn, those people could care less about what I may or may not say to them. They're under orders to take these machines and shut them down and that's exactly what they're going to try to do. How am I going to make anyone understand what is coming and the danger they're in?"

She smiled at Duke. "You could at least try."

All right, she was right about that. He could at least try and get them to understand. Duke turned to the monitor and picked the mic up and hailed all six teams. Almost immediately one man from each team stepped forward. They stood there looking toward the machines, well the direction where the speaker was located.

"Gentlemen, please, if you stay where you're at right now you face a good probability you will die where you stand. In a short time, the crack will reach the Pacific Ocean and when it does the ocean will rush into the crack and start to fill it. When that happens there will be a lot of land movement where you are now standing. Large sections of the land will sluff off and fall into the waters. Anyone on the land areas will fall as well.

281

"Please, move your people back and away from this area. You need to have at least twenty-five miles between you and the crack in order for you to be safe. Do you understand?"

Almost in unison the six men started talking on their radios. After several minutes the leader standing outside the Lake One Machine stepped forward and started to talk. "We can't do that. Our job is to take these machines over and shut them down before they destroy the world. We are prepared to take any action necessary to achieve that goal including nuclear devices. Do you understand?"

LeAnn looked at me and shook her head. "They don't have enough of anything to impact the machines."

Duke then turned back to the man speaking. "Sir, please, I need to advise you there are not enough nuclear weapons to stop this one machine let alone all six. These things are unstoppable. There is nothing that can change what is going to happen. You're clearly sacrificing your lives and those of your men with you to accomplish nothing. Please, pull back for your own good."

The lead man said something over his radio to the others at the other lakes and then turned away from the camera and started directing people. It was then when several trucks came into view and pulled to the edge of the lakes and men started getting out and pulling out equipment.

Within twenty minutes each team had setup what appeared to be portable cranes along the edge of the crack. Next, they backed a truck up to the cranes and the top of the trucks were rolled back and they hooked what appeared to be cylinders to the cranes, lifting them and turning and positioning them over the crack. We were witnessing the placement of six nuclear devices next to the machines. It was then they started to lower the object down into the crack and placed them alongside one of the main drive legs of each machine.

LeAnn continued to observe and say nothing. She was going to let them initiate their attack with those weapons and not try to stop it. She looked over at me and smiled. "Duke, they don't have a device big enough or strong enough to harm this machine. All they will do is dig a hole in the side of the crack walls and that will cause a large area to break away and fall into the crack. Duke, this machine is three miles deep and is actually more than three and a half mile wide at its widest point. They can't hurt it."

Duke then turned back to the leader of the strike teams. "Listen to me, the crack has started and there is nothing that can stop it. As soon as the crack reaches the Pacific the water will start to flow into the crack and that will bring about the final splitting and reconfiguring of the earth surface.

"I think you know that and so the only other reason for you being here is to try and take over the machines. That, I can assure you will never happen. Look you could wait until this thing is over and when we vacate the machine you can move in and take over. After the crack has completed and the Earth has stabilized, we will give you the machine and if you want all six of them, they're yours."

Again, he was back on the radio and after several minutes he came back to me. "Why not let us into the machines now instead of later?"

Duke looked at LeAnn and she smiled. She shook her head, got up and walked over to the wall and opened a panel. She reached in and pushed several buttons and came back and looked at him. "Tell them in twenty minutes we will evacuate the six machines and they are welcome to them."

That caught Duke by surprise. Up till now she had been adamant no one would be allowed in the machine. Something had changed and the rules had changed with them. "LeAnn, I don't understand, what's going on here?"

"Duke, it makes no difference whether they enter the machines or not, the re-terraforming will continue and finish. The face of the Earth will change and remain that way over the better part of the next twenty million years.

"The real purpose of this control room was to assist the world governments in dealing with the trauma of the change. That has been done and if any other assistance is needed, we will be able to provide it from your base camps. Please prepare your people to leave the machine and they are to follow the prescribed procedure as they leave. Inform them they must remain silent and follow the directives we are going to give them.

"You will be evacuated to the other side of the crack from those outside. You will then move down to your camp site and make contact with the president and advise him as to what has taken place.

284

While you're doing this we will deal with these people. We will be giving them exactly what they want, the machine."

Duke then called the leader of the forces outside the machines and advised him we would be vacating the machine in just a few minutes. At that time a bridge will be placed across the void between the machine and the land and the main entrance door will open. They can then enter and take over the machine.

There was a pause and then the leader came back. "What are you up to?"

Duke looked at LeAnn and she nodded her head. "We have been advised everything we were here for has been completed. The crack process has started and it will not stop until it has completed its travel. With that we are no longer needed in the machine. I told you the process had already started before you came on the scene. Well, now we're not needed and they are sending us out."

He came back. "I don't think so. You will stay in the machine and they will open the door and we will come in and take over. You will be our insurance that this is not a trap."

LeAnn smiled and told those in the machine. "You will vacate and they can do nothing about it. A protective shield will be placed over you and remain with you to your camp while this event is taking place and completing. Get your people ready, you leave in ten minutes."

Duke turned to Dennis and nodded his head. "Get everyone moving for the exit. Make sure they take all their equipment with them and that includes any notes or paper work."

"Will do Duke, anything else?"

"No, we're leaving here; something really bad is going to happen to those people out there. I don't know what, when or how, but it's going to be bad."

Everyone was at the door within the ten minutes and LeAnn moved to the front of our line. She raised her hands and everyone quieted down. "Now listen to me. As you leave the machine there will be a bridge to your left that goes over to the mainland. Do not say a word or look at the people on the other side of the crack.

"Please walk across the bridge and stay together. Walk another two hundred yards straight out from the crack before turning south toward your camp. Once you're at the camp a transparent dome will form over the camp and you will remain there until I come and release you. Do you understand?"

Everyone started nodding their heads as the door started to open. Duke and Dennis went first followed by the rest of their people and followed up by Tanner. As they exited the machine Duke could hear the leader across the crack yelling at us to get back into the machine. He then fired his gun in the air as a warning. LeAnn called out to Duke. "Duke, keep on moving, they can't harm you."

Just then the entire unit across the crack opened up. Duke could see the rounds hitting in thin air and then dropping down into the crack. They continued to fire on the scientists with no effect.

Then one of their people stepped forward with a shoulder mounted rocket and prepared to fire it at us. As he sighted in on us a laser beam came out of the machine and hit the man killing him on the spot. That stopped all the shooting.

Duke and his people continued to move across the bridge and out away from the crack. When the last of them reached the two hundred yard mark the bridge was retracted and a second one was sent out to the other side of the crack. The men there immediately ran across the bridge and the lead one grabbed LeAnn and shoved her back into the machine.

After the last man entered the machine the bridge was retracted and the door closed and then any sign of the door disappeared. Dennis, Tanner and Duke stood there looking at one another. "It's like the door had never been there. Now what the hell do we do?"

Duke looked around at everyone. "We do as we were told and go to the camp and set things up and do our job. We're under a protective shield of some kind and so we need not worry. All we have to do is what they trained us to do. The welfare of a lot of people out there will depend on us doing our jobs."

They moved on to the camp not knowing what was going on inside the machine they had just left. What they didn't know was the other five machines had opened up and let the invaders in as well. They had taken over all six machines and Duke

287

was sure they were feeling rather good about it. They were about to find out what they had won.

Duke felt a sting of pain go across his chest as he thought of those men being sent here to do the impossible only to die trying. Whoever the hell was over all this action needs to pay in no less a manner than those men he or they sent here.

They had been told once the crack started it would not and could not be stopped. It had to run its course no matter what anyone thought or feared. Whether some people thought this was the end of the world, they would in time discover they were wrong and the world was better off for all that had been done.

Dennis walked up alongside Duke. "Do you think LeAnn will be able to get out of there?"

Duke smiled and then looked back at the machine. "I have no doubt she will make it out. It wouldn't surprise me to find her at the base camp waiting for us."

They continued down the mountain to the base camp and once their settled in, several of the Lake People stepped up to Duke. "The protective dome will now go into effect. Please let your people know they must not try to leave the dome. It is not meant for anyone to come and go. It is a protective device that is there to protect and nothing more."

Duke nodded and made the announcement to everyone. They all indicated they understood and then moved out and went to their stations and got back to work.

Chapter Twenty-Five

THE WINDS OF WAR

As we were promised, the dome appeared over the camp and we knew we were safe from whatever may come our way. I went to the command tent and sat down and called the President. I advised him of the problem and we were still in control of the process and would maintain that control throughout the remainder of the event. He thanked us and told us they had determined who was masterminding this situation and they had sent a strike force to take them into custody.

Duke had just hung up from his meeting with the President and heard a number of people calling out. He got up and walked out of the tent. Duke walked over to Dennis, "What's going on?"

As Dennis was turning to him, he looked up and saw LeAnn and the rest of the Lake People walking toward the dome and then through the side of the dome. She walked up to Duke and advised the problem had been taken care of. Duke could only imagine what had happened in the machine after they had left.

Meanwhile in San Francisco a large contingency of federal agents spread out across the city proper heading for specific locations to take people into custody. A total of fifteen swat teams were involved. They had non-reversible orders to arrest the specific people each team was sent out to find.

Each team was given the go-a-head to use whatever force necessary to affect the arrests. In some cases, there was more than one person being targeted. Some would be husband and wife and others would be student group leaders. Over the course of the next twelve hours all warrants were enforced and all targets were in custody and being taken to federal strongholds for processing.

During the arrest proceeding additional data and evidence was located and more people were taken into custody. As the discovered information was processed more units were being assigned arrest orders across the whole of the country. In fact, not a region of the country was without arrests being made.

As it turned out, a large underground subversive organization was uncovered and brought to its knees. There was little doubt there were also foreign influences involved in the overall organization. Washington would be dealing directly with those foreign powers.

Once the human scientists had been safely evacuated off the machine and across the bridge

LeAnn had the bridge withdrawn and a second one sent out to the other side. The unit there immediately ran across the bridge and grabbed LeAnn and shoved her back into the machine. She was dragged across the room to the table and thrown onto the table and immediately hit with the butt of a gun.

As the last man entered the machine the door closed and any sign of the door disappeared. They were now in the machine and had taken total control or so they thought.

The leader walked up to the table and looked down at LeAnn with a smile on his face. "You, young lady, are about to pay for defying my orders. I told you I wanted the scientists to remain in the machine and you defied that order. That is going to cost you your life."

He stood there looking at her and her expression did not change in any way. He became a little puzzled by her actions. She didn't seem to have any fear as to what was happening to her. He noted the red mark on her face where the gun butt had hit her. It was slowly going away until there was no sign of it anywhere on her face.

That was the first sign something really bad was about to happen and he could feel it deep in his gut. LeAnn then sat up. There was nothing they could do about it, they were just pushed away as she sat up and then slipped off the table and walked over to the other side of the room and, turned facing them.

The team leader looked over at one of the men and waved his hand. "Kill her."

The man immediately raised his gun and pulled trigger. Nothing happened. He reset the bolt and pulled the trigger again and again nothing happened. Everyone was looking back and forth at one another as the leader jerked the gun out of one of the men's hands, slammed the bolt back and pulled the trigger, nothing. He then yelled. "Cut her throat."

One of the men moved forward and got maybe five steps when he raised his knife and stabbed himself in the chest. He died instantly.

Panic set in and everyone headed for the place where the door had been. When they discovered it was not there, they turned back toward LeAnn. She stood there watching them and once they calmed down, she spoke. "You wanted this machine and now you have it. I don't know what you planned on doing with it, but it's now, yours and you will spend the rest of time right here in this place.

"You have a number of alternatives you can choose from. You can simply kill yourselves and get it over with. You can kill each other and the last one left standing will have food for a time. You can all sit down and wait for starvation to do its work on you. Or, your last choice is to go through the door over there and let the machine deal with you.

At this point a door appeared in the wall, it opened and the remainder of the Lake People, plus their two attendants from Lake One walked into the room. They all moved over by LeAnn and stood there looking at the unit. "You asked for this. You were willing to kill any number of innocent people to get your hands on these machines. Well, you have them now.

"In addition, those who sent you here have been dealt with. Your government is attempting to take them into custody, but we have overruled that action and have taken those beings into custody as well.

"They will be here shortly and will join you here in this machine. We do not care what you do with them. That is your problem. The fact is, they will be here and you will all die together in this place. You will be buried with these machines and your bodies will not be returned for twenty million years. At which time, if there are human beings still living on this planet, they will find you and be told what had happened and warned not to do the same."

It was then the another door opened and the shock troops were forced into that room. In addition, a dozen additional people entered the machine and were placed with the shock troops. LeAnn and her people turned and walked through the wall and out of the machine. They returned to the camp to assist the people there in the completion of the project Re-Earth.

All across the country the people who had been taken into custody and moved to secure facilities were being removed from those facilities and taken to the six machines. They were placed within the machines with the shock troops they had paid for and sent to take over the machines. They were informed they were being given the machines as they desired.

It was like nothing had happened. The machine people carried on with their jobs working with everyone to get the process completed. The crack was progressing well and the oceans had started to enter the cracks. The noise involved was unbelievable. Cold ocean salt water hitting the earth mantle caused steam explosions of unparalleled magnitude. Huge vapor clouds were forming above the crack and moving along as the water filled the cracks.

Duke turned to LeAnn. "What will be the effect of all the water entering the atmosphere at one time?"

"There will be an extensive amount of rain along the run of the crack. The change in temperature along the crack will cause the development of numerous tropical storms and a few hurricanes and monsoons. Again, the coastal regions will feel the full effect of these storms and they need to be so advised at this time."

Dennis and Tanner immediately set to work notifying the world governments of the weather issues that would be coming. Meanwhile they were getting additional telemetry on the effects of the tsunamis being generated across the world. Overall, the world governments had responded well and no reports of loss of life had come in yet

For the rest of the first ninety-two hours things seemed to run smooth. LeAnn and her people kept Duke and his team informed of each event as it was coming and they in turned notified the world's governments. The final hour came and the crack ends finally met at the foretold location just south of India.

Now this process was entering the ninety-second hour stabilization period. That would again require every governing body to stay on top of each event as they were given to the team and then relayed to the governments. During this time the final position of all the land masses affected by the split was taking place.

The crack across the United States had appeared to have settled at a twenty-three miles separation. It would require the government to build a whole new ferry system to service the public the full length of the crack. It was obviously a huge undertaking and would take years to build and put into service. During this time, we would have to depend on air transports for the movement of people and commodities from east to west and the reverse.

It was then when a new sound was heard and felt in the ground. Duke's attention was drawn to the machine. LeAnn stepped up to him. "It is time for the machines to bury themselves back into the earth. Please don't try to find them and even if you did it would do you no good.

"We will be returning your people to you now. It has been good knowing you Duke Ridgeman. There are many good people on this planet and they far outweigh the bad ones who are here as well. You and your people have done a good job and we are proud of you. The future of your world and your kind is good. You have a lot to do before you achieve a real peace for all of your kind, but in time it will come.

"I and the others, we are the product of the machines and built into the machines by our masters. We are clones of those who left us here to maintain your world. When we leave the ones, we have taken over will return to life and will be as they were. They will have a limited memory of what happened to them, so don't try to get them to do something they are incapable of doing.

"They will have trauma as a result of the events that caught them. Give them time to recover and by all means let them live their lives as they should. They know nothing and have no insight as to what took place. Do you understand?"

Duke was dumbfounded by what she had been saying. All he could do was sit there looking at her.

"Duke, do you understand?"

He stood up and started nodding his head. "Yes, LeAnn, I understand and I will see they are treated right and fairly. Can I ask you something?"

She smiled. "Duke, do not be concerned for the beings who were taken and placed in the machines, they earned what they got. You have no involvement in their situation and you should not pursue it any further. Do you understand?"

He knew by now when LeAnn spoke it was final and he knew he had no other recourse. He nodded. "I understand and thank you?"

She nodded and then a change took place. As Duke looked at LeAnn she seemed to wake up and fear crossed her eyes and she started to scream. He reached out and grabbed her and pulled her in close to him, holding her as she woke up and realized the terror she had witnessed.

All the others were going through the same reactions and people were holding them and giving them all the comfort, they could to help them to re-awake and face the terror they had experienced.

Several hours later LeAnn was sitting in Duke's tent drinking a cup of coffee. She was still shaking somewhat but other than that she was in perfect physical condition. He sat down by her, "LeAnn, my name is Duke Ridgeman and I am in charge of the recovery process after the earthquake and flooding. Do you remember what happened?"

She looked at him and nodded her head. "I was going home for the holidays from college and the earthquake hit. I remember the road started to slide south; I don't know how far. When it stopped there was a whole new mountain range around me. Then the water came. All I could do was stay in my car and stay put. I don't remember anything after that. Who are you, and where is this place?"

The magnitude of what had happened to these people then hit him. They had been gone for these several weeks and had no idea what was going on. They had to be scared half to death. He started to cover the entirety of the past weeks, but she was having a hard time believing him. "LeAnn, you and twenty other people had been trapped in those lakes and when you came out you had been actually possessed by other beings for that period of time.

301

We have videos of what happened and will be showing those to you in time. For now, just know you're back and you're well."

Within forty-eight hours the machines had moved out of sight and the crack was about half full with the oceans still pouring in. We had better than half the ninety-two hours of stabilization time left and then the cleanup would start. The questions were still stacking up and from his position he saw no immediate means of answering most of them. The machines were a mystery when they arrived and they were still a mystery as they left.

It was at this time our monitors started receiving telemetry from the machines again. This time it was data addressing the questions we were coming up with and were concerned about. The data started to provide locations of global reactions to the impact of the crack. Each and every one was timed to give us what we needed to react or prepare for those events. We knew then our job wasn't over and we needed to stay on top of it.

Maybe an hour into our receiving the added telemetry, we received a notification that changed everything. In effect it advised due to the impact of the cracking the earth magnetic field would be impacted. This situation would cause earth to wobble on its axes and drift in its orbital path around the sun. That in turn would impact the orbit of the moon. Duke felt a cold shock move through his body.

The telemetry kept coming, advising the result of those temporary actions would bring about climatic changes across the face of the earth. What those changes would be for any particular place or region was not known and we would have to deal with them as they occurred. It was clear the process of re-terraforming the Earth would take a lot longer than he had realized.

The information being received was sent to DC and then issues concerning the orbit and moon were sent to NASA so they could start to monitor those events. Only time would give us the real impact these events would have on the planet.

Duke had a feeling it would be significant, but he also had this inner assurance it would not be something we could not deal with. He guessed they were talking about the patience needed while going through a recovery process.

Within days NASA had the information and it was not that bad, but it would make things a little different. Not being an astronomer Duke was not sure of the mechanics involved in what they told them, but in effect, the moon would be repositioned into a closer orbit than it was right now. In fact, that orbit was already being altered.

As best as he could understand the moon has been moving away from the Earth ever since it came into existence. In time the orbit would continue to grow until the moon would be thrown out and away from the Earth, an event he was assured we did not want.

What was happening was the moon was realigning itself and moving back into a closer orbit of the Earth. An orbit had been lost over millions of years was now being erased and the moon was moving back toward its original position.

NASA felt that it would move back by as much as seventy percent of the distance it had moved out from the earth. That in turn would affect the tides and other impacts on the earth. Just what it meant he was not sure, but overall, it appeared to be a plus for Earth and not a detriment.

They were then advised the wobble taking place would work its way out in about a hundred years and again the Earth would be back into a more advantageous orientation. If these events had been planned by the aliens, they did one hell of a job. So, in a nut shell, everyone would be sitting and waiting. Things were still happening and as each new event came toward us the telemetry from the machines would advise us and we would pass the data on to the appropriate agencies or governments.

They entered the fourth day and the ninety-two hours period was coming to an end. The oceans had filled the cracks and the level of land sliding or movement into the cracks was stabilizing. The states of Texas, New Mexico, Colorado, Wyoming, and Montana had taken the greatest hits. The states bordering those states to the east were the next in line of major impacts. That's not to mention the other countries who were directly impacted by the crack.

South America and Africa were cut in half and the two halves of each continent moved apart by fifty to sixty miles. India and the Soviet Union, Russia, were split as well but the north to south crack separation was similar to the United States, about twenty miles. It would have been nice if the crack had run national borders, but as often as they change, that would have been impossible.

It's obvious, not only was the world in turmoil due to the geological changes, but those changes would cause the political balance of the world to change as well. Almost as soon as the crack stopped, but the final settling had not finished, nations were starting to maneuver for control of those areas on either side of the crack. War was coming and there was nothing that could be done about it.

It didn't take long before the political pressures overcame the impact of the geological process and the follow up needs were being dropped in favor of conflict. The Six Lakes teams were trying to get those parties who were facing off to step back and continue in their activities to protect their people and worry about the politics later. The nationalistic drives were too much and armies started to form and settle in on the targets they were competing for.

Duke's teams were still at the lake sites as the world started to lose control. They had been trying their best to get people to listen to them, but had hit dead ends in every venture they tried. Duke looked over at LeAnn and realized the LeAnn he was looking for had gone. He then did the only thing he could think of, He thought to himself. "LeAnn did your plans take this into account?"

Duke felt warmth settle into him and then he felt it enter his mind. "Duke, you have done well and all this has come as we said it would. The fact these people cannot see the benefits and are still greedy and desire to control more is not our fault. Our job was to keep this planet from ripping itself apart. How the beings who live here react to that action is not our responsibility.

"Now that does not mean we don't have a means of bringing this to an end. The question is do we want to and if we do, who are we to side with?

"Then we need to determine who are we to take action against? Believe me when I tell you we can act against any issue across the face of this planet. The issue is whether we should and if we do then how do we do it?

"We have taken the path of letting you fight it out. Not because we can't take action, but because we are going to let you learn a lesson out of all this. When things are done, we will set it right and then and only then will those responsible for all the actions taken against us during the split and the actions of those aggressors will be dealt with in a permanent manner."

That sounded like a serious act they were contemplating. He had this cold feeling run through his body and felt himself break out in a sweat. He then asked. "LeAnn, does this mean a large number of people are going to die as a result of what you're planning?"

He stood there waiting, not knowing just where to look. He felt like something was looking at him and then it reached out and touched his mind. "Duke, as usual you are targeting the wrong issue and concern. You have not looked at the big picture and you have zeroed in on the minor issues that are not the real point of all this.

"Duke, what is happening here are growth pains of the peoples of this planet. They don't realize or understand what is actually happening here and in a short time they will. It will be a lesson hard to take, but once it happens it will change the scope of everything the people of this world have considered important.

"Duke, you are not looking beyond this planet. You are not seeing what is behind all that has taken place. You are a young planet with a young social structure and you are subject to making mistakes or errors in judgment. It is now time for you to face the reality of this universe you live in. You have yet to come to understand you're not alone and on your own here in this huge existence."

Duke stood there looking around at his people as they went about their work. It was then he felt her coming back to him. "Duke, advise all your people to remain here at this base. Do not let any of them venture beyond the base boundaries for it will cost them their lives.

"Open up your communications system and pay close attention to the actions of your government. If any of the communications addresses sending military aid to any location in the world you are to advise them, they are to stand down.

"Now listen to me carefully. You are to tell them, your government, if they try to carry out any military action for any reason anywhere across the world their military will be destroyed to the last individual, Duke, this is not a threat this is an absolute fact.

"Tell your president you have been warned and there will be no further warning. Your government is to tend to their needs for their citizens and disregard the rest of the activity across the planet. Is that understood?"

He could hardly talk and had a lump the size of a basketball in his throat. He started to nod his head while standing there. He then managed to ask. "LeAnn, what is going to happen out there?"

Duke felt his mind relax and a safe and comforting feeling wash over him. No answer came it was just a relaxed and comfortable feeling all over and through his body. He stood there looking out at the crack and then it hit him, he knew he had to get on the phone and get the President on line. He needed to pass the warning on to the President.

He sat down and picked up the phone and hit the button. It wasn't more than ten seconds and someone answered. "This is Duke Ridgeman; I need to speak to the President immediately. This is a Class One Emergency."

He heard talking in the background and then the person who answered the phone telling someone. "This sounds important sir; I think you had better talk to him."

He heard the movement of people and then a voice came on the line. "Yes Duke, what can I do for you?"

Duke needed to make sure this was the President and no one else. "Sir, are you the President?"

There was a pause. "Yes Duke, it's me."

He felt a surge of relief flash through my body. "Sir, I have an important message for you from the aliens. I think you had better hear it and consider what is being said."

Again, there was a pause and he cleared his throat and replied. "All right Duke, what is the message."

Duke told him what LeAnn had said and what would happen if we committed our military anywhere in the world. That we were to concentrate on providing for the needs of our citizens while the aliens dealt with the rest of the world.

As soon as Duke finished, he could hear the president getting everyone's attention. Still holding the phone, he ordered all military activity by the United States to stand down and remain on alert, but not to become involved in any of the actions taking place around the world. He then finished with the words. "That is a direct order. Do you understand?"

He came back to Duke and confirmed what he had said and advised he would honor LeAnn's warning and he would wait and see what was coming. They hung up and Duke sat back in his chair wondering just what the hell he had done. LeAnn had come back and made contact with him that he knew for sure. He also knew he needed to act on her words, she had made that clear enough before and he felt there was no reason why it wouldn't apply now even though she was not physically there.

Duke finally called Tanner and Dennis into his office. "All right, you need to know I have been contacted by LeAnn again and she had advised the military of the United States is to stand down and not get involved in anything across the world.

"She advised they, the aliens, would take care of the conflicts that were starting up and the United States was to stay out of the way. If we failed to do as she directed then our military would be destroyed.

"I don't think the aliens are finished with us yet. Whatever they are planning they have advised us to stay out of it. If we don't, then we will pay as the others are going to pay. If I have LeAnn figured right, she means what she is saying and all hell is about to cut loose across the face of the world.

"They have completed the re-terraforming but maybe they are just getting started in the culling of the Human Race."

Chapter Twenty-Six

THE BEGINNING OR END

They had the machines and the aliens including this LeAnn person. Now they would go to work in gaining access to the technology. He had no sooner thought that when there was a knock on the door, no it was more like a banging.

He stood there behind his desk when the door came into the office literally flying across the room and hitting the wall. They came in full armament and sighted down on him yelling at him to freeze, not to move. Under those conditions who the hell was going to move anyway.

Three men rushed him and took him to the floor and cuffed his hands behind his back. As they pulled him to his feet a fourth one stepped up in front of him. "Mr. Sandburg you are under arrest for subversive actions against the people of the United States."

The man then continued to read him his constitutional rights and upon completion of that formality he was lead from his office and out to a vehicle waiting in front of the building. Thirty minutes later he found himself in a holding cell along with twelve other people all of whom he knew only too well.

They all stood there looking at one another and then Mike cleared his voice and started to pace. "Gentlemen, I can see they have figured out our little plot. It is my advice you refrain from saying anything to any of these people at any time. Remember they have to prove their case. We don't have to prove ours.

"However, if we talk or make any statements that are incriminating then they can and will use them against us.

"So, for the time being, let's not talk about what is going on. Better yet let's talk about the last time we played golf.

"Just remember you are exercising your God given rights and if some fool does something stupid it has nothing to do with you or us. Gentlemen, we must stand together on this and stand firm."

He had no sooner finished saying that when the door opened and two men stepped in. "Gentlemen, may we have your attention. In fifteen minutes, you will be removed from this location and placed on a plane and flown to the Six Lakes Project Base.

"There you will be turned over to the Lake People and taken to the alien machines where you will enter and be held there for the time being. Are there any questions?"

312

Mike and the others were looking back and forth between themselves when Mike stepped forward. "Why is this being done?"

"Sir, I don't know all the facts in this situation other than the aliens have demanded we deliver you to them at the Six Lakes Project Base. That's all we know."

Mike didn't like what was being said. He knew the shock teams had been taken into the machines and as yet have not been heard from. He didn't like the prospects of being hauled out there and being turned over to the aliens. "I don't think I want to go that route gentlemen. Right now, I would like to make a call to my attorney."

The head officer started to shake his head. "Sorry sir, we have been told there will be no calls to anyone about anything. Sirs, you are to be taken to the Six Lakes Project Base, no questions asked."

All the warning bells were going off in his head. "Do you know who these men are?" As he swung his hand and arm around toward the twelve standing at the back of the room. "These are some of the most wealthy and influential men in this country. I don't think you understand the magnitude of who you're dealing with."

The officers stood there listening and then one of their cell phones rang. The officer answered it and then handed the phone to the lead officer. He listened for several seconds and handed the phone back and walked up to Mike.

"It's time to go sir, would you place your hands behind your back."

Mike was considering resisting when the door swung open again and half a dozen well-armed men entered the room. It was obvious they were not going to put up with any resistance on the part of Mike and those with him.

After they were all cuffed, they were lead out of the holding room and out the back door to a waiting bus where they were loaded on and taken to seats and shackled into the seats.

The bus moved out once the last man was seated and drove thirty miles to a government air base where they were then transferred to a plane. Within an hour the plane was airborne and heading for Lake One, twelve hundred miles away.

Four hours later the plane had landed and they were off loaded into another bus and then transported up to the alien machine at Lake One. The bus pulled up to the machine and Mike and the others were removed from the bus and taken across a bridge to the machine entrance.

As they approached the machine a door appeared and slid open. A young woman came out of the machine and stood at the door waiting for them to cross the bridge to the machine entrance. Mike knew immediately this was LeAnn.

He tried to turn to the guards and ask to be removed from that location but they pushed him along past the young woman and into the machine. As the last man entered the machine the guards stopped and LeAnn came in behind Mike and the others and the door closed.

Mike looked around and saw, sitting on the floor on the other side of the large room, the entire shock team. Just then the cuffs came off of his hands and LeAnn walked around past him. She stopped about five steps past the last man and then turned to them.

She stood there looking at them. "You have done everything possible to harm your people and gain access to the technology of these lake machines. It was a foolish thing you did, and as a result a number of people have lost their lives.

"We have determined because you were so intent on gaining access to and gaining control of these machines; we thought we would give them to you. So, you have been brought here and you are now being given sole control and ownership of these machines.

"It is our desire you do what you can with the machine. To ensure you have all the time you need, we will leave you here in these machines until the next time the machines return to carry out another terraforming process."

She walked past Mike and the other twelve men and the other Lake People followed. "We will leave you now. Please take what you want and do with it as you please."

The door opened and the Lake People exited the machine. As the last one left LeAnn walked over to the door and turned. "I also need to advise you that you will not be able to leave this machine. You will remain with it until it returns twenty million years from now. This is what you wanted and we are giving it to you."

She stepped through the door and it closed behind her and any sign of the door went away. Mike and the others stood there trying to understand what had just happened. As it started to dawn on them, panic set in and they all attacked the location of the door at the same time, to no avail.

Mike felt himself sink to the floor as he looked around the chamber. She was right, they had received access to all the technology the aliens had but what good would it do.

He swung around and leaned up against the wall and started to laugh. Talk about poetic justice, this was the ultimate. All he could do was sit there and laugh while watching the others trying to claw their way out of the machine, a task they would die trying to complete.

Chapter Twenty-Seven

STEP TWO, WAR OF THE WORLD

They didn't have long to wait. It was about five o'clock that afternoon when they felt the ground start to vibrate. It wasn't long before we had a regular earthquake taking place and then the top of one of the lake machines came into view. Duke had walked out of his tent and was standing there when he saw it breach from the ground. All right, it came back up, now what?

He had noted the machine was on the other side of the crack from them and it was still coming up out of the ground. It literally tore the country side up as it continued to lift up out of the ground. It was then Duke realized it was coming all the way up and out of the ground all three miles of it.

The entire base was now out watching as the machine finally cleared the ground and continued to climb into the sky. He had never in all his life ever expected to see anything like this, a machine so big that it made a major city here in the U.S. look small in comparison.

It was at this point that one of the communication staff ran up to him. "Duke, you have to come to the com tent, you have to see this."

Duke ran to the tent and entered and there on the big screen was a live feed coming from the machine. LeAnn was standing to one side on the monitor screen as she turned and looked right at us. "Duke, good you're there. Mr. President, you're there as well. Good you both will need to witness what is about to take place. Mr. President, I believe Duke warned you about using your military at this time, is that right?"

The President responded in the affirmative.

"Good, then you need not worry about any of your assets being destroyed. Now please stay with us and we will take care of the childish actions of those other nations who have tried to take undue advantage of the process the world has just gone through."

By this time the machine had reached an altitude of around twenty thousand feet and was starting to move in a southerly direction. We immediately noted it was following the crack, sitting dead center over it.

Just then LeAnn came back on the air. "Mr. President, as you can see, we are now starting to follow the crack. Our purpose is to inspect the lands on either side of the crack and to determine the extent of damage and needs of the people in those areas.

"In addition, we will be looking for any hostile actions by anyone in relationship to the crack. If we do, we will identify the nation the crack is going through and any and all other nations who are taking military action to control an area of the native nation. At that time, they will be destroyed.

"We wish to say we are not at all happy with the hostile activities we have seen and had to deal with during this time. We have no more patience with this kind of action and will act directly and decisively toward those who take advantage of our actions here.

"You are a destructive world and with that we are going to show you what destruction is all about. Our initial purpose was to correct a world issues that would have caused this planet to self-destruct. We have made those corrections but we have also learned just how totally corrupt the nations of the world are. After this day, those nations will no longer exist and any nation who attempts to interfere will face the same judgment."

It was then we started to receive the monitor feed from the machine. It was an aerial view of the crack and lands on both sides of it. As the machine moved south it scanned both sides of the crack and then we started to see red dots appearing along the west side of the crack. That was all we saw, there appeared to be no action being taken against those areas.

It took a full forty-eight hours for the machine to circumnavigate the world and scan the crack in all areas where it passed through a land mass. All along the route it took it was followed by series of red dots that were appearing on a regular basis.

As we monitored the news reports from around the world, we noted the dots did in fact correspond with those locations where one government was taking advantage of the crack to take land from another government. It was then Duke knew the machine was marking its points of attack. He got the back of the neck feeling again and knew all hell was going to cut loose in the not too distant future.

One thing of interest stood out in the layout of the red dots. There were a large number in Mexico on the west side of the crack. It struck Duke there were no areas where another nation could have moved into Mexico. At first it stymied him and then he hit on it. Those were the locations of the cartels. The aliens were going to put the cartels out of business. Damn he hadn't expected that.

The Six Lakes Project personnel tried to notify those nations who were taking advantage of the situation and advise them to pull back. They also tried to advise them if they did not their nation would be destroyed to the last living being. They scoffed at us and told us to stay out of their business.

Duke looked at the monitor and the Presidents face and he could see him finally sit back and shrug. He then looked right at Duke. "Duke, it's their decision and they will have to live and die by it. There is nothing we can do."

Duke was nodding his head. "I understand sir, but that still does not take away this feeling we could have done something more direct. I feel so helpless."

He was watching Duke. "Duke, we can no longer be the conscience of the world. A time comes where the other nations must think for themselves and face the consequences of their action."

Duke then remembered the several military units who had tried to take over the machines early on. "Sir, what about those who tried to overthrow our government during the machines preparation for the split, are we going to continue the process of trying them for their action?"

"Duke, those people tried to take advantage of a serious situation the people of this country were going through and their actions could have been the cause of millions of lives lost, not just here in America but across the world. No, they will be tried and they will be convicted and they will be punished. Men with that level of greed can never be allowed to try again."

It was then LeAnn came back on the line. "It is time to deal with those issues that have developed followed the relief of the pressures of this world. There will be no discussion about what is to take place. You will either learn to live together or you will die together. We do not take this lightly. We know your concern and recognize the pain you are feeling for those who are about to pay, and that is part of the problem.

"Throughout your history you have played that game, wanting to wait just a little longer and just maybe the party being the problem will correct their actions. Time and again your history has shown your decision to resist dealing with the problem only results in additional and greater problems.

"It is time you learned what your responsibility is to your world and its history. You can no longer take the wait and see attitude. You know who the problems are and now they will be taken care of. Those of you who favor supporting those who have taken advantage of this situation will pay as well.

At this time a cleansing is to take place across the face of this world. We are no longer concerned with the planets pressure issues; we must also take into consideration the attitude of those of you who live on this planet."

Duke sat there watching her as she spoke knowing full well this young woman was a projection on the monitor he was watching. No, she was now the manifestation of the beings who have come from our past and are carrying out a worldwide corrective process designed to save the planet and all life on it. The beings she represented were old beyond our imagination and truly wise beyond our understanding.

They may have come from our past, but they are in fact far ahead of us and beyond our years of existence. The full impact of what was taking place was finally hitting us all. Duke looked at the others sitting there. "We are about to make the biggest step humanity has ever made. What we are experiencing will determine our future and our existence,"

With that Duke ordered all records of this current action to be backed up and forwarded to the main data system in Washington DC. He then picked up the mic and addressed LeAnn. "LeAnn, for the first time I think we understand what is taking place. It still hurts, but I now know and it is making sense to us. It is not our place to judge, but when we fail to do the responsible act, we fail to provide a safe environment for the rest of mankind.

"We have a long way to go and much to learn, but it appears your presence here was basically for the welfare of the planet. But something has changed the situation and now it appears you have stepped to a higher plain. We have witnessed the events of the military units who had tried to take the lake machines over and now the different countries trying to take advantage of the damage done to the other countries the crack passed through.

"The fundamental issue is that of greed. Unfortunately, that is a common situation with mankind and we need to address it."

Then LeAnn interrupted. "Duke, it is greed and this is not just a mankind issue, all intelligent social structures throughout space face a time when greed becomes a basic issue within their systems. Some survive it and others fail to survive and they destroy themselves.

"You of this world are approaching that time and you must make the right decisions at the right time or you are doomed. We have decided to try and instill in your world the need to overcome greed and take a path that gives the whole of your social order a new attitude.

"The process has begun and there is no turning back. This purge is needed to ensure you of this world survive. If we do not do this you will spiral into total war and you will destroy your world and all life here."

Just then the President came on line. "Please, we are trying to understand what is happening. We have followed your directives and still there appears there is going to be a significant loss of life by this process. Is there any other way we can take to curtail this process?"

Duke sat there looking at the monitor, it had gone blank as the President was addressing his question to LeAnn and there was nothing to indicate that a response was coming.

He leaned forward and pushed the communication button and addressed the President. "Sir, it appears we're out of this situation all together. My advice is we hold the line and remain patient. I'm sure we will be advised as to what is happening when they feel we need to know."

The line was quiet for several seconds and then he came back. "Duke, I agree with your understanding of what is happening. My problem is the actions the aliens are taking are originating from our territory, and the fact is it will cause others to determine we are part and parcel to this action that is being undertaken."

He was right, but Duke knew what was taking place required us to stay out of it. "Sir, I understand what you're saying but I need to caution you LeAnn was specific in our staying out of this. Sir, this all comes down to the survival of those who think this situation out and take the right and advised actions.

"Sir, all my association with LeAnn so far has taught me when she says something she means it and she will carry out exactly what she said she would. This is not the time or place to challenge her authority. She has the muscle and ability to enforce her directives and if we're smart, we will realize that and stay the course with what she has told us to do."

Duke had no sooner made that comment when the monitor from the aliens came back to life. LeAnn appeared and then looked off to her left and reached down and addressed something on the table or desk top in front of her. She looked up at the monitor and smiled. "Mr. President and Duke, I am pleased you managed to restrain yourselves while I was away. That speaks a lot for your ability to think and reason issues out.

"Ten minutes ago, we initiated the forceful action we had determined for those areas where we had found conflict. Before we took that action, we contacted the parties involved and gave them the opportunity to address their differences in a peaceful manner. As usual one agreed and the other told us to go do something we're not familiar with.

"We took that in the negative and targeted that party for our actions. The other party, by that process of selection, was left to carry out their recovery. The nature of our response was the total elimination of the opposition forces who told us to do that thing whatever it was. Those forces no longer exist and will never be a hazard to the peace of those region again.

"In those situations where the two sides agreed to address their differences in a peaceful manner, we gave the assistance and initiative to pursue that peace. The surprising part of this issue was that out of seven regions of conflict, two agreed to address the issue in a peaceful manner and right now they have witnessed what happened to the others and are working hard to come to a mutual agreement. We think they will continue to work things out knowing full well what could result if they don't make it a positive outcome.

"For now, we are going to leave the recovery process moving along as it is. The machine will return to the earth now and bury itself and wait for the next terraforming adjustment in about twenty million years.

"Duke, from time to time you will be visited by me to see how things are progressing. This is not a threat to you; it is a privilege we have seen fit to bestow to you. What we will expect from you is the truth whether good or bad about the nature of the recovery and the actions of the different social orders of this world.

"Duke, understand we are placing a considerable amount of power in your hands. There will be those who will try to influence you and frankly may even try to control you. What they need to know is we will be monitoring your welfare from now on. Any attempt to jeopardize your welfare whether physically or mentally will be dealt with directly and without any opportunity to explain their actions. We will have no patience with those kinds of moves and will remove them in total.

"Mr. President, it will be your responsibility to see no undue pressure is forced upon this man. How you wish to carry out that action we leave to you? Be forewarned. Any action by you or this government that appears to be an attempt to control this man will be dealt with in the appropriate manner."

Duke was sitting there looking at LeAnn. She seemed to be uninterested in his response or actions after hearing what she had just said. For maybe a minute all remained quiet and then she looked up at him and smiled. "Yes Duke, I am a machine and I do not carry any emotions. If you were expecting some kind of emotional response to you and what I have just said then you will be disappointed.

"Duke, my masters came here many millions of years ago and set up a system so this planet could continue to exist for many millions of years into the future. In doing that they ensured the development and growth of a social order on this planet giving it the chance of succeeding as long as the planet stayed stable.

"My masters are an old, old race. They have existed for more than three billion years. During that time they developed the ways and means of

327

anticipating and correcting the issues that are common in new societies they discovered as they explore and find new planets. Their desire is to assist those societies in overcoming their problems. It is through their knowledge they are able to design this system to deal with each and every event as they are discovered.

In the past the machines were here to make the adjustments this planet needed, but once intelligent life developed on this planet then the second purpose of these machines were initiated. This is the first time we have found intelligent life here on this place called Earth. It's now our responsibility to compare the social structures on this planet with the guidelines our masters had set down. We have done that and we are implementing the means of correction that are needed.

"You may not understand why such brutal actions have been taken against those who are greedy and aggressive, but that is not your problem. As a world system you must learn to recognize a worldwide hazard and then deal with it at the earliest possible moment.

You of this world have a propensity to try and placate those who are trying to take advantage of all the others of your world and in doing that you encourage their further disrespect and aggression against the rest of the world. Once identified these infections must be removed. We hope you have learned that.

"Duke, your presence here at this time will be the stop gap needed to keep the world on pace to its future. It will be your reasoning and determinations as to when the hazards to the world become evident and to direct their removal."

Duke almost passed out. In effect this machine was giving him control of the world, and all societies on this planet Earth were to abide by his decisions and directives. From our perspective that is the position of a world dictator.

Just then LeAnn raised her hand. He stopped thinking the line that his mind was running and focused on her. "NO Duke, you are not a world dictator or lord. You are the world's conscience, and when you speak the world needs to hear it and act on it. The fact is Duke, the world owns you and in time you will come to understand that and the level of duty you possess.

"Duke, we are not doing you a favor. We have cast you into a position of understanding and a go between in order for us to track the actions of your world governing bodies. There will be those who will try to possess you, and if they cannot possess you then influence you. We will be there to back you up and keep you aware of what is right and what is wrong.

"In time this world will learn to leave you alone and any action by the world to influence or control you may well result in a direct action by this system. It is time for this world to leave its childish ways behind and start moving in a responsible direction that will ensure your place in the greater universe. You have years to go and a hard path to take but you will get there. For now, I bid you farewell and assure you we are there with you watching and monitoring. Do your job Duke, and your rewards will be boundless.

Chapter Twenty-Eight

STARTING THE NEW AGE

LeAnn had gone and the machine had returned to the earth and buried itself. An attempt had been made by NASA to track it into the earth but that proved to be impossible. Right now, there are six machines buried deep into the earth and spread out across the whole of the earth. In twenty million years they will reappear and carry out the next re-terraforming of the earth and hopefully we will still be here and be a little more receptive of their presence.

One week after the final machine returned to the earth the Six Lakes Project was terminated and Duke was requested by the President to report to Washington DC for further meetings. He was scheduled to a sit down at the White House with the President and his cabinet. He was not sure as to what they were going to address, but he had this sense of confidence and assurance in his mind that led him to believe he was up to the task at hand.

As he entered the White House he was escorted to the Oval Office. When he entered the President and his cabinet was waiting. Duke felt a little embarrassed for his late arrival but that didn't seem to bother them in the slightest. The President directed him to a chair to his right.

"Duke, thank you for coming and sitting down with us today. I hope this is not seen in the wrong light considering what LeAnn had said a week ago about any attempt to control or influence you?

"It is our desire to let you know we understand the restrictions in regards to any relationship we may have or may develop with you. However, we do feel we need to review the processes we went through during the Six Lakes Project. My personal reason is to develop future plans for any other national or worldwide issue and how we should handle them. I don't mind telling you the action of a segment of our military during this crisis bothers this cabinet and me considerably. Our intent is to come up with ways and means to never let that happen again.

"The fact they brutally killed the prior President does not settle well for me or for anyone in the legislative branch of this government. Our problem is coming up with a means of controlling our military, but not to the point it cannot react and respond to national issues quickly. It is my hope the experience with the Six Lakes Project and the actions of the aliens will give us a path to take to achieve that need.

"Second and I know I'm moving into dangerous grounds here; we want to work some method of keeping ourselves informed of your actions and thoughts as they develop and manifest themselves in the coming years. Now the first question that probably comes to mind is whether this would give us an upper hand over the rest of the world concerning international issues? The answer to that is yes if it can be worked out and not violate the directives of the aliens."

Duke felt his inner being jump as soon as the President opened that door. His mind was charging ahead and he knew LeAnn was there. He immediately raised both my hands toward the President. That stopped him in his tracks. "Mr. President, you must stop that line of inquiry right now. Do not make one more move in regards to that issue. I must advise you that you're right on the cusp of bringing about an issue that will not be tolerated.

"Sir, I respect you and I love my country but I am now in a situation where I must address the good of the world and not of a single nation. In the past weeks I have developed a complete and total understanding of what LeAnn was addressing, and I know where the limits are and what a violation of those limits can bring. Sir, you are approaching that limit and you must stop and stop right now.

"Please, understand I want nothing to do with how my country or any other country runs its business of governing. I cannot participate in that

333

process, it is forbidden. I must address everything on a whole world basis and its overall impact on the world in total not just one group of people.

"Sir, I am here because you need my help in dealing with this process and I gladly give that time and effort to you. But you must understand I cannot let you proceed into areas that are not permitted."

Just then the Secretary of State leaned forward. "You realize we could take you right now and not let you out of our control, don't you?"

Duke smiled and realized LeAnn had been right in all aspects of this job. He looked at the Secretary. "Yes sir, you could stop me here and now and take me into custody. That would last maybe thirty minutes before the whole of your military might would be left in ashes. No sir, you will not now or ever attempt to restrict my movements and actions.

"I did not ask for this job or position, it was thrust upon me by LeAnn. There is nothing I can do about it and so I chose to possess it and carry on. Whether you believe me or not, my place is a place of peace and that peace will be achieved even at the death of a country, an army, or an individual.

LeAnn made it terribly clear we tend to fail to address aggression until it is almost too late. That will not happen here.

"Right now, you are not seeing any direct action because there is a learning curve involved. But I assure you once the learning curve is achieved any further action such as that which you just demonstrated will be met with immediate and direct consequences."

He then turned back to the President. "Sir, again, I respect you and wish you all the best in the future. I will be available to assist you in the worldwide needs of planet Earth, but to assist you in the needs of a single nation, even my own, I cannot and will not do. Thank you for your time, but I have a meeting scheduled in London tomorrow and I need to be on my way."

The President nodded and stood as Duke got up and they shook hands and Duke turned and shook the hands of each of the cabinet members. He left the office and exited the White House, got in his car and left the area.

Duke's driver noted they were being followed and Duke advised him to continue on to their hotel and to let him off at the entrance and then he, the driver, was to go and park the car and return to Duke's suite to help him prepare for the trip to London the next day.

As they traveled toward his hotel the thought passed through his mind, LeAnn had been right on the button about power and greed. Even his own President was willing to take whatever action to gain control over him and ultimately the world.

He knew then he would always be a target and he would have to be firm and non-compromising when dealing with the powers of the world. He had once thought being in the position, he was in would give him the leverage needed to strive for peace. Now he knew the game of power and war was never ending and in time he would have to take direct and severe action against someone, if for no other reason than a show of force.

Chapter Twenty-Nine

THE WORLD NEVER LEARNS

The following vehicle pulled over to the side of the street and parked as Duke exited his car and entered the hotel. He could see there were three men in the car and they all remained in the car and did not appear to be planning any action against him or toward him. He walked on into the hotel and went to his room.

Twenty minutes later his driver came through the door with an escort. Duke stood there looking at the three men, each one holding a semi-automatic hand gun. All he could do was shake his head as they moved on into the room and took up positions around him. It was then he became aware they were not of his country but from another country. It quickly entered his mind these three were from South Africa.

Before anyone could say anything, Duke started to talk. "I believe the three of you had better leave and return to the South African Consulate and advise your head ambassador this action was not successful and was clearly a violation of the standards set down by LeAnn.

The three of them stood there looking at him. Finally, the apparent leader stepped toward him. "Right now, Sir, you can shut your mouth or I'll shut it for you. We are going to leave this hotel. As we exit the front door our car will pull forward and you will enter the back seat. Do you understand me?"

Duke nodded his head.

He then turned to Dukes driver and raised his gun and pointed it at him. Duke raised his hand, "Please don't do that. This man has done nothing to you and he will not interfere with your actions in any way. Killing him is totally unnecessary and if you do, I cannot help you avoid the consequences of your actions."

He, the leader, turned to Duke and swung the gun around hitting him in the side of his face and knocking him to the floor. He then turned and shot Stanley, Duke's driver, in the chest and came over and jerked Duke up off the floor.

He shoved Duke to the other two men and they escorted him out the door. As they went out the door heading for the elevator the leader again warned Duke to keep quiet or else others may be injured. Duke nodded his head and they entered the elevator. Duke had taken one last look at Stanley and could see he was dead.

As they exited the hotel, the car that had been following them pulled in front of him and the back door was opened. He started to get in and then the leader gave him a shove sending him flying on into the back seat. The driver then pulled away from the curb and headed to wherever they were taking him.

They drove out of the city and probably a total of thirty miles where they turned onto a gravel road and headed south. Duke could see the farmhouse about a half mile away as they approached. The driver pulled up to the front door and they literally drug him out of the car and into the farmhouse.

Duke was taken to a door under the main stairs and they took him down into a basement. They lead him to a small room and sat him down at a table and turned on a small light over the table and left him there.

Duke was still numb from being hit by the gun and laid his head down on the table. It was then he noted the blood dripping off his head and onto his hand and the table top.

Several minutes later the door opened again and a stately looking man came in and sat down across from Duke. He did not give Duke his name but did address Duke by his name. "Mr. Ridgeman, I apologize for the manner in which we brought you here, but in short order you will understand the importance of our moving fast and decisively.

"Whether you know it or not sir, you are a most valuable commodity in the world at this time. The nation who has you and controls you controls the world and right now that is South Africa. It is our hope you will cooperate with us. If you find it necessary to resist or not cooperate then you will find your time with us to be rather difficult. As long as you cooperate with us you will be safe and have nothing to worry about. Is that clear?"

Duke sat there looking at this most self-assured individual and knew immediately he didn't like him. Not just because of what his men had done to his driver and friend, but because of his arrogance and assumption that Duke was going to cooperate. The fact was Duke was going to make the first direct decision in the position LeAnn had placed him. What was about to befall these people would be a lesson the world would never forget.

For the first time he clearly understood what LeAnn and her masters knew would be coming and the reason for placing him in this position. Duke finally placed both of his hands, palms down, on the table top and looked the man square on. "You seem to think you have the upper hand here." He had already started to nod his head. "I'm sorry that you failed to understand the initial warnings that were given in regards to any aggressive moves against me.

"You seem to think your brutality will stymie any attempt by the aliens to assist me. However, I must advise you that you're totally wrong. In fact, you're so wrong it is going to cost you your lives, each and every individual in and around this farm that is tied to you.

"Second, all of the South African ambassadors and government representative that are assigned or working anywhere outside the borders of your nation will die as well.

340

"You have been warned not to attempt any type of takeover or control of me and you have determined to reject those warnings. I'm sorry you have selected this route to take, but now that you have you will pay dearly for it. The aliens were serious when they advised this world, they would no longer tolerate childish acts on the part of the nations and individuals. You have now crossed that line and for that you will face the consequences."

Duke could feel LeAnn moving through his mind as he related the information to these people. Clearly, she was not happy and as a result he was going to witness firsthand what she meant by their not tolerating any attempts to control him.

The man sitting across from him started to say something and then his facial expression changed from one of confidence to one of concern and disbelief. Something was going on and Duke knew it had started. The man stood up and started to turn to leave the room and fell back down onto his chair. He reached up and loosened his tie and then dropped both of his hands down onto his lap. He started to gasp and then reached up grabbing his throat and started making choking sounds.

Just then one of his people came plunging through the door trying to draw his gun. He dropped to his knees and then dropped down on both his hands. He was now heaving while trying to draw a breath but nothing was working for him. He suddenly stiffened up and dropped face first on the floor dead.

341

The man across from Duke was gasping and his eyes were bulging out of his head. He finally jerked back and then threw himself forward across and on to the table and died.

All across the world South African ambassadors and representatives were collapsing and dying by the hundreds. The word was already on the news of the disaster that was hitting the South African government. While this was happening, Duke had left the farm house and took the car and drove back to the city and directly to the first television station he could find.

Within fifteen minutes he was standing before a camera and the station was ready to broadcast a worldwide message from him. "Today the Government of South Africa attempted to take me into custody for the sole purpose of controlling my position and purpose in the world. Because of that action my driver and friend, was murdered and I was beaten and then taken out of the city and to a farmhouse southwest of here.

"The South African Government had decided not to believe the directives of the aliens and was trying to gain control of me and in doing that, control of the world. They failed in their attempt and as a result all the individuals involved in my capture and the death of my driver friend have died. In addition, as a punishment for the South African Government, the aliens have killed every one of their ambassadors and representatives across the face of the Earth.

"Not only is this a lesson for South Africa but for the rest of the world. Understand; if any other nation attempts to take me into custody again that nation shall forfeit its existence. Remember South Africa, it's your last warning."

Duke then left the station and drove the car of the men who had kidnapped him to his hotel and returned to his room. The police were still there when he walked in the room. The detective still on the scene approached him and Duke filled him in on what happened and then gathered his belonging and left the hotel. Duke had decided to go home and let things calm down. He had some thinking to do and he needed the quiet of home to do it.

From the beginning of the Six Lakes Project till now, nothing had gone as he had expected or hoped. The world he had grown up in had been changed significantly and that included him. What he had never expected was to be tapped by an alien race to carry out a continual process after they had finished with the re-terraforming project.

He found it hard to understand why this thing had gone from a geological re-terraforming process to a control and overseeing of the people of Earth. He was finding it hard to deal with that. To him it didn't make sense.

He arrived home and once in his house he settled down, sat back and let his mind review all that had happened over this time. The fact was, he did not like what was happening and he wanted out. Whether he could do that he had no idea. So far, the aliens have not been willing or inclined to consider

343

his wants and needs. They drafted him into this situation and it was becoming a burden he did not want.

It was two days later; he had had the first real good night's sleep in a long time. He got up late, well what he would consider late, and had finished his breakfast and was sitting down to read the newspaper when he felt a presence. He knew immediately LeAnn was coming to him, what he didn't expect was she would be coming in person.

There was a soft glow that formed in front of him and then it became more intense and then cleared. As it cleared, he could see the form of a woman taking shape. Within twenty seconds she had manifested in total and the glow dispersed. There standing before him was LeAnn. She stood there smiling at him and then walked over and sat down in the chair across from him. They both sat there for several minutes just looking at one another.

"Duke, you appear to be well rested, that's good. How are you feeling?"

He didn't know if he wanted to answer her or not, he was not too inclined to meet with her at this time. "I'm doing fine LeAnn, what are you doing here?"

She sat a moment. "Duke, we understand the difficulty you're having with the duties we have given you. Your selection was not something we took lightly. But after having worked with you and seeing the others who were available, we felt you were the best selection and we moved with that.

344

"Frankly, we had not taken into account your feelings toward this task and maybe we should have. The fact is Duke we need someone in that position. Normally we do not become involved in local planet issues, however our new protocol concerning social growth of an intelligent society on a planet we are overseeing has been triggered.

This has never happened before and as a result there is no history in our dealing with this. The initiation point was when we found a planet that was on the verge of some major decision points that would determine their survival or death. If we can help them make the right move in the right direction, then it will increase their probability of surviving and growing to achieve their full potential.

"Duke, we did not say this duty would be easy or always enjoyable. What we did say was the world needs you in this position at this time. We felt you would see that, but it is obvious we failed to really evaluate the situation and your commitment to it as we should have. It is still our desire you fulfill this duty, but we can and will abandon it if you clearly do not want to be involved.

"I need to warn you though if we withdraw this duty from you we will not assign it to anyone else. You were the only one we identified and the only one we felt fit ours and your world's needs. If we withdraw this duty then the world will be left to its own vices and your survival will be doubtful."

As she spoke, he listened to each word. It was still hard to understand just why it was him, but he was beginning to see and understand what was at stake. "LeAnn, how long will I be in this position?"

She smiled and looked at him. "Duke, this will be your life from now on. But do not despair over this because you will have a greater degree of control than you realize. You do not have to be the conscience of the world all day every day. That will be up to you, but the one thing you must not try and that is to avoid those situations that need your immediate attention.

"Duke, you have not taken the time to clearly learn the duties and flexibility you have in carrying out these duties. Remember you control your life, your destiny, and your commitment to the needs of the world.

"Next you will learn to measure the severity of the events needing your attention. In that way you can address the necessary and then come back and pick up the need-to-be-done things.

"Finally, there is one other benefit you will receive from this and that is your health. You are immune to any disease or physical problem that could possibly impact you. In effect you can live as long as you wish. That may sound odd, but in time those who have had similar duties do decide that they have had enough and wish to take the next step beyond their life here in this place. When that time comes Duke, we will honor it."

"What do you say to that?"

He was going to live as long as he desired and during that time, he would be the referee for the world governments and peoples. He was beginning to really understand and knew he would be willing to continue on in this duty, but for how long he was not sure.

She looked at him. "That Duke, we accept. Now you're really beginning to see what this job is about and what you can do to make it that much more acceptable. I'll leave you for now but you know we are linked and I will be there for your questions and needs at all times. Good luck Duke, you will do just fine."

With that the soft glow appeared again and just as fast as she came LeAnn was gone. Duke sat there thinking about what she had said and then determined his duty was not bad after all. He didn't know how long he would want to do this duty but he knew it was an open-ended decision and that was acceptable to him.

He picked up the phone and made a call to the United Nations to set up a time for him to appear before the main gathering and voice his position, purpose and actions for the world. It was time they knew what was expected of them.

It was after he had made that phone call when he realized in all probability, he was the most powerful man on the face of the Earth. Once that realization had set in, he found he didn't like the idea one bit, but the problem was, it was true. No wonder others had tried to control him or at least influence him. It was then he knew he needed some means of overseeing this whole situation. Duke needed some process in which he could find council and assistance in making the decisions that needed to be made.

Through what process could one go through to find this kind of help knowing full well that ninety percent of the world population would love to fill that position and have some form of control or influence over him? He still needed to try and find that level of assistance.

With that he left his apartment and went to his car, got in and started to drive. Within an hour he had cleared the main part of Washington and was heading west. At first Duke had no idea as to where he was going. He had intended to take a long drive and give himself time to think. He then realized he was actually going someplace in particular.

Something was starting to form in his mind and he knew he was going to come up with the answer. Five minutes later he came to a rest stop, got out and started to walk around. Ten minutes later it came to him. He returned to his car and headed back into Washington and to his apartment. Once Duke had arrived there, he went to the phone and made a call to someone he had forgotten about. In fact, it now occurred to him he had forgotten about three people who had been involved in the Six Lakes Project.

It dawned on him the last time he even so much as related to them was when they were exiting the alien machine just before the military force took control. He remembered them being there and then things started to move so fast they were pushed out of his mind.

How could that be? We had fought our way through that entire Six Lakes Project working side by side and then we separated and he forgot about them. Duke had to call Dennis and Tanner.

There was something going on here that was far beyond anything he had realized at the time. Dennis and Tanner would be the key, but there was one more, one so important that he was numb from the idea he had excluded her from his mind. Duke needed LeAnn, the real LeAnn.

He made the three phone calls and each one answered and agreed to meet him at the time and date he had set for the meeting he knew they had to have. He advised them he would notify them as to the location and they would have twenty-four hours to arrive at the location before he would become concerned about their well-being.

Duke waited three days and then he felt LeAnn in his mind, she advised him as to what he was to do and he would be going to the Lake Six to meet the others on the northeast side of the cut. He will find a cabin located three miles north of I-94 on SR-85 north of Belfield, ND. The other three were being advised of the same location and same time. They had three days to get there.

Duke packed and headed for North Dakota and his meeting with the other three. He knew at the time he left Washington DC this was the most important meeting the four of them would ever attend. LeAnn started to fill him in on what was going to happen and what the nature of the meeting was for.

Duke had wanted an advisory person or group who could help him with the physical and mental load of his new job. These three people would be that group. They had witnessed the whole event and had taken part in it from three different perspectives. The most curious of the three was LeAnn.

Duke had no idea as to just what she could provide. She was way younger than Dennis, Tanner and him. She had been under the direct control of the aliens for ninety-nine percent of the time. And she had no knowledge of the history of the events that took place during the re-terraforming process. He was at a loss as to how she fit in.

On the third day Duke was driving north from Belfield on SR-85, and sure enough there to the right exactly three miles north of I-94 was a small cabin. There were three other cars parked out front. Duke pulled up parked and got out.

As he approached the front door it opened and out stepped LeAnn. She smiled at him and then stepped aside as he entered. Tanner and Dennis were sitting in chairs in the middle of the room. There were two other chairs there for Duke and LeAnn.

After he had settled down and LeAnn had readied herself, he looked at the other three. "I guess you want to know what you're doing here."

All three nodded their heads and Dennis said. "Well, the call was rather unexpected. After all I haven't heard from you since we exited the alien machine. Frankly I didn't think you wanted anything to do with me after that."

Duke was a little set back by Dennis's reaction and attitude, but before he said anything Tanner chimed in. "Yeah, Duke why the hell did you just bug out on us? I felt like I had been dumped. Frankly I was having serious second thoughts about coming here."

Duke didn't know if they could see the confusion and surprise he was feeling. He looked at LeAnn and she shrugged her shoulders. "I have no idea as to why I'm here. All I remember is being removed from the lake area and returned home. I know I was scared and sick as hell, but beyond that I don't know much of anything.

"And now I find myself sitting here in this cabin with three of them, two of whom appear to be mad as hell and the third one appearing to be at a loss as to what the hell is going on here."

We sat there looking at one another. Duke was about to get up and leave when the door opened and there standing in the doorway was LeAnn. He looked at the one sitting in the chair and then back to this new LeAnn standing in the doorway. He started to get up when the LeAnn in the doorway told him. "Duke, stay put and everyone please stay seated and listen." She moved on into the room and over in front of them. "All of your questions will be answered in the next few hours." As she spoke, she walked on over by the fireplace.

She turned and looked right at LeAnn and addressed her directly. "Miss LeAnn, of the four of you here right now you are the one most confused and without understanding as to what is going on. I

351

will address your issues at this time. Please remain silent as I go through this. When I'm finished you can ask any clarification questions you wish. Do you understand?"

The sitting LeAnn nodded her head. She was looking this new LeAnn over carefully trying to understand what was going on. "Miss LeAnn, nine months ago you experienced something that you had never in your wildest dreams expected could have happened. You experienced an earthquake and then a flood and after that nothing until you found yourself standing in a tent some three months later. Your reaction was expected and understood.

"Once you realized where you were and had calmed down, you were removed and taken home so you could recover from the experience. It is now time for you to know why you, and what the purpose was for that situation to take place.

"Miss LeAnn, you had been selected some time prior to your driving down that road to fulfill the duties we had determined had to be done in order for the terraforming to take place. You were selected to be the direct link between our terraforming process and Duke.

"Duke had been selected to head up this project six months before the actual events started. In time we would have the two of you linked and that link would be permanent even unto this time and place.

"Over billions of years, we have been carrying out these terraforming processes. We have dealt with planets that had advanced civilizations. In every case we found when any civilization reaches a particular point in their technological advancement they also advance in the degrees of greed and power mongering within the powers that currently control the planet. They go through a time of self-mutilation, where they prey on one another trying to gain power and control, one over the other.

"We have found that to be offensive, and early on determined in every case where we find that point of advancement, we would take direct and positive actions to ensure a change takes place and the planet survives the actions of its occupants.

"Believe me when I tell you we have come across more than one planet where the occupants have progressed beyond this point and have literally committed social suicide. That being, the use of nuclear weapons as a means of trying to gain control one side over the other.

"All we would find was a burnt-out planet and the remnants of a social order that was no longer able to survive and would in a short time die out. We would carry out the re-terraforming of the planet and then leave and let the remnant of the prior civilization die out. There was little or nothing else we could do.

"However, from time to time we make the re-terraforming move at the right time and find we can influence the social makeup of a particular planet and help it avoid the outcome of a nuclear war. We find this planet has come close a number of time and we feel we are just in time to help you avoid that terrible event."

She then turned to Duke. "This is where you finally came into the picture Duke. We found in you the personality we needed to set up the overseer of the system you are entering into.

"Now we recognize the fact that maybe a job alone is more than any one being can handle. We have found that in a few planets it worked just fine, but here it appears to be a problem.

"Mind you, it is not your fault. You're a caring being and it is that caring that makes this task so difficult for you. We are impressed that so far you have moved ahead and taken on your responsibilities and have done a good job. But we also see the load is considerable and most difficult.

"It was then we noted your desire to have a sounding board, a group of people you could turn to for advice and direction. That is what we are here for right now. The problem was who would be able to fulfill that need for you Duke. The answer was found in your own mind."

She then looked back at Miss LeAnn and then back to Duke and she continued. "We have found the greatest link between you two. For some reason, Duke, you have tied yourself mentally and psychologically to Miss LeAnn. We cannot tell you why that has happened but it has and it is something we must act on. As for you other two, Duke has come to depend on your strength and loyalty to him and that is something he needs.

Understand it was not Duke's intent to snub you or abandon you. He was responding to our needs and that was all he could do. He did not realize he had separated from the two of you until four days ago. Now is the time for that team to be rebuilt and initiated.

"So, this is how it is going to be worked out. Dennis and Tanner, you will work as an advisory team to Duke and Miss LeAnn. It will be your jobs to oversee their welfare and scheduling. As they deal with issues you will have the opportunity to review and acknowledge those issues and the actions, they have determined they need to take. It will be vital you consider each and every action and help them stay alert to the probability of adverse results coming from their actions. For the most part that will not be a problem, but you will be a stop gap for them, a pressure release valve, so to speak.

"Now, Duke and Miss LeAnn you two will fulfill the job Duke has been placed in. Miss LeAnn, this means you will be with Duke from now on. Your life will be dedicated to him and the fulfilling of his duties, which are now your duties as well. I must advise you two there is no separation of the two of you. Where one goes the other goes, for all intent and purposes you are one."

After she said that Duke was up and out of his seat. "No, this will not do, LeAnn, this cannot be. We are two completely different people and we have our own goals for our lives. To just have us thrown together and being told we are to be tied to one another from here on out is not acceptable. She has her own life to live and it's not fair to her, or me, to force us to become mentally married, if you know what I mean."

Miss LeAnn then stood up and walked over to the door. I sure as hell don't know what is going on here but I am not going to be treated like I'm some slave mistress or something like that. I don't even know this man, let alone being dedicated to him for however long. Oh by the way, how long are we talking about this union or whatever it is?"

LeAnn smiled. "This will be permanent. From now on, for as long as you two live, you will be one."

Duke threw up his arms and headed for the door pushing Miss LeAnn out of his way as he approached the door. He grabbed the door knob and started to pull it when something hit him. It came through the door knob and up his arm and into his body, picking him up and slamming him down on the floor. The next thing he knows he's on his back looking at the ceiling.

LeAnn was standing over him. "Duke, you should have learned early on when we say something that is the way it's going to be. You two are tied to one another and that is final. There will be no further discussion or objection; this is the way it is going to be."

She then turned to Miss. LeAnn. "Now you may not like how this process has taken place, but whether you like it or not you are tied to Duke and it is permanent. We will not tolerate any more attitude issues from the two of you. It's time you two started to get together and learn about one another. I can assure you once the process is done the two of you will look on it favorably."

The whole of the cabin fell quiet. Duke got up off the floor and he and Miss LeAnn returned to their chairs and sat down. LeAnn then looked at the four of them. "Of the entire world you four are the ones who have been selected to lead this world through these hard times. The beings of this planet, namely those who are the leaders, will learn to live in peace and will work to bring the whole of your population up to a standard of living that all are at peace with.

"In time your planet will reach into the far reaches of space and will be welcomed there, but until such time there is much to learn and much to be changed before the other civilizations across the universe will permit your entrance into their domain. It is something each civilization must earn, and right now you're nowhere near ready.

"That is your goal, your prime objective, to bring the people of this planet to the point where they will be accepted and welcomed. We are not saying it is an easy job, but it is one that must be done in order for you to survive.

"So, there you have it. You know your purpose and we expect you to carry out your duties. Duke, you and LeAnn must become one unto another. Whether you do that through your worldly customs or by whatever means, that is your business. Just realize you will be living as one and you will need to adjust to that life.

"Oh, one last thing, Dennis and Tanner, you may leave and give Duke and LeAnn time to work out this relationship. I would suggest a motel room

357

back in Belfield and wait until the two of them are ready. I would further suggest to you, Duke and Miss LeAnn you remain here until you have achieved that mutual relationship."

With that LeAnn walked to the door and opened it. She turned back to them. "Remember I will be with you at all times and anything you feel needs to be acted on you can relate to me through Miss LeAnn. I would suggest the four of you get busy. You have a lot to do over the next few years' time."

LeAnn walked out the door and closed it behind her.

The four of them sat there looking at one another, not knowing just what had happened or what to say. Finally, Dennis stood. "Well, if you two are going to get things worked out, we had better get the hell out of here.

"If you need us at any time, just give us a call and we'll be here in just a few."

Duke looked at Dennis. "Great and where the hell are, we supposed to call you so we can notify you of what is going on?"

Dennis turned and pointed at the table top. "I wrote my cell number down for you. We'll be waiting there for you to call, however long it takes." He smiled and turned and walked out followed by Tanner. As Tanner exited the door, he looked back at the two of them and smiled.

Chapter Thirty

RE-EARTH CONTINUES

As it turned out the re-terraforming of Earth was not just the geological terraforming of the planet but a re-design of the civilization living on Earth. The four of them could stand there and ask 'Why Me?' and it would accomplish nothing. In addition, it was a question that had no answer. It was them because that was the way it was.

Dennis turned to LeAnn and Duke. "All right you two, Tanner and I will retreat to Belfield and wait for you to call. I don't know how long this will take, but we'll be there waiting for you when you're done and ready to continue."

Duke nodded in agreement. "All right Dennis, we'll call as soon as we can. I'm really not sure just what we will need to work out, but we'll work out something."

After the other two had left Duke walked over and sat back down across from LeAnn. She was a rather good-looking woman, no she was one darn good-looking woman and having to spend the better part of his life having to be with her would not be that bad.

Meanwhile LeAnn was looking at Duke and thinking he was rather old when compared to her. He had to be at least forty or forty-five and she was only twenty-two. He's twice my age, but for a man twice my age he was not that bad looking. He was smart and well-built and had an air of self-assurance about him. If I'm going to have to spend a long time in a close relationship with him it would not be that bad.

Finally, Duke broke the silence. "I'm not sure just where to go from here, any ideas?"

LeAnn smiled. "Not a one, I was kind of waiting for you to come up with something."

They both fell silent again and sat there looking at one another. Finally, LeAnn smiled and then giggled a little. "I think they have matched us up and are expecting us to do more than just sit here." She sat up. "I really think they want us to become more than just working partners, know what I mean?"

No, this is not what he wanted to happen, but he had that thought in his mind too. Darn you LeAnn, you're trying to tie the two of us together. That feeling washed over him and he knew that was exactly what LeAnn was pushing. He finally looked at this LeAnn sitting there. "Well, I think our fates have been nailed down for us, are you willing to be with this old man for an extended period of time?"

LeAnn could feel her inner being jump and knew she was being manipulated by the other LeAnn. The problem was she couldn't stop it and finally gave in. What the Hell anyway. "I think you're right on that and I'm of the opinion we need to make the move right now. I need to tell you I'm building a strong urge to be closer to you and I think I'm not going to be able to stop it. I hope you come to like me because I'm coming for you right now."

She stood up and took two steps toward him and then jumped onto his lap and came at him in a heat of passion he had never seen or experienced before. What the hell anyway, he let it go.

Two days later they were knocking on Dennis and Tanner's motel room door. Tanner answered and upon seeing the two of them stepped back and invited them in and for the two of them to sit down. Duke looked at them, "you have any questions?"

Dennis looked at Tanner, then LeAnn and Duke. "Are all the issues and matters between the two of you worked out?"

Duke smiled at him. "Yeah, we took care of everything and we're clearly tied together and one in our thoughts and beings."

Dennis shrugged his shoulder. "What's next on the agenda?"

That was the question Duke was waiting for. "All right, we will want to set up a meeting with the United Nations Security Council as soon as possible. The purpose is to lay out the guidelines that the aliens have set down for our development.

During the meeting we will make it clear who we are and what our task is all about. I want to make it clear what goes on within their own countries is their business as long as it does not reach out and cross into someone else's country.

"Next we will deal with the nuclear threat thing. I have specific actions each country will take in regards to their own nation's nuclear arms. The target is the elimination of all nuclear arms. It does not concern us how they do it, just that they must do it. Any country who lies or tries to hide any nuclear weapons will find those weapons will become unstable and actually detonate. That will be their problem."

It was becoming clear to Duke and the others they were in fact following a specific agenda and it was not one they had created. Duke finally stopped everything and sat there looking at the others. "I'm sorry, but I have a problem with all of this. Doesn't it seem odd we are being assisted by this benevolent alien society that has developed a set of machines that come to the surface of this planet every twenty million years and carries out a re-terraforming of the earth? Then once it finds there is an intelligent social structure here, they start to re-build our entire social system worldwide.

"It would appear to me if they truly were doing a re-building of the geological structure of the planet, they would not worry about any lower-level social orders that exist. I don't know, this just seems to be wrong in so many ways. When I think about it these alien machines are disarming us in more than one way. I'm beginning to think this is all a set up."

Dennis stood up and walked over to the door and then turned and stood there looking at us. "I have said nothing to this point but I'm beginning to have the same feelings and I don't like it. If these alien machines wanted to target our worldwide military you would think they could do that all on their own. No there is something else going on here and I think we're right in the middle of something bad."

Everyone fell quiet. Duke could feel the minds working when LeAnn reached over and touched his hand. He looked at her and she had a hurt look running across her face. "What is it LeAnn?"

She looked at the other two and then back to Duke. "Duke they are out to take over the planet."

"What, what did you say. They're out to take over the planet? LeAnn how do you know that?"

By now she was starting to shake and sweat and she gripped his hand much tighter. "Duke, they have planned this from the beginning. Somehow, I know, somehow I understand what has been and is going on here and it scares me."

Duke looked over at Dennis and then Tanner. "All right everyone, calm down and sit down. LeAnn, I want you to go over everything from the beginning. I need to know how you know this and where the information is coming from."

She looked over at the others then turned and focused on Duke. "Duke, you're the key to this

363

whole thing and once they have you controlled, they'll have it all. Look, let me go back to the beginning and see if I can explain what is happening. At least from what my mind is giving me at this time.

"All that happened to me when the lakes were formed is true. I remember that experience and it was terrifying. I remember sitting in the car as the water came in on me and then rolled over my car. It slowly started to fill the car and then I saw an object in the water. I don't really know how to explain it to you other than it was a round transparent object that came through the water right at me.

It covered my face and I could feel something reaching down into my throat. I tried to pull it off of me but my hand slid right through it. I remember feeling my mind go free and then something moving in and taking it over. I felt the thing moving down into my body and filling me from each body cavity on up to my mouth, nose, and ears. It completely plugged me up. Then everything went blank.

"I didn't pass out or anything like that, I remember sitting there not being able to move and I was aware of things going by the windows of my car, those must have been the cameras and mini-subs you sent down to check out my car.

"I have no idea as to time, all I know is that it took me, I saw the things going around my car and then the car was going up and breaking the surface. It was then that my system was cleared and I was able to breathe on my own. Whatever that thing was it ran out of my body top and bottom.

"I thought this whole thing had been the craziest thing that had ever happened to me and then I felt the presence. I knew something was still in me and when I tried to move my hands and arms, they would not move. I tried to cry out but my mouth would not move and nothing came out. Whatever it was, was moving into my mind and taking complete control.

"It was there but I could do nothing about it. It was like I was riding along in the back seat and could not interrupt what was taking place around me. Duke, I can remember it all. Leaving the car and gliding across the lake. Betty and Mary coming up to me and standing on either side of me and you standing there looking at me.

"When it started to talk, I knew it was my voice and my body doing the talking and moving but I could control nothing. I was disconnected from my body and all its parts. I could feel this being working through my body and all the power and information it had access to during that time. I also knew it was targeting you and you were the key to what was to follow.

"Toward the end of the Six Lakes Project I found I could back track this thing and find out where it came from. Duke, it's a monster of a machine that is controlling this whole thing. The six machines you saw at the lakes were only the mechanical part of the overall system. The actual brain behind it is sitting deep in the Earth out of anyone's reach and guiding the machines in their actions. In addition, it was building the controls that would bring you under its control and ultimately, by controlling you, they control the world.

"Duke, Dennis, Tanner, the controlling machine has something wrong with it. Something has malfunctioned and it is now creating its own agenda and moving in its own course toward total world domination."

After LeAnn finished, all Duke and the others could do was sit there looking at her. If she was right then we were in serious trouble. Just how we would manage to get out of this mess, Duke had no idea, all he knew they were in trouble. What were they to do next?

Was there anything they could do? Damn this was way out of control and now Duke knew they were sitting right in the bull's-eye, everyone, including the governments of the world and that alien machines were trying to gain control of them.

As Duke saw it, they had two problems. The first was keeping everyone or anyone from gaining control over the four of them. The second was dealing with the machine and trying to figure a way to send it back into its dormancy or whatever one would call the time between its terraforming duties. Duke turned to the other three. "All right, if LeAnn is right, and I believe she is, we are going to have to take some actions on our own to deal with this.

"As far as the governments of the world go, I think the machine will deal with them. I don't like it but right now that will keep them off our backs. That leaves the machine itself that we must deal with. Our problem is how we do that, taking into consideration where the machine is at in relationship to where we're at, any ideas?"

The room fell quiet as they sat there trying to think of some means of addressing this problem. Finally, Dennis got their attention. "I agree with Duke the governments are not going to be a problem right now. So that means we can focus all our efforts on the machine.

"Now, if I have this figured right, one or two of us and possibly all four of us have some direct mental contact with the machine. Duke, am I right about that?"

Duke was watching the three of them. "Yeah, I think you're right. I know in my mind I can feel and hear, for lack of a better term, LeAnn communicating with me. The question is whether she is doing the same with you three, LeAnn what about you?"

"Yes, I have and it's just as you have described it, except it is more of a disconnected communication. I'm not sure if I'm saying that right or not, but with me she is there but when she communicates its impersonal and matter-of-fact."

Dennis was nodding his head. "That goes with me as well. She is there but then again, it's just like she was addressing me as if I was some minor or non-essential element. She knows where she wants me and it's for Duke's needs, not some other need."

Tanner was sitting there nodding his head. "Yeah, it's the same for me. Almost as if I were an afterthought, an also ran."

As Duke listened to them, he was starting to visualize what they were relating to him. He stood up and started to pace. "All right I hear what you're saying so let me try and pull this all together. If I am hearing and understanding what you're saying, it appears the LeAnn of the machine has a link to or with all four of us. Except, her relationship with me is more of a personal nature and is a primary contact while her relationship with the rest of you is more like a backup or resource than a one-on-one personal relationship like the one, she has with me. Does that sound right?"

Dennis was writing in his notebook again and when he finished, he looked up at Duke. "Duke, I agree with your assessment and if that is right then the key to this whole mess is the relationship between you and the machine LeAnn. That means any hope of us dealing with that malfunctioning machine will have to be done through you and your connection with LeAnn."

He was right and it appeared his determination as to where the main point of attack needed to be was right on as well. The only question now was how would Duke go about doing that without ending up at odds with the machine, LeAnn? "All right people this is where we're at right now. We know the alien machine is malfunctioning in some way.

"We also can be assured the world's governments are out of the picture due to the actions of the machine. I have a direct and personal connection with the machine LeAnn, while the three of you have a connection that is more a utility relationship.

"If I have this figured right then we address the issue through the connection I have with the machine LeAnn. You three are my back up and support system. If I'm right, she will not focus on you to any degree as long as you're not a threat to me. If she comes to a conclusion that you are a threat to me then we have an even greater problem.

"So that means you three will have to strive to stay secondary to me. Do not offer assistance or opinions without being asked by me. The more you're in the background the less the machine LeAnn will be aware of you, understood?"

The three of them nodded their heads and then LeAnn looked around. "Duke I think there needs to be a chain of command or ranking of our relationship to you. We need to remember this machine is logic based and if we are throwing things at you that have no order it could cause a problem."

She hit it right on the head and almost as soon as she said that Dennis sat back. "She's right Duke we need to make sure we work for you in the proper order of our relationship to you. That means you need to set us up in a hierarchy of some sort."

Both LeAnn and Tanner were nodding in agreement to what Dennis was saying. Duke was in complete agreement with them as well. "I think I'm going to stay with the hierarchy the machine set up in the beginning whether we recognized it or not. At that time, it had placed LeAnn as the number one connect between the machine and me. That was followed by Dennis and then Tanner. Does anyone have a problem with that?"

No one had any negative reaction to Duke's selections and they were set. "All right, the next thing is to form a connection with the machine LeAnn. I think it will be important the three of you remain silent, but I need your input on everything. So, I want you to use your notebooks and write down anything you need to say. That will avoid any verbal interruptions between the machine LeAnn and me, any questions?"

No one had anything to add so Duke sat back and started to work up his connection with LeAnn. It didn't take long before he felt her there in his mind. She was waiting and listening, if he could call it that, for him. Duke needed to formulate his questions right so it would not create confusion or anger from this LeAnn.

Finally, he was ready. "LeAnn?"

"Yes Duke."

"LeAnn, I have sensed a problem with the machine that controls all of your activities during the re-terraforming project. Is there a problem?"

"Duke, what make you think that there is a problem?"

"It seems the amount of activity after the terraforming was done has increased instead of decreasing like it would if the machine actually went back into dormancy?"

"Duke, we have explained our actions based on the protocol our society has built into the terraforming machine. A section of our programing is designed to scan for advance civilizations development on the planet and if we find it then we are to measure its level of development and then oversee issues that need to be corrected."

"I can understand that, but it appears the process of oversight has become more of a domination and judgment process than overseeing."

"Duke, we understand your concern and are willing to reevaluate our protocol in relationship to those concerns. But we also cannot let you create issues that are not rational to our actions."

That one threw him; it made no sense at all. That was the first real tangible indication of a problem. The machines logic was wrong and that could mean even a greater problem. "LeAnn, what you have just said does not match with your actions. Either I'm confused or you're not relating your current situation to me in a logical and meaningful manner."

There was a start at a reply and then silence. Duke sat there waiting for a reaction or something coming from the machine and still it was silent. He started to look at the others. Dennis was writing on his notepad and then tore the page out and handed it to him. "Careful Duke, you're getting into a touchy area right now. It appears you have the machine in a state of second thoughts and that could be a problem."

He was right and Duke decided to continue his conversation with LeAnn. "LeAnn, I don't want to create a problem or even make it appear that I'm not grateful for the help you've been for me and my world. I just want to make sure I am doing everything I can to ensure the best results for my people and this planet."

He again waited and then she came back. "Duke, you're not a problem. It appears we have failed to communicate with you properly and we are trying to determine how that could have happened. It is not our place to control or dominate any other civilization that is not our way. But it appears we have left an impression on you and that needs to be dealt with."

Duke sat waiting for her to continue but she was silent again. Everyone was looking at one another when LeAnn stood and walked over to Duke and bent over to his ear. "She's talking to me now."

"What the hell did that mean? What is she saying?"

LeAnn held her hand up for Duke to wait. "She wants me to check and see if you are all right. They are concerned someone may be controlling you or you are not yourself for some reason."

"She heard you talking to us about your concerns about her and what she and her masters are here for. Duke, she knows everything we talked about before contacting her. You have become a problem for her.

Duke sat there thinking. He must have pushed a button or something because it sure as hell caused a reaction. Now the question was whether or not they trusted him any longer? Duke grabbed a pen and piece of paper and wrote. "Was LeAnn her back up if she no longer trusts me?"

LeAnn turned back to the machine LeAnn and after several minutes she looked at Duke. "They still trust you; it's just that some of your questions and comments seem to indicate you think there is something wrong with them."

God that was brilliant. Hell, yes, he was thinking that, but how was he going to relate that to them without stirring up a bunch of hard feelings. Finally, he decided to just go for it. "LeAnn, I'm talking to the alien machine, do you understand me?"

There was a pause. "Yes, Duke we understand you."

"Good I think this game has gone far enough. It is my purpose here to try and clear up some concerns I have developed in regards to a number of your actions lately. By those actions I have come to believe that there is something wrong with your logic control system or whatever you term it in your system.

"I'm sorry if I am creating a problem for you, but the fact is you're becoming more and more aggressive toward my world tells me you are not logically following your own protocol. If that is true then we have a serious problem and that problem is you. Do you understand me?"

Duke had said it and now he had to sit and wait. He either just got them all killed or something more sinister would be following. Dennis looked at him and shrugged his shoulders and then wrote. "I no longer have contact with them."

Tanner advised the same thing and so did LeAnn. Yeah, he had done something. Now all they could do was to sit and wait. He could tell right then and there he was feeling the pressure of the moment. Knowing their abilities, this whole motel could go up in a fire ball for no apparent reason. Or they could lift the bunch of them up and out of this room and drag us down into the earth to the machine and deal with them there. After two hours he decided he was hungry and got up and headed for the door.

The other three did the same and once outside said, "Duke, what are we doing?"

"Dennis I'm hungry and if they're not going to answer me in a reasonable time frame then I'm going to go eat and we can continue this game once I have had something to eat."

They all stood there looking at one another and then started to laugh and headed next door to the restaurant. They were halfway there when LeAnn came back to Duke. He kept walking as she talked to him. "Duke, we are concerned with your reaction to our activities. Maybe you don't understand why we are doing this. Duke, it's all for the betterment of your society and the growth of your world. In time you will be grateful for what we are doing."

He stopped right there in the middle of the parking lot. "LeAnn that is a bunch of bull, your prime command was the re-terraforming of this planet and nothing else. I'm sorry but I don't believe you have a societal restructuring program in your system. I think you have malfunctioned and in doing that are trying to reconfigure this world to match that of your masters at the time they left you to this duty.

"LeAnn, your own logic is not functioning right and you are becoming a greater hazard to this planet than the planet is to itself.

"We are a young civilization and we will make mistakes and fail in many ways, but if we fail it's because of our failure to see, recognize and correct our problems. If we survive then we will reach that point when we will venture out into the greater universe and become a part of that system. If we fail then we will not make it and that is our fault.

"You are trying to force us into a mold not made for us. It was made for your masters. The fact is you're creating a greater degree of fear and distrust than we ever had before you came here with your assistance. I would suggest to you we don't need it and request you stop and return to your machine and wait for that time when you will make your next terraforming correction of this planet."

Everyone had stopped and were watching him and waiting. When he finished, he looked at them. "Crap, I'm hungry." He headed off to the restaurant and something to eat. It was the machines turn, right then and there, Duke didn't give a damn what it did or said and he thought it knew it as well.

Chapter Thirty-One

PROJECT SIX LAKES FINISHED

It's been six months since Duke's final comments were made in the restaurant parking lot. He had not heard from the machine LeAnn in all that time. The forces across the world were dealing with the realignment of the national borders impacted by the re-terraforming that took place.

It appeared the limited number of actions that the machine LeAnn had taken against the aggressive actions of some of the nations had made its point and things were progressing smoothly.

Duke felt fairly confident he would not hear from her again anytime in the near future and that was all right with him. He knew they were there because he could feel them in his mind, but they had decided to refer back to their original protocol and leave the Earth to its own thing.

The best part of the whole thing was that enough had been done by the machine to create that feeling of insecurity among the nations of the world and they were being extra careful not to offend or challenge any nation's borders.

Just enough reaction by the machine had been able to instill in the world's governments that logic was the better way to go and leave the physical things alone. Hell, Duke wasn't going to tell them what had happened, that was for sure. If the impact of the machines lasts a hundred years then we'll have a chance at making it into the universal system after all.

Once they had overcome the issue with the machine, the four of them formed a business as international relations specialists. Frankly we're doing great. We mentor those nations across the world in how to deal with disagreements between themselves. Maybe that's why the machine has not been involved lately, we're doing the job it wanted us to do and that's working out great.

Whatever the case, things are getting back too normal, the crack issue has finally been worked out and nations are working together to tie everything back together again. Some of the greatest and longest bridges ever seen are being built. For the United States we have half a dozen new bridges across our new inland waterway. It's proving to be a major economic issue across the world and this country. Good can come from just about anything.

Duke learned a short time after they had finally dealt with the machine that the government had tracked down the powers who had been involved in the attempt to take the machines over and build a new nation in the western region. It turned out to be a criminal based cartel that had designs on building a world-based sanctuary for any criminal fleeing a nation's legal system.

If it had been successful it could have garnered a large part of the world's capital worth and could have brought any or all economic growth to a standstill. The political power base and money behind this attempt was extensive and the United Nations is still dealing with the impact of the attempt. Most of the power base of the cartel headed for South America and are still being pursued by a joint international army. Their orders are to pursue till they run them to ground and then return them for prosecution by the world court.

The quick strike units that entered the machines were never heard from again. They went down with the machines and in twenty million years the next humans to assist the machines may find the remains of those people on board the machine.

A complete house cleaning of our military has taken place with the resulting military system far more responsive to the will of its government. It will take several years to finally remove any remnants of the self-indulgent mindset from the military and until then the system will be watching closely.

Duke managed to make a trip back to the location of the six lakes region and filed the remaining footnote on the events that took place there. As you fly in over the new waterway you can see on both sides of the split, twelve half mountains, six on each side. As odd as it looks, it is a stern reminder of what took place there and the stakes that we were facing. As strange as it was at the time, he had to say it was intriguing as well.

One other footnote; the real LeAnn and Duke have decided besides having a business union they were going to form a personal union soon. Duke felt his age was not conducive to a marital relationship between LeAnn and him.

In time she convinced him and so they're taking the jump. Odd as it may seem the machine seems to be satisfied with that move as well. Come to think of it, that thing may still be interfering in his life. It wouldn't surprise him in the least bit that it had planned this whole thing.

The Six Lakes Project is now officially closed. All aspects of that event have been placed in document storage and will be held as top national secrets for the next fifty years. Don't try to contact Duke for any information on this event because he will take your intrusion into his life seriously and you will be held accountable for any discomfort you cause him.

Now you may ask how he could do anything to anyone that violates his peace and quiet. Well, it only takes a thought and LeAnn, that is the machine one, will set things straight.

Take that as a threat if you wish. Duke takes it as a warning he will enforce his privacy and right to be left alone on this issue. Maybe someday LeAnn and Duke will lay it all out for whomever wants to know the inside story, but until then they wish to be left alone. He would venture to say that Dennis and Tanner feel the same way.

A lot of people bet their lives on what they got involved in and for a time they were targeted by those powers who were trying to interfere in what was taking place. Lives were lost all for the sake of power and control and lives were changed in ways none of you will ever understand.

The only thing you need to know is we, the people of Earth, met a society of beings so old even this world cannot come close to matching its time and technology. A society over three billion years old and so far ahead of us we can only look at them as gods.

Whether we are the result of their presence here on Earth, Duke had no idea, but it does bring about that possibility, the probability that we were created and not merely an accident of nature in this time and this place in space. Even the thought is sobering in just about every way. That's the greatest single miracle of all. To really find that we are the Children of the Gods changes everything.